LOVE IS IN THE AIR

Rowie found her key. "Thanks for walking me home."

"Anytime." Drew stared at the damp ringlets around her face. His eyes grazed the curve of her neck, and drifted upward until they locked eyes. "Good night," he said, unable to leave.

Rowie didn't say a word, but her breath quickened. The air between them was as thick and sweet as honey. Their energies danced, and zapped, and nipped at each other.

"I should...go in."

Drew instinctively stepped between Rowie and the door. "Wait..."

His hands closed around her as he pulled her toward him. His mouth crushed down on hers. She kept her arms frozen at her side. Her eyes remained open, waiting...waiting...*waiting*...

Finally, she pulled back, shocked. She grabbed the handrail for support. Something was wrong. Really...wrong.

She didn't see anything.

FORECAST

Jane Tara

LOVE SPELL  NEW YORK CITY

For my beautiful boys, Indy and Raffy.

And in memory of the real Rowie...who told me to write.

LOVE SPELL®

November 2007

Published by

Dorchester Publishing Co., Inc.
200 Madison Avenue
New York, NY 10016

ISBN-10: 0-505-52744-8
ISBN-13: 978-0-505-52744-8

Printed in the United States of America.

10 9 8 7 6 5 4 3 2 1

ACKNOWLEDGMENTS

Writing is supposedly a solitary occupation, but there was nothing solitary about my journey with this book. I am completely indebted to the following people:

Rosemary Serluca who first saw the potential. Thank you for your support and belief. L&L always! To everyone at AEI, especially Ken Atchity and Mike Kuciak and Chi-Li Wong. I feel absolutely blessed to have you in my camp. Also Andrea McKeown from Writer's Lifeline. And everyone at Dorchester, especially my editor, Leah Hultenschmidt, whose magic wand helped make this book a fabulous reality.

My father Rod Hinchey (from whom I inherited a passion for books) and stepmother, Shirley, and my brother Sean Hinchey, who have all sup-ported me unconditionally. A huge heartfelt thanks also to Hiromi and Gerhard Linzbichler, and to Warren Gibson, for never complaining about the mileage.

To all my gorgeous, aristocratic, understanding friends for putting up with me when I disappeared for weeks at a time to write, or into my head midconversation. "What was I saying…?" Oh yes. The drawbridge to the castle is always open.

Special mention to Viscount Willis, Marquis Mark, the lovely Lord Locust, Dame Drinkalot Ruwhiu, and my fabulous NW, Olivia Pigeot. Also, Sue Scannell, Robyn English, Michelle Frost, Margot Dunphy, Linda Larcan, Sam Beeston, Rachael Denniss, Markham Lane, Ulrike Sturm, Assheton Whiley, Thorsten Eckhoff, Paul Bishop, Vince Paul, and Joe Brownlee. I thank you all!

To Chicky: ironically, words will never express what your support means to me. Thank you for everything. This wouldn't exist without you. And Indy and Raffy, for putting up with a mother who forgets to do normal mother things be-cause she's in front of the "poota."

And last, but certainly not least, my incredibly patient mother, Yvonne Pfeiffer. Thank you for your support and encouragement, the many road trips, plane trips, and the countless hours of babysitting. But mostly, *thank you* for showing me what a magical place the world is. No matter what else was happening in your life, you always, *always* took time to show me the faeries.

For that alone, I am *eternally* grateful.

FORECAST

Chapter One

Every morning a mishmash of people gathered outside a crumbling, ivy-covered brownstone in Manhattan's West Village.

This morning, as always, everyone mingled patiently on the pavement. Sunny from the local fruit and veggie shop waved to Ned, who ran the cafe. Officers Luke O'Hare and Justice Washington double parked their patrol car and joined the others. More people arrived. Everyone chatted about the weather and waited.

Suddenly the bright red door of The Grove—as it was affectionately known—swung open and Rowie Shakespeare trotted down the stairs.

"Morning. Everyone ready?"

The crowd murmured that they were and a hush fell over the street.

Rowie stared skyward. Her exquisite face softened, her tiny body relaxed, and her emerald eyes focused somewhere beyond the earthly realms. Only her bright red hair moved as it fluttered slightly in the warm breeze.

A minute passed, and then another. Someone had the

nerve to ask what was going on and received a number of silent glares in return. Obviously a tourist!

Officer Washington edged over to the tourist and whispered, "She's predicting the weather."

"The *New York Times* says it'll be hot and sunny all day," said the baffled tourist.

Officer Washington nodded. He too had once relied on the newspaper, Internet or CNN for his weather forecasts, but since discovering Rowie, he was never again without an umbrella when he needed one.

The tourist looked quite disturbed by the whole scene. "How does she know what the weather will be like?"

"She's psychic."

The tourist started to laugh, but stopped when he realized the cop was serious. "Psychic?"

"Yep. And goddamn accurate too. These reports are a bit of a neighborhood tradition."

The tourist looked uncomfortable for a moment, and then started to edge toward the street corner. New York was full of weirdos. He still had the Empire State Building and Toys "R" Us to check out, but after that he was catching the first flight back to Salt Lake City.

Officer Washington returned to his partner's side and pulled a dollar out of his pocket. "I say it'll be sunshine all day."

"You're on."

"Got it," Rowie called as her gaze refocused.

She walked over to a whiteboard attached to the wall outside Second Site, the metaphysical bookshop and healing center her family owned next door. For sixteen generations, psychic abilities had been passed down to all the Shakespeare women, including her grandmother, Gwendolyn, and her mom, Lilia.

Rowie grabbed a big red marker and wrote, *High of 80. Rain later! Take an umbrella.*

Officer O'Hare laughed at his partner. "You'll never be a farmer, buddy."

Rowie opened a cardboard box full of umbrellas and offered them around. "Don't forget to return them," she reminded.

Sunny from the fruit shop waited patiently until the crowd petered off. "Rowie, I hate to bother you . . . it's just . . ."

Rowie placed her hand on Sunny's shoulder. "She'll be home soon. A couple of months. Until then, she's safe."

Tears of relief filled Sunny's eyes. His granddaughter had run away from home, and no one had heard from her all week. "Thank you. What you have . . . No wonder they call it a gift." He gave Rowie a hug and headed back to his shop, feeling happier than he had in a long time.

Rowie tidied the umbrella box, then walked toward the shop. She paused, glancing at the huge billboard that had recently been installed across the street. The picture of the man on it gazed straight back at her, a huge smile on his handsome face. He looked confident, smart . . . well flossed. Underneath were the words: *Drew Henderson, He's hot!*

"You're not wrong." Rowie sighed.

Every night, women all over the tri-state area were glued to their TV sets while USBC's Drew Henderson delivered the weather. Tall, dark, handsome, he was enough to raise temperatures in the middle of winter. He'd become an overnight sensation the minute he hit America's TV screens. Some of his detractors felt his piercing blue eyes and slightly ruffled brown hair belonged on a daytime soap, not reporting on the forces of nature. But Rowie liked him. Sure he was smooth, and he probably had the substance of a soda, but out of all the weathermen, Drew was the most accurate. He wasn't as good as her . . . but he did well with the tools available.

Rowie glanced at the sky. It was still deceivingly blue. She wondered if Handsome Henderson—as her grandmother had christened him—had picked up on the incoming storm. Unlikely. He was probably still in bed, curled up with a supermodel. Men that hot usually enjoyed a high turnover of naturally airbrushed woman.

Rowie turned back to the billboard and searched Drew's face. Are you up, watching the weather? she wondered. Unlikely. A man like Drew Henderson? He was definitely flat on his back somewhere.

Chapter Two

Jess Walker was having a shit of a day, and it wasn't even nine A.M. The Christopher Street Station was closed for track repairs, so she was rushing down to Houston. Why they had to suddenly fix the tracks the day before Fourth of July weekend was beyond her, but then the MTA was never known for its timing.

Unlike her. Jess was never late for work, and she didn't want to start today. She quickly scanned the street for a cab. She noticed a large crowd of people blocking the sidewalk in front of her. Probably gawking at a dead body, she thought. She'd seen a number of jumpers and drug addicts clock out on Manhattan's pavements. Not that she stopped to stare. She was too busy.

Jess glanced up to see how high the buildings were and saw a billboard of Drew. Goddamn it! Wasn't her day bad enough already? Wasn't it sufficient that she had to work with the guy every day?

Every billboard, every magazine cover, every inch of gossip column devoted to Drew was just another nail straight through her heart. Oh yes, she pretended to be friends with him. They'd agreed to remain friends when he dumped her. But she wasn't his friend. She barely liked him. She just wanted to have his babies. Totally different.

Thankfully, she wouldn't have to see Drew in the flesh today. He was on assignment in Florida. Another huge hurricane was brewing offshore, so Jess had made the call late yesterday to send him down there. Sometimes being a producer came in handy, especially if it meant you could get an ex-lover out of the way for a few days.

Not that Jess would ever admit it, but she'd found it hard working with Drew since their bust-up. Work had always been the most important thing in her life, but lately she'd found it difficult to concentrate on her job. With any luck, Drew would be overcome by Florida, decide to stay there, and she'd never have to set eyes on his rippling biceps again.

Her phone rang. "Jess Walker."

"Jess? It's Dario. There's been an accident."

Jess froze. Fear shot through her legs. Dario Volteri was the cameraman she'd sent to Florida with Drew.

"What's happened? Is it Drew?"

"Yeah. He fell through a roof. He's . . ." Dario was shouting. Jess could hear the wind howling through the phone.

Jess staggered over to a parked car and fell against the trunk. A moan escaped her lips. "Oh no, no, no, Drew, not Drew, he can't be dead."

"Dead? No, he's not dead. But I think his leg is broken."

Jess pulled herself together. "What the hell was he doing on a roof?"

"We were shooting. He decided to stand on top of a boat shed to get a good shot of the hurricane coming in from sea."

"Is he insane?" And then a thought occurred to her. "Did you get footage?"

"Of course."

"Good. Send it through. Where's Drew? Can I talk to him?"

"He's at the hospital. We're waiting for the X-rays to come back and then we'll know more."

"Unbelievable. The biggest predicted hurricane all year and no one to cover it."

"Eva Sanchez is here," Dario yelled. "She can do it."

"What's she doing there? I didn't send her on this assignment."

Dario stalled for a moment. "She's not here for work. She came down with Drew."

"What do you mean?"

"You know. *With* Drew," said Dario.

Jess wanted to be sick. How could he hurt her like this? Obviously this news would get back to her. She thought their relationship had meant something to him. It certainly had meant something to her. And while she knew Drew would date other women, this won him the two-minute noodle award for moving on. It had only been three weeks.

"Fine, use Eva." She'd deal with that little tramp later. "Get back to me as soon as you know more about Drew's leg. And don't forget the feed." Jess turned her phone off and slipped it into her bag. She hoped she could air the footage of Drew's fall before he tried to quash it. There was no way he'd allow his female fans to see him looking anything but controlled and cool.

Falling through a roof wasn't cool.

Jess moved closer to the crowd and noticed that it wasn't a dead body, but a gorgeous redhead who was the center of attention. The woman was tiny, but had a commanding presence. She was standing completely still, gazing skyward. The crowd around her was silent, respectful, and obviously in awe.

Suddenly the redhead walked over to a whiteboard and scrawled a weather prediction across it. Not just any weather prediction, but an incorrect one. There was no way it was going to rain today.

Jess pushed her way past the crowd. What a bunch of freaks. She noticed a cab, double parked in front of a police car, and walked over to the driver. "Are you working?"

"I am now. I've got my weather report for the day." The driver waved to two policemen. "See you tomorrow, boys. Don't get wet."

Jess slipped into the backseat as the driver started the ignition.

"Where to?" he asked.

"Fifty-fourth and Sixth." Jess stared out the window at the redhead now handing out umbrellas. "You don't really believe that woman, do you?"

"Who, Rowie? Sure. I've been getting her reports every day for the past three years and she's never been wrong. Ever."

"Is that so?" Jess turned and watched Drew's billboard disappear from view. All thoughts of the redhead slipped her mind, replaced by images of Drew. She couldn't believe he'd been injured.

Damn him, she thought.

Jess bowed her head and, despite being a self-affirmed atheist, said a little prayer for Drew: *Dear Lord, I don't ask for much, but if you could, have a look at Drew Henderson . . . and please make sure he's in a lot of pain.*

Chapter Three

Second Site was a jumble of an establishment next door to their home, affectionately known as The Grove. Rowie's grandparents had initially held readings and séances at home, but the business expanded so rapidly that they decided to search for another premise. Around the same time, the house next door became available. Isn't synchronicity marvelous?

Gwendolyn and her husband Dorian had bought the building and christened it their *Second Site*—because that's what it was—and before long it blossomed into one of Manhattan's leading centers for metaphysical research and education. The entrance, which was at basement level, was easy to miss. Many people couldn't find it at all, but that just meant they weren't ready for spiritual investigation.

Neighbors often dropped by to ask advice about a family member, or where they should spend their holidays. And every year around Yule, the doors to both brownstones were thrown wide open for the

Shakespeares' annual winter solstice party. It was an event not to be missed.

The shop was filled with books, crystals, tarot cards and tools of the occult. There were sofas and comfy chairs scattered around so customers could relax and read. The rest of the brownstone was a maze of rooms used for healings, counseling and psychic readings. It was warm and inviting, the kind of place that was difficult to leave, providing a safe haven for people to search for, and often find, answers.

Gwendolyn was greeting a nervous client when Rowie arrived. "Morning, Rowena. That delivery of wands needs to be unpacked."

"Excellent, another challenging day," grumbled Rowie as her grandmother disappeared out the back.

Lilia was curled up on a sofa, surrounded by a pile of books.

"Aren't you supposed to be pricing those, Mom?"

"I was . . . and then this charm of a book sucked me in and I haven't been able to put it down. *The Truth About Faerie Magic*. An important and timely book."

Rowie watched as her mother turned a page and resumed reading. There was no point trying to reach her until she put the book down. Rowie had learned at a young age that it was best to leave Lilia alone when she had her head in a book.

Lilia was an unusual parent. She loved immensely, but never showed it the same way other parents did. She didn't worry about Rowie; she considered worry a useless emotion. She didn't set rules, enforce discipline or push her daughter. It didn't occur to her that most parents did. And Rowie didn't miss having a more involved mother. Besides, she always had Gwendolyn to nag her.

"I'll do the accounts," said Rowie.

"If you like," said Lilia, vaguely.

If you like! Actually, no, Rowie didn't like. She hated bookkeeping. But seeing as Lilia had to be pulled down by a string just to talk, there was no way she could do it. Lilia wasn't capable of running Second Site, so when Gwendolyn died, which she constantly promised was going to happen soon, it would be Rowie's turn to take over. The thought depressed her.

Lately, each day was an effort. The same conversations with countless different people, all on a desperate search for happiness. How was she meant to help others find their paths when she was having difficulty finding her own? She felt like such a hypocrite, advising people to follow their destinies when she was busy ignoring hers.

All her life she'd been assured that her path was the same as countless Shakespeare women before her. But if that were the case, why did it make her feel so empty? Like she was missing something important? If Lilia would assume more responsibility, then Rowie could have some much-needed freedom to see what she really wanted from life.

She longed to march up to her mother and boot her dipsy ass off the couch. But Rowie didn't, because one look at her mom lying there and her anger faded. Her mother had a way of commanding protection without saying a word. Lilia was truly beautiful. It wasn't just the auburn hair, flawless pale skin or the petite frame. It wasn't even the clear emerald eyes that possessed answers to questions most people feared. It was something else, something magical.

Lilia looked like one of the faeries she was reading about.

The doorbell jangled and the Shakespeares' dear friend and most loyal customer, Petey Morris, bounded in carrying a tray of coffees.

"Coffee break!"

Rowie grinned and pulled out a stool for Petey.

"Skim milk latte for Madam Lilia," he said.

Lilia put her book down and looked surprised at his kindness, even though he'd been bringing her the same coffee every day for a year. "Thank you, Petey. Aren't you a gem?" she said, peeling herself off the couch to take her coffee.

Petey beamed, as he did every time Lilia noticed him. "What are you reading about today?"

Lilia stared into space for a moment, then smiled. "I forget."

There were many regular customers who had become friends over the years, but none quite like Petey. He thought of himself as a Shakespearean disciple. He loved all three women like family, but also treated them with a degree of awe and reverence. His life was one big "if only." *If only he were psychic.*

Goddess knew he tried.

He knew the tarot deck by heart, he could tell you the colors of every chakra, he had studied the Bible, Kabbalah, A Course in Miracles, the Tibetan Book of the Living and Dying and everything by Deepak Chopra. He meditated, was attuned to Reiki, and practiced yoga. He even knew Shirley Maclaine—well, okay, he saw her at a restaurant once and threw himself at her, begging for an autograph—but none of it made him psychic. It only made him confused.

He finally realized he'd never make a living channeling astral masters, and made do with being as useful as possible to the women he adored. He brought them coffee every morning, even though they preferred to make their own. They let him think he was helping because he always made them laugh, and that was priceless.

Petey perched on the stool. "Not long until the All-Star Game. Who do you think will win?"

"No idea," Rowie said, sipping her coffee.

"No point being psychic if you don't know the important answers in life."

"Perhaps it's not the answers that are important, but the questions we ask." Rowie nudged him, teasing. "So what's happening today? You're all dressed up."

Petey grinned, thrilled Rowie had noticed. "I've got a date. For lunch."

"That's great. Who is she?"

"I met her online. She seems nice. She's a dental nurse. Likes French films, yoga, reality TV . . . she's also a Libra."

"Sounds promising," said Rowie.

Lilia nodded enthusiastically. "Yes. Pity it won't work out."

"Mom," Rowie chided. "Why do you do that?"

"No point wasting his money on the wrong girl." Lilia took Petey's hand. "It's only because I care about you."

Petey looked devastated. "Why won't it work out?"

"She's very superficial. And you lied when you described yourself."

Petey went sixteen different shades of red. He *had* lied. But he was scared that if he were honest with dentalnurse69 she'd never agree to meet him. And surely once they met and talked, she'd realize what a nice person he was. . . .

"In future when they ask for a photo, send one," Lilia recommended.

Petey looked horrified at the thought. A photo was out of the question. He'd never even get a first date, and his self-esteem would take a battering it didn't need. It hobbled him at the best of times. No amount of positive thinking or mumbling affirmations was enough to lift his self-image out of the doldrums.

Petey knew he wasn't Brad Pitt—although he felt they had been brothers in a past life—and there was nothing he could do to change that. He was tall, skinny and slouched, with a long hooked nose and lank brown hair. He wasn't exactly a blank canvas that could be improved upon. But during those moments when he actually liked himself, usually after listening to his Louise L. Hay tapes, he realized that while not handsome, he was interesting. He was a walking caricature, which was better than being bland, forgettable. Anything but that.

Petey knew he lived in a superficial age, but he also believed in the power of love. He knew that when he met his soul mate, his looks wouldn't matter. So he kept putting himself out there, steeling himself for rejection, while praying that the next woman would be the one to welcome him home.

Rowie patted Petey's arm. "Are you okay?"

"Yeah. I guess 'tall, dark and handsome' was a bit of a stretch."

"I think you're just lovely," Lilia purred, "and so will the gorgeous brunette you eventually fall for."

Petey's eyes lit up. "Really. You can see someone for me?"

"Of course," Rowie assured him. "There's someone for everyone. You just have to be patient, that's all." She certainly was.

Lilia gave Petey a sly smile. "She's not far off."

Petey jumped off the stool and gave Lilia a hug. "I'd better ring the dental nurse and cancel. Then I'm off for a haircut. Don't want to look scruffy for the brunette." With a wave and his usual optimism, Petey rushed out the door. Each day alone was one day closer to his soul mate.

"Stop interfering, Mom."

"No. The dental nurse is a cruel little vixen, and I don't want Petey to get hurt."

"Fair enough," Rowie sighed as she turned back to

the accounts. Something was off. "Did you already pay for the delivery of moonstones, Mom?"

"Yes. I gave them cash," said Lilia. "And a free aura reading."

"You have to tell me, okay? No wonder the accounts are out."

"Sorry . . . I didn't think it was that important."

Rowie shook her head in frustration. Lilia thought faerie magic was important, but money could be ignored. She had recently admitted she thought the stock exchange was a place to swap cattle.

Gwendolyn entered with her beaming client. "Are you sure you don't want to finish the whole hour?"

The woman handed Gwendolyn some money. "No, I got the information I came for. As long as that bastard isn't getting custody of the kids, then I'm happy." She smiled at the three women. "A good lawyer and a good psychic . . . it's what every divorcée needs."

"Don't forget that younger man, with the surname starting with R. He'll be giving you what you need too, my dear."

"Bring it on. After twelve years with a sexually challenged caveman, I'm ready." The woman snapped her purse shut. "Thanks again. I'll definitely be back." She exited with a confidence not present when she entered.

Gwendolyn grabbed a handful of her ever-present Post-it notes. "I did the Wedgwood this morning. There'll be no squabbling over that when I'm gone."

"That's good to know," Rowie said, humoring her.

"The last thing you need when you're grieving for me are arguments about who gets what."

"Too true," Rowie agreed. "And I'd fight a duel to the death for the Wedgwood."

"You'll be surprised what holds sentimental value when I'm dead," sniffed Gwendolyn.

Gwendolyn was a walking obituary. Despite perfect health and a history of family longevity, she was constantly preparing for death. Being in regular touch with the spirit world meant she had no fear of it. Having loved and lost a lot of people over the years meant in some ways she was looking forward to it. It would be quite a reunion.

But mostly, she used her pending death to manipulate her daughter and granddaughter. Constantly reminding them of her fragile mortality meant they wouldn't stray too far away from the fold. Death didn't frighten her, but being alone did. So Gwendolyn's days were filled with notes and instructions and preparations for her passing. When it arrived, she would be ready. Really ready: She had been preparing for it for years.

With a dramatic flourish she stuck a Post-it on the cuckoo clock. "I think I'll leave this for Nathan the florist. So, Rowie . . . how's Brad?"

"Fine."

"I like that boy. So handsome," said Gwendolyn. "He hasn't been 'round much lately."

"No, he's busy . . . I'm busy . . . you know."

"No. Busy with what?"

"I don't know. Work and stuff."

Gwendolyn looked affronted. "You're hardly overworked."

Rowie burst into tears. "We broke up, okay."

Lilia and Gwendolyn both rushed to her side.

"Oh no! He was so nice." Gwendolyn grabbed a hanky from her pocket and shoved it at her granddaughter.

Lilia hugged Rowie. "Did you . . . ? You didn't . . . ?"

Rowie nodded and a fresh wave of sobs exploded. "I did."

"Oh darling, I told you not to kiss him," Gwendolyn said.

"I had to kiss him sometime."

Gwendolyn and Lilia comforted Rowie as best they could. It didn't help. Rowie wasn't just crying over the loss of a perfectly likeable boyfriend, but because she was sick of having her hopes shattered.

It was clear from the moment Rowie was born that she had inherited the family gift of clairvoyance. What no one knew then was she had been blessed (or cursed, as she often suggested) with a couple of extra gifts as well. One gift became apparent the day she first spoke. They were all sitting down to dinner when, as clear as day, Rowie said, "A hurricane is coming."

Everyone laughed and commented on how clever and sweet she was, until the following morning when they found themselves hiding under the beds as strong winds ripped off part of the roof.

They used Rowie's knack for forecasting the weather to their advantage after that. The Shakespeare women were never caught without an umbrella when it rained, and Rowie's predictions helped Gwendolyn gauge when she should plant her seasonal vegetables. Predicting the weather was harmless and helpful. Not a day went by that she wasn't thanked by one of the locals for her morning reports.

The second, more unusual addition to Rowie's clairvoyant repertoire was the reason she was now crying. It was the reason David Packer, the first boy she ever kissed, made the rest of her school years a living hell. It was why Rowie's romantic life had been one premature breakup after another.

Thanks to her extra gift, one kiss was all it took for Rowie to know a guy. One kiss and she could clearly read him, his desires, his secrets, his past, his present and, most importantly, his future. No matter how great the guy was, his future played out clearly before her—and her visions always starred other people. Rowie stayed detached from the men she met because she didn't see the point of getting too involved with someone she had no future with. She'd learned years before how painful that could be.

Erich Lennox had been her first real boyfriend. They'd met in college and fell madly in love. She tried desperately to ignore the future she saw for Erich when they kissed. She didn't ever want anything to come between them. Not their separate destinies, not the man for her, the one shrouded in mystery, and certainly not the blond lawyer he'd eventually marry.

They shared two bittersweet years before he met Darna Mattel, a pretty blond law student. He returned home to the small studio he shared with Rowie, packed his bags and hugged her tightly before he left.

"I still love you, Rowie . . . but I belong with her." With that, Erich walked out the door and disappeared from her life.

All night Rowie had sobbed at the unfairness of life. She wailed the twist of fate that had burdened her with a gift which stole the most treasured of human experiences from her: first love. With her clear second sight, only the truest of love would be blind. All others would be nothing but glass and completely transparent.

That night Rowie had promised herself to never get seriously involved with another man unless they had a future together. A future she couldn't see.

"What did you see for Brad?" asked Lilia.

"The bank will transfer him to Hong Kong in the next couple of months."

"Good silk in Hong Kong," Lilia offered. Then she added, "Cruel trade, silk."

"He'll marry someone from mainland China."

"How lovely for him," sighed Lilia.

"Yes, remind me to send chopsticks," Rowie snapped.

"Why don't you continue seeing him until he leaves?" asked Gwendolyn.

"What's the point?"

"We may see the future, Rowie, but we must live in the present."

"Thank you, Confucius, but it's over. He's already signed up to study Cantonese."

"I still think you should give him a chance."

"It's too late. You don't understand what it's like, Gran."

"That's not true. Both your mother and I have experienced the same thing . . . granted, a much milder form."

"I've just got to face it; I may never meet anyone."

"Rubbish," said Gwendolyn. "These things are fated. You will meet your One True Love, you will have a daughter and you will take over this business."

Rowie grabbed a pricing gun and started attacking some wind chimes. "And I obviously have no choice in the matter."

"Unfortunately for you, no." Gwendolyn shrugged. Who was she to buck tradition? Each new generation was raised knowing she would carry on the family traditions, as well as the name. It had been a fight to even continue the lineage. Historically speaking, the Shakespeare women weren't breeders. There had been no surviving boys since the 1600s, and each generation bore only one or two girls. The Burning Times had wreaked havoc on the line, as had a wild pig at a family reunion.

The women were part of a matriarchal line descending from William Shakespeare's great aunt Sylvie. (In fact, Sylvie had been better known in those days than

Shakespeares' her literary nephew. With her bright red hair and extensive herbal knowledge, she had always been in demand to deliver babies and heal the sick.) Sylvie bore one child, as did her daughter, Olivia. In the 1700s there was a surge in births, but by 1975, only Lilia and Bettina, a distant relative in England, were left to provide for the name. Lilia had Rowie, and around the same time, cousins Calypso and Nell were born in London.

Rowie knew the fate of the Shakespeare line was in her hands, but things didn't look too hopeful. She was roaring toward thirty (okay, she was twenty-eight) with no romantic prospects on the horizon.

Rowie felt overwhelmed. "Why me?"

Gwendolyn spoke slowly, as though to a child. "Well, who else will take over? Your mother couldn't organize a bucks' night in a brewery. Tell me, Rowena, who else is there? It's important we sort this out now, because I may be dead tomorrow."

"You're not going to die," said Rowie.

"We're all going to die," Lilia offered.

Rowie locked eyes with her grandmother, begging her to understand. "I need to find my own path."

"Your path was laid out at birth, Rowie. Accept it."

"How will I ever meet a guy when I'm stuck working here? All I meet are desperados and aging hippies."

Gwendolyn and Lilia both gasped, shocked at Rowie's rudeness and blatant disrespect for their beloved customers.

"Keep your voice down, young lady. I'll have you know, our male customers are a cut above the rest simply because they walked through that door. It takes courage to change." Gwendolyn fanned herself with the Post-its. "I can't talk about this right now. I feel a turn coming on."

Rowie picked up the wind chimes and stalked to the

front of the shop. Most women her age had proper careers, were having families, or both. She was always with her mother and grandmother, fighting over cuckoo clocks and hanging wind chimes.

Yes, it took courage to change, and Rowie desperately wanted a change. But sometimes she wondered if she'd ever have the courage.

Chapter Four

Drew Henderson couldn't remember the last time he'd cried. It hurt when the Marlins had whipped the Yankees in '03. He'd shed a tear or two at Yankee Stadium that night. But this? This pain was in a whole new ballpark. Could he help it if he was crying?

He'd been lying on a hospital gurney for three hours. Around him, total chaos reigned. Hurricane Hilda was roaring through the area and the emergency room at Plankaville Medical was bursting at the seams.

Drew was more scientific than religious. He didn't believe in God, but was open to admitting he was wrong. All he needed was some proof of existence. Yet suddenly, he found himself praying for help.

"Please . . . sir, I know there's a lot of people here who are worse off than me but, if you do exist, could you arrange for some pain medication or something . . . ? The shot they gave me didn't work. If you have time, that is . . ." Drew shook his head. The pain was obviously making him delirious.

"Mr. Henderson, I'm Dr. Hinchey."

Drew looked up at the doctor and smiled. Was that a glimmer of wings and a halo with that white coat? "Great to meet you, Doc. I'm in a helluva lot of pain. Do you think I could have another shot of something?"

The doctor closed the cubicle curtains, then removed her glasses and rubbed her eyes. She was obviously exhausted. "Yes, sorry about the wait. As you can see, things are out of control today. And we needed to see your X-rays before giving you anything else."

"Is my leg broken?" Stupid question really. He'd felt it snap.

"You have an open tibial shaft fracture."

"Which means what in English?"

"You've made a mess of your leg. The bone is broken, but there's also the risk of infection. When was your last tetanus shot?"

"I don't know . . . a couple of years back when I went to Cambodia." Drew looked faint. "So what's the deal?"

"Unfortunately, our options are limited. This area is in a state of emergency. Normally we'd airlift you, but we're going to have to deal with the injury here, with the resources we have."

"It'll be okay . . . won't it?"

The doctor took Drew's blood pressure. "Yes, but we'll have to put the leg in skeletal traction."

"Sounds painful."

"You'll be under general anesthetic."

"Can I be flown back to New York first?"

Dr. Hinchey shook her head. "The airport is closed. You're not going anywhere today . . . or for a while, actually."

"How long? A day or two?"

There was a beat before the doctor spoke. "At least six weeks."

The room started to spin. "What? I can't. I have a life. I have to get back to New York. To work."

"We'll consider transferring you back home once the bones knit, but there will still be months of rehabilitation."

Drew was flailing about like a fish out of water. "Months? But . . . but . . . I . . . there's things I need to do . . . I have a dog . . ."

Dr. Hinchey placed a hand on Drew's shoulder. The poor guy had been waiting for hours without complaining, only to be told that his life was going to be on hold for a long time. Not that she balked at the thought of having him around for a while. Drew Henderson was the most exciting thing to happen to Plankaville since *J. Lo*'s jet had been rerouted on the way to Miami. "It's a very serious injury, but you're lucky. You could've been killed."

Drew nodded. She was right. Death would have sucked, but this option wasn't much better.

Dr. Hinchey handed Drew a clipboard and pen. "You need to sign this."

"What's that?"

"It's a release form for surgery."

"I'm having surgery now?"

"You got something better to do?"

Drew began to panic. He felt like a five-year-old who wanted his mother. "Are there any other options?"

Dr. Hinchey slid her glasses back on. Good lord, he was handsome. "We're a small hospital and are operating with minimal resources today. We either get this leg in traction, or you can stay on this stretcher . . . or we can amputate."

Drew wasn't sure if she was joking.

An orderly entered the cubicle and released the brakes on the gurney. "Where to, Doc?"

"Mr. Henderson needs to go to pre-op."

The orderly grinned at Drew. "I'm Winston. Ready to roll?"

Drew felt a surge of fear. "I've got to contact my boss."

"Winston will wheel you past a phone on the way there. Do you have any allergies?"

"I'm allergic to pain," Drew joked.

"In my experience, most men are," chuckled Dr. Hinchey. Drew Henderson was a bright and incredibly hot-looking spot in a grueling day. "I'll see you up there."

Winston started wheeling Drew out the door. What had he done? How the hell could he put his life on hold for so long?

Drew stared at the ceiling as Winston whizzed him out of the ER and toward the elevator. He stopped at a desk and passed Drew a phone.

"You'd better make that call."

Drew started to dial his boss. Slowly. He rarely felt regret, but it filled his body now. Climbing on that roof had been one helluva bad idea.

Chapter Five

Drew was standing on top of a boat shed, yelling into the microphone. It was a fabulous shot. Behind him Hurricane Hilda roared toward the mainland. The ocean rocked under a black sky. Drew looked handsome and wild.

"As you can see, it's already volatile here. But this is nothing compared to what it'll be like later today. This part of the coast is experiencing king high tides, which will result in massive storm surges when Hilda hits. My advice is to stay indoors and don't do anything stupid."

Suddenly there was a loud crack and the roof fell in. The last word from Drew was a terrified, "Shiiiiit!"

Mac Roberts switched the TV off and turned to Jess.

"Ouch, that hurt," she said. "Excellent shot, though. We could use that as a promo for tonight's news."

Mac glared at her. He sat back behind his desk and scratched his head. "We've just lost our guaranteed number-one spot," he said.

Jess stared at the wall above her boss and pretended to be thinking of a solution. All she could think of was

Eva running her claws down Drew's back. Mac had already updated her on Drew's surgery. He'd also made it clear that he was furious to be left without his star weatherman. Worst of all, as far as Mac was concerned, it was all Jess's fault.

His voice was measured. "Any ideas for a replacement?"

Jess steadied her voice. "Eva is down there. She'll fill in for Drew at that end, and we already have Ray Wilson on for the long weekend."

"Excellent," snarled Mac. "That's three days covered."

"Can't we keep Ray on?"

"Nope, he's committed to that program on global warming. What about John Price? Women like him."

"Lobotomized women," Jess said. "He's got the presence of a brick."

"Jennifer Kelly's already on her summer break. So is Delice Robinson." Mac looked stressed. "Jesus, it's July. We're already working without most of our big names."

"Bill and Tina are on most of the summer, so we can afford to replace Drew with someone fresh."

"We could bring Eva back. She's got a solid fan base, and she's proved herself on weekends."

Jess gritted her teeth. "I don't think she's strong enough. Plus, the stats show the female audience hasn't really warmed to her."

Mac looked amazed. "Really? I've always thought she was cute."

"You would, you're male. Besides, cute is for puppies. We need someone special."

Mac was worried. "We need a goddamn miracle."

They sat quietly, desperately searching for a solution. Mac mindlessly played with the snow globe on his desk. He'd picked it up on a trip to Cairo. He liked shaking it and watching snow fall on the pyramids.

Jess glanced at her fingernails. She needed a manicure. She thought about Eva. Eva always had perfect nails. She was also the obvious choice to replace Drew, but Jess wouldn't let that happen. Not now.

Suddenly a crack of thunder broke the silence, and they both jumped.

"Holy shit," cried Mac. "Where'd that come from?"

Jess stood and walked to the window. It was raining. Pouring. Absolutely bucketing down.

"Did anyone predict that?" asked Mac.

Jess stared out the window and thought of the beautiful redhead she'd seen that morning. "Yes, actually, someone did." She turned to Mac, excited. "Mac, I have a brilliant idea."

"It'd want to be better than the last one you had."

Jess ignored his dig. "We need someone different to replace Drew. Someone who won't steal Drew's thunder, but will create a bit of her own."

"Her?" Mac asked, warily.

"Yes, her. There's this woman . . . it's a bit of a gimmick, but I think it could work."

Mac leant against his desk, his arms folded. "Is she a meteorologist?"

"Ah . . . sort of. Apparently she hasn't been wrong once in the last three years."

"That's impossible. No one is that accurate. She'd have to have a crystal ball or something."

"Funny you should say that." Jess paused for a moment. She could feel it in her gut. This would be a ratings winner. "How about . . . a psychic weather woman?"

Chapter Six

Rowie had an appointment for a reading. The client had never been to a psychic before but had nowhere else to turn. She stood at the counter and glanced warily around the shop. She was quite tall, with brown hair pulled back into a neat ponytail, and her features, while not beautiful, were pretty. In her simple tan skirt and cream shirt she looked practical and confident—an illusion shattered with one glance into her eyes. They gave the appearance of a deer caught in the headlights of a rather large truck.

Rowie led the woman upstairs to the Edgar Cayce Room, Rowie's favorite room to read in. It was a small windowless room, but thanks to a spell cast by a family friend, it was always filled with sunshine.

The woman didn't seem to notice the room's quirk. Rowie motioned for her to sit in one of the chairs placed on each side of a small table. Rowie then sat opposite her and popped a blank tape into the cassette recorder.

"What did you say your name was?"

"I didn't," said the woman. "I figured you could work that out yourself."

Rowie sighed. Why visit a clairvoyant if you intended to be difficult? There was nothing wrong with a good dose of cynicism, but it was unacceptable to be downright rude when you were the one who made the appointment.

"Your name is . . . you were named after your grandfather . . . starts with a G . . . ?" Rowie began.

"Georgette."

"Well, Georgette, I'm clairaudient, clairvoyant and clairsentient, which means I hear, see and feel things. Please remember, everything I tell you is written in sand, not stone. If you don't like something, go out there and change it. Use what I say here as a guide to assist you to make your own choices."

"Okay," Georgette murmured.

Rowie calmed herself. "To start with, I'm receiving a message from someone called Isabel who wants you to know she is around and looking out for you."

Georgette's eyes filled with tears.

"Isabel is your mother?"

Georgette nodded. "She died of . . . she died ten years ago."

Rowie paused, not sure how to continue. Isabel was speaking a hundred miles an hour, relieved to finally have someone listen. But Rowie wasn't sure how to relay the message to the distraught woman in front of her.

"Tell her to go straight to the doctor. It's not too late for her, but if she waits any longer it will be," Isabel screeched.

Rowie looked at Georgette. "What did you want to ask? Did you come about your boyfriend?"

Georgette nodded as a fresh set of tears began to flow.

"Okay," said Rowie. "But first there's a more pressing issue to discuss."

"What could be more pressing than catching Jay in bed with his ex?"

Rowie decided to cut straight to the chase. "You said your mother died of breast cancer."

"No, I didn't."

"Oh . . . that's what I'm picking up."

"Well, you're right," Georgette conceded.

"Do you have regular checks?"

"No. Why would I?"

"I'm not a doctor, Georgette, so I can't diagnose, but your mother is telling me you need to see one," Rowie explained.

"That's ridiculous," Georgette said. "I'm fit, healthy . . . I eat organic . . . I live on tofu."

Rowie sighed. "I'm passing on a message. You really need to see a doctor as soon as possible."

"Are you saying I have breast cancer?"

"You'll have to ask your doctor that."

Georgette laughed, not mentioning the tiny lump she had recently found and chosen to ignore. "That's great. I'm paying you sixty dollars to tell me I'm going to die."

"I never said that. I don't normally go into all this in a reading, as it's not my place to predict death. If I clearly saw your death, I'd keep my mouth shut and just give you a vague reading." Rowie tried to remain as detached as possible, but she ached for the girl opposite her, who was about to embark on the toughest journey of her life.

Rowie felt Georgette clam up, as though all that she had just told her had been locked in a vault for later.

"And what about my boyfriend?"

Rowie gritted her teeth and delivered yet more bad news. "He's not coming back. There is a man for you, though. You will meet him soon, and he'll love you in a way you never thought possible. I like the feel of him very much. He's tall. He might have something to do with children . . . You're a teacher, aren't you?"

Georgette nodded and looked shocked that Rowie had known.

"A good one, from what I gather." Rowie paused briefly, trying to decipher the images she was receiving. "This man may also have something to do with education . . . I'm not certain, but I see a red balloon, which would normally symbolize a child to me."

"A red balloon?"

"Yes," said Rowie. "It's very clear."

"So I'm not going to die?"

"We're all going to die, Georgette. I presume the fact that I see a man in your future means you won't be dying right now. Why don't you ask me some questions and we'll see what else comes up?"

"No, thanks. We'll leave it at that," Georgette said, reaching into her handbag. "Do you take Visa, or do you want cash?"

"Either is fine." Rowie removed the taped recording of the session for Georgette to take home.

Georgette placed the money on the table, then stood and straightened her skirt. She looked around the room and noticed that, despite the light, there were no windows. "How strange," she whispered before turning and holding out her hand. "Thank you for your time."

Rowie stood and shook Georgette's hand. "Good luck."

"If any of what you just said is true, then I'll need more than luck."

Rowie led her back into the shop, and Georgette left without saying another word. Gwendolyn looked at Rowie and smiled sadly, while Lilia patted her shoulder.

"Breast cancer?" Gwendolyn asked.

"I had to tell her."

"That's okay. Sometimes these messages are a warning."

Rowie nodded. "I just hope she goes to a doctor. She may have a chance."

The shop door jangled and a woman rushed in, shaking off her umbrella. She stalled when she noticed the three Shakespeare women standing together.

"Wow! Triplets." She made her way over to Rowie. "Was it you outside this morning? Predicting the weather?"

"Yes."

The woman grabbed Rowie's hand and shook it. "I'm Jess Walker. Can you really predict the weather?"

Rowie glanced at the umbrella dripping all over the counter. "It would appear so."

"Excellent. Can you show me how you do your . . . thang?"

Rowie glanced down at the appointment book. "I have a client in half an hour."

"That's fine. I don't need much time. Half an hour is great."

Rowie looked over at Gwendolyn, who nodded. The girl was obviously desperate. Rowie led Jess out the back and motioned for her to sit. She took a pack of cards and shuffled them. "Is there anything in particular that you need me to look into today?"

Jess shook her head. "Nope. Just show me how you do it."

Rowie pressed record on the tape deck and started laying out the cards. She spoke gently as she did so. "Remember, nothing I tell you is set in stone. You have the power to change things."

"Yep," said Jess, as she peeked at her watch.

"It's all about work at the moment. I see here that you're good at your job."

Jess rolled her eyes. Didn't need a psychic to tell her that.

Rowie continued, "You're in a tough field . . . journalism . . . TV?" Rowie paused and concentrated. "I'm getting both."

Goosebumps shot up Jess's arms. "Yes. TV news."

"You'll go far . . . if . . ." Rowie paused.

Jess leaned forward. "If what?"

"There's a guy connected to your work. You need to let it go."

"Is that a fact?"

Rowie looked up at Jess's piercing emerald eyes. "I believe so."

Jess felt hot. She squirmed back in her seat. "I have. Let it . . . him go."

Rowie saw straight through the lie. "No, you haven't."

"Well, I'm not a quitter."

"You're wasting your time. He's moved on. And so should you, before it affects your work."

Jess felt completely exposed. "Do you know everything?"

Rowie smiled, which helped ease the tension. "No. Not everything. Unless I kiss you."

Jess looked horrified. Was this witch hitting on her?

Rowie laughed. "It's this thing that happens when I kiss someone. I see their whole future in my head. Like a movie."

"That must make for an interesting sex life."

Rowie nodded. "I've had to dump some really great guys because of it."

"Why?"

"No point in wasting time with someone else's man. If I see that I'm not a part of his future, I might as well move on."

"Sounds like good time-management skills to me,"

said Jess. "So have you ever starred in one of these movies in your head?"

"No. And I won't. I'm waiting for a man I can't read."

"Someone mysterious?"

"Exactly."

Jess glanced at her watch again. Down to business. "So how does this relate to the weather?"

"The way I just tuned into you, it's the same, but on a grander scale," Rowie explained. "I tune into nature."

"How fascinating," said Jess, who thought it was anything but. Nature, shmatcher! Could she do this stuff on live television?

Rowie realized that Jess was humoring her. "It's just a silly neighborhood tradition."

"No, it's great. What else do the cards say?"

Rowie turned three more cards, and then looked at Jess in surprise. "You're not here for a reading at all. You're here to offer me a job."

Chapter Seven

Rowie was closing the shop when she heard a familiar shriek behind her.

"I came as fast as I could . . . or as fast as Qantas could!"

Rowie's heart leapt at the sound of Angel Sorrenti's voice. She spun around just in time to feel the full impact of Angel's curvy body hurling into her.

"I missed you," Angel howled. She held Rowie tight, pushing Rowie's face into her own enormous cleavage. "I got your e-mail. How dare you break up with Brad while I was back visiting the homeland. Are you okay?"

Rowie nodded. "I am now."

Angel Sorrenti was the type of woman who compelled men to paint and write poetry. She was tall with jet-black wavy hair, flashing blue eyes and lips that made Angelina Jolie look in desperate need of some collagen. In fact she looked a lot like Angelina Jolie, only over-inflated. She was a delicious mix of big breasts and big hips that didn't sag or dimple, but jiggled and swayed and made people think of sex, and sweat, and summer fruits. She was positively ripe and looked as though she had stepped straight off a Botticelli canvas.

They'd met when the magazine Angel worked for sent her over to Second Site to do a piece on psychics. Angel had admitted that while she didn't doubt Rowie's abilities, she thought it was "all a bunch of crap" anyway.

"Nothing like living one day at a time to see what the future has in store for you, darl," she had declared. "But hey, next time I want to bet on a horse I'll call you up."

Her honesty had been refreshing; her lack of interest in Rowie's clairvoyance was like a breath of fresh air. Rowie was used to people being nervous around her, or overly friendly in the hope that she would constantly feed them information about their futures.

Angel was different. Angel didn't care. She was a loud-mouthed Aussie girl who had been Rowie's friend, confidant, and line to all things wicked and wild for the past three years. She entertained Rowie for hours with stories of the poor heartbroken men she left in her wake; for although her name was Angel, everything from her looks to her husky laugh to the way she roared through life, reeked of the devil.

"I'm so sorry I wasn't here for you. How are you handling things?"

Rowie smiled. "Better, now you're home. When did you get back?"

"This morning. I can feel jet lag creeping up behind me like a Catholic priest. Want a beer? Beer is the best thing for jet lag . . . and broken hearts . . . and anything, for that matter." Angel pulled a six-pack of Bondi Blondes out of her bag, opened two and handed one to Rowie.

"I've got a friendly merlot in there as well," she giggled.

Rowie locked the shop door and the two friends curled up on a lounge with their drinks. Angel plopped her feet up on a coffee table, guzzled back some beer and let out an obnoxious burp.

"God, I love beer," she sighed.

"So how was Sydney?" asked Rowie.

"Brilliant, darling. The Aussie peso is so bloody weak that when I converted all my money I felt like a well-fed Hilton chick. I shopped, I shagged, I partied. I'd love you to come back with me one day."

"I will, definitely," Rowie said.

Angel rolled her eyes. "That's not one of your hokey pokey little insights, is it? A little flash of the two of us cruising around Sydney in a convertible filled with party-loving surfers?"

"No." Rowie laughed. "Just hope."

"Thank God for that because I can't stand surfers. They have small willies. I think it's because of the pressure from the wetsuit. It stunts the growth," said Angel. "So are you totally devastated?"

"No," Rowie admitted. "I'm used to it."

"I didn't like him."

"Thanks for telling me now," Rowie laughed.

"I mean, he was nice enough, but he was a bit insipid. He had small feet and you know what that means?"

"Small shoes?" Rowie offered.

"Exactly," Angel said. "And also that you were lucky you didn't do more than kiss him."

"You're obsessed."

"No, just particular. So, what else has been happening?"

Rowie took a sip of her beer and tried not to sound too excited. "I've been offered a job."

"No way!" Angel shrieked. "Where?"

Rowie told her about Drew's accident. "It's only temporary, while he's away."

"That's amazing. Brilliant." Angel paused for a moment. "Will you get to meet handsome Henderson?"

"Unlike you and my grandmother, I'm not obsessed with the guy." Rowie looked at Angel and they both giggled. "Although he is hot."

Angel threw her empty bottle into the trash. "How did Gwendolyn react?"

"I haven't told her yet," Rowie admitted.

Angel slapped Rowie's arm. "You've got to stand up to her. I love Gwennie, but she's a manipulative old cow. You have every right to do this."

"I know," Rowie said.

"Go tell her. Get it over with now. I'd better go home anyway. I'm a bit pissed."

"Who with?"

"Pissed. Drunk," Angel translated.

Rowie smiled. She still got confused by some of Angel's Australianisms. "You're losing your touch. We only had one beer."

"You had one, my princess. I, on the other hand, have been drinking for twenty-six hours straight, courtesy of Qantas."

"The spirit of Australia."

"And my spirit of choice was vodka."

Angel fell silent for a moment and stared at the resident statue of Ganesha, who, as always, stared right back. Gwendolyn had discovered the statue in India after it had called her name as she passed. He was shipped back home and had taken a place of pride next to the counter at Second Site ever since. It was rumored among New York's New Age community that he brought great luck to whoever kissed his trunk during the first full moon of summer. It was a tale that had lines of tie-dyed quasi-Hindus lining up for hours with their best beeswax lip balm.

"What's his name again?" Angel asked.

"Ganesha. He's the patron god of artists and writers. You should ask him to help you write that book you're always talking about."

Angel rolled her eyes. "Yeah, I'll do that."

"He's also the remover of life blockages."

"Then you'd better ask for his help when you speak to Gwendolyn."

"I was going to," said Rowie seriously.

"And I thought I was weird." Angel turned back to Ganesha. "Hey, big boy, is that a trunk on your face or are you just glad to see me?" She chuckled and, with a wicked gleam in her eye and a lick of her plump, pouty lips, she sauntered out the door.

Chapter Eight

The Grove was a grand old home, with creaking floorboards, rickety stairs and a hodgepodge of floors and furniture. Unlike many of the area's brownstones, which had been renovated or turned into apartments, the house stood exactly as it had the day the Shakespeare family bought it.

Spread over four floors, the house contained a labyrinth of rooms, many never used. People regularly gathered in the kitchen, the heart of the home, or the attic, which was used for séances. In summer the garden, the family's constant and vital link to Mother Nature, teemed with friends. Surrounded by walls and tall trees, the garden gave the Shakespeares the privacy people of their kind needed. It shielded them from the prying eyes of neighbors who, through lack of understanding, feared them. For their own kind however—psychics, spiritualists, Witches, students of the old ways and the new ways—the door of the rambling old house was always open. In a city where it was unheard of to leave windows and doors unlocked, they had no worries about intruders. Not since a Romany friend had placed the Mark of the Gypsy over their house forty years earlier.

Gwendolyn wandered the house dusting and occasionally placing a Post-it on something she'd forgotten she owned. She drifted into the lounge and noticed Lilia curled up reading.

"Can I get you anything, love?"

"Yes, thanks, that would be nice," Lilia said, barely glancing up.

Gwendolyn looked to see what Lilia was reading and realized the book was upside down. How she'd ever given birth to such a strange creature was beyond her. Lilia's entrance into the world had nearly killed Gwendolyn. Lilia had refused to leave the fluid world of her mother's womb, and Gwendolyn had screamed and cried and pushed to no avail for two horrific days. The midwife and the spirits failed to coax the child out, so it was a bespectacled doctor and a huge set of tongs that finally dragged Lilia into the world.

Stubborn and aloof from the very start, Lilia refused to breathe until the doctor gave her a hard whack on her milky white butt, which shocked her into taking her first gasp. But she never cried, never whined. She even bottled in the despair of her birth. Lilia still bottled everything away, so much so that she often forgot what was bothering her and would wander around worried about something she couldn't quite recall.

Gwendolyn sidled over to a table laden with family photos and picked up one of Lilia as a child. Lilia's burgundy hair fell in gentle undulating waves over her shoulders, and her skin remained so translucent that it was almost blue, like the sea she appeared to be floating under. Lilia had been, and still was, the most stunning creature Gwendolyn had ever seen. Fifty-odd years after her birth, Gwendolyn was still surprised that such perfection had sprung from her own body.

She put the photo down and reached for one of Rowie, undoubtedly the greatest love of her life. She looked just like Lilia, but without the hazy edges and liquid eyes. Rowie worried Gwendolyn. She seemed unhappy, restless, although Gwendolyn couldn't understand why. Hadn't she provided everything the girl needed?

Dorian was always telling her to get off Rowie's back, but that was easy for him to say. He was rarely around, and Lilia couldn't raise a rabbit. Someone had to take responsibility for Rowie. Gwendolyn had always been the responsible one.

She picked up a framed photo of herself and Dorian on their wedding day.

"You're not getting melancholy on me, are you?"

Gwendolyn jumped and realized her late husband had appeared behind her. "I didn't know you were at home."

Together they peered at the photo. "You looked beautiful in that dress."

"It's still in the attic somewhere." Gwendolyn sighed. How quickly time had passed. It seemed like only yesterday that she'd first locked eyes with him.

When they had met, Dorian was struggling with a small funeral parlor he'd inherited from his father. He'd never liked the hushed tones and morbid colors of his father's work, but endeavored to keep the business afloat out of respect for his parents. During the week he spoke in subdued, considerate whispers as he buried and burnt his customers. Then on his days off he sang loudly as he tended his garden. Dorian's garden was as Mother Nature intended, with a mass of flowers and plants supporting one another's existence and where weeds were equally admired.

He carved tiny chairs and tables and placed them underneath bushes and hanging plants. He painted small signs that invited wood folk and elementals to feel at ease in his garden. Faeries, elves and mystical animals—creatures that now hid in other realms, wary of the human race and its fear of the unknown—grew to trust him, and their festivities in his yard could be heard late into the night.

It was the nature spirits that had orchestrated Dorian's first meeting with Gwendolyn. Her mother, the world famous Rosina Shakespeare, had just died when Gwendolyn discovered a leaflet in her mailbox. It said: *Feel like you're six feet under with all the decisions to be made? Trust is a must and in us you can trust. Call Cunningham and Sons for all your funeral needs.*

To Gwendolyn it was a sign and, to the delight of the watchful spirits, she went straight over to Cunningham and Sons.

Dorian answered the door and felt a lightning bolt of love hit him straight in the chest.

"Are you Cunningham or one of the sons?" Gwendolyn asked, aware she had just met her future husband.

"Cunningham Senior is dead. I'm his son."

"What about his other sons?"

"There are none."

"Then why the name?"

"My father always lived in hope," Dorian explained.

"Then he must have been a good man," Gwendolyn said. "I'm looking for someone to bury my mother, but I don't want any hushed voices, morbid speeches or black clothes. I would rather bury her in the backyard than subject her to that crap."

Dorian had led her into his life, and she stayed. The next week was a busy one for the new couple. They mourned Gwendolyn's mother, then celebrated their own marriage. They bought The Grove, and a short while later Second Site. A year later, Lilia was born, and they felt their life was complete.

Of course, their relationship had changed over the years . . . as relationships do, even true love. Then Dorian had left her for a while, which had been devastating. And although he'd eventually returned, it was never the same again. Gwendolyn was used to feeling lonely now, especially when he was around.

Gwendolyn placed the photo back on the table. "Where have you been for the last week, Dorian?"

"Here and there."

Gwendolyn turned on him, her green eyes flashing angrily. "Sometimes I don't know why you bother coming home at all."

"Oh, don't start, woman. I'm doing the best I can."

"Well, your best isn't bloody good enough."

Dorian looked like he was about to say something, but stopped. Instead he turned and left the room.

Gwendolyn gulped back her tears. She refused to cry. She made her way to the four urns, on what she called the "mantel of marital mortality." Dorian hadn't been the only man in her life!

Urn number one was husband number one: Ed. Gwendolyn and Ed had met and married when they were too young and too stupid to know any better. He had been killed when he fell down a manhole, the first recorded death of its kind in New York State.

The second urn was Tedious Tom. He had been the dullest man on earth, although this fact hadn't transpired until well after their wedding. Tom had choked to death on a fishbone, despite Gwendolyn pleading with him to turn vegetarian, like her. She'd contacted him during a séance not long after he died, and he admitted she'd been right.

The third urn was a boy Lilia had married just out of high school. He'd been conscripted to go to Vietnam.

Lilia had known he wouldn't come home, and he'd been so in love with her that she felt marrying him was the least she could do.

Gerry had gone off to war with a smile on his face and the naive belief that everything would be okay. Under the circumstances, and with no choice in the matter, it was the best way to be. Lilia had grieved, but only for a lost life, not a lost husband. It would be six more years before she met her one true love: Rowie's father.

And then finally . . . there was Dorian, or his ashes, anyway. More often than not she labeled it pain encased in ceramic. Sometimes Gwendolyn had the overwhelming urge to pour the ashes over her head, to rub them into her skin. Just to find some remnant of something physical to connect with. But she was practical enough to know it wouldn't work . . . and she hated vacuuming.

Gwendolyn wiped a tear from her eye. Sometimes she felt her life was rather empty. It was why she continued to cling to tradition and to her family, past and present. The walls of The Grove were lined with portraits of redheaded women: the glue that held her together. There was Rosslyn Shakespeare, burned at the stake in 1642; Ariadna Shakespeare, who bore the illegitimate child of King James VI of Scotland; Muriel Shakespeare, who wrote poetry that healed the reader; Yvonne Shakespeare, midwife to Queen Victoria. It was an illustrious history, a difficult one to live up to. Even Gwendolyn recognized that.

The front door slammed and Rowie entered. Gwendolyn grabbed her Post-it notes and stuck one on a portrait of ancestor Margot.

"You look so much like Margot Shakespeare," she said to Rowie. "She took over the family business when her mother was burned at the stake, and she was only twelve at the time."

"That's interesting," said Rowie, who'd heard it all before. She noticed her mother in the corner. "Weren't you going out on a date tonight, Mom?"

"I had to cancel," said Lilia. "He arrived wearing the most awful shoes. Brown slip-on things."

Rowie glanced at Gwendolyn, who nodded. "They were awful."

Lilia was constantly being asked out. She was a bright flame and every man who met her was a dull flapping moth. She found it difficult to refuse the suitors and was often quite excited by the prospect of a date. But when the day arrived, she usually found a reason for not going. No man was good enough. No man quite right. No man lived up to Rowie's father.

Not that Rowie would know for sure, as she'd never seen him. Her parents had met briefly when they were young, and were torn apart by circumstances—or so Lilia said. But in Lilia's mind and the stories she told, Rowie's father was the man to end all men. There was no one else, and she was just biding time until fate threw them back together.

Rowie steeled herself. "I need to talk to you both. Something happened today."

Lilia put the book down and sat up. She was up to a difficult part anyway and really couldn't understand what she was reading.

Gwendolyn sat beside Lilia on the couch. "We're listening."

"That girl today . . . the one who had the short reading . . ."

"The desperate one?" Gwendolyn asked.

Rowie nodded. "She's a producer with USBC news. The weather, actually."

Gwendolyn looked excited. She loved USBC's weatherman. "Oh, does she work with Handsome Henderson?"

"Yes. And he's had an accident. He fell off a boat-shed roof." Rowie noticed her grandmother's distraught face. "He's fine, but he'll be in the hospital for a while. They need a replacement." She spoke slowly and clearly. "They've asked me."

Gwendolyn smiled. "How kind. Were they upset when you said no?"

"I said yes."

Gwendolyn looked like someone had punched her in the gut. She doubled over and started gasping. "I can't breathe. . . . oh . . . oh . . . help!"

Rowie and Lilia rolled their eyes at each other. They'd seen this act before. Rowie ran to the kitchen and returned with some Bach Rescue Remedy and a bottle of peppermint oil. Lilia held the essential oil under her mother's nose.

"Just breathe, Mom."

"Oh Goddess, don't take me yet," gasped Gwendolyn. "There's no one to take over the shop."

"Don't be so melodramatic, Gran," Rowie said as she squirted the Rescue Remedy near Gwendolyn.

"Melodramatic? Shakespeare women have been in the business of healing and predictions for over five hundred years. Fighting constant persecution to honor The Gift."

"I know. Boy, do I know," snapped Rowie.

Gwendolyn was genuinely at a loss. "How can you not respect such a great history?"

"I do respect it . . . as my past. I just don't see why it has to be my future as well."

"You can't escape your Gift."

"I'm not trying to. I'll be reaching more people than ever."

"By turning it into a freak show."

"You admire John Edwards, Mom," Lilia reminded. "And you've always said Drew Henderson is an excellent weatherman."

"Al Roker is better."

Lilia stroked her mother's head. "You were thrilled when they put up that billboard across the road. You said he was the perfect man to keep watch over us."

"Only a fool would fall off a boat shed."

"The job is only while he's in the hospital," Rowie explained. "Please, Gran."

Gwendolyn thought about it for a moment. Rowie looked so excited. And business was slow at this time of year. "Oh, okay. But then I need you back at the shop. I'm not long for this world and I need to know the business is safe before I go."

Rowie nodded and walked out of the room. She didn't have the strength to fight for total freedom. This would have to be enough.

Chapter Nine

Jack Witterspoon stared at Drew's sleeping face. He looked so peaceful. Who would think that the guy was a complete and utter idiot? For as much as Jack loved Drew, only a complete and utter idiot would take on a category 5 hurricane.

"Drew . . . buddy . . . wake up. C'mon, Drew, open your eyes."

Drew's eyelids fluttered.

"That's it, open them. C'mon, Drew."

Drew was thrust out of a dream about Charlize Theron into the harsh reality of his hospital room.

"What the . . . where . . ."

"Drew, it's me. Jack . . . your favorite agent. Wakey wakey."

Drew took a moment to settle back into his body. Everything was fuzzy and confusing. "Where am I?" he mumbled.

"In the hospital."

"In New York?"

"No, buddy, you're still in Florida."

"Then what are you doing here?"

"I came down with the Air Force. On a media flight," Jack said.

Drew closed his eyes for a moment as he relived the fall. "How's Hilda?"

"She's moved on, leaving nothing but a trail of destruction behind."

Drew smirked. "I've had a few girlfriends like that."

"Haven't we all," Jack chuckled. "How are you feeling?"

"Better now that the morphine's kicked in." Drew noticed the frame around the bed and his leg, now in traction. "Guess I won't be dancing for a while."

"You're lucky you're breathing, you dipshit. I'm so mad at you. You nearly killed yourself."

Drew looked up at his agent and grinned. Jack didn't get angry. He was too laid-back. But Drew could tell he was worried.

Jack was a big bear of a man with a heart to match. A devotee of transcendental meditation, he looked much younger than his sixty years. He was an interesting combination of hard-hitting businessman and heartfelt hippie. His appearance was smart and neat, a man comfortable in his own body. His mind was a razor-sharp, eclectic mix of beliefs and ideas. He relied on his gut instincts in business and only took on projects that meant something to him. He didn't work for the money, but because he was passionate about his job, yet the money came anyway, as it often does when people follow their dreams.

"I spoke to your doctor," Jack said. "They rarely use traction anymore. Looks like you got lucky."

"I can't believe I'm stuck here," Drew groaned.

"Perhaps we can find a way to speed up your healing

process," said Jack. "I know a great Reiki healer . . ."

"No, no, no," Drew interrupted. "You are such a closet hippie. I bet you wear tie-dye boxers."

"I'm serious."

"No, thanks."

"He's been on *Oprah*," Jack continued. "The guy is gifted."

"So are the doctors here."

A pretty blond nurse entered and checked Drew's chart. He raised an eyebrow and grinned. Maybe being stuck in the hospital wouldn't be so bad.

"Hi, I'm Drew."

"So it says on your chart."

"Are you my nurse?"

The nurse slammed the chart shut. "This isn't the Hilton, although you're obviously used to special treatment."

"What do you mean?" asked Drew.

The nurse glared at him. "The rest of the hospital is packed, yet you have your own room. Someone pulled some major strings for you, Mr. Henderson."

Drew looked at Jack, who shrugged. "It's like a zoo out there. It's a win-win situation: you get your own space, they get a new incubator in maternity."

Drew turned back to the nurse. "There's plenty more room in here for other patients."

"I'll let the doctors know, Mr. Henderson."

"Just Drew." He upped the flirt factor. "Are all the nurses here like you?"

"You mean overworked and underpaid?" She was determined not to give in to Drew's charms. It was better to keep a professional distance when bedpans were involved.

Drew checked her nametag: Ingrid Linz.

"I have so much respect for nurses. It's the toughest job around."

Ingrid softened slightly and took Drew's wrist.

Drew relaxed back into his pillows and grinned. "If my pulse is faster than normal, it's because of you."

Ingrid cracked and blushed. Jack shook his head. He was used to the effect Drew had on women.

"I'll check on you later," Ingrid promised. "If there's anything you need, just buzz me."

Ingrid left and Drew turned back to Jack. "Where were we?"

Jack shook his head, amazed. "I can't believe you just hit on your nurse. You realize at some point today, she'll have to check your bedpan."

Drew blanched at the thought. He suddenly felt depressed. "Get me out of here, Jack."

"The only way to get out of here is to heal that leg. How about acupuncture?"

Drew held up a hand. "Enough with the hoodoo voodoo."

"You put way too much faith in western medicine, Drew."

"It's a science worth trusting, Jack."

"Okay, fine. How else can I help? Can I get you some magazines or something?"

Drew's face filled with worry. "Can you swing by my place when you get home? My dog, Norm, needs to be fed."

"How do I get on?" Jack asked. Drew lived on a boat, so it wasn't just a matter of opening an apartment with a key.

"I'll call the boat basin and tell them you're coming," said Drew. "It's just until I can arrange for someone to take him."

"It's no problem."

"When do you fly home?"

"I'm still waiting to hear," said Jack.

"My neighbor has been feeding him, but I told her

I'd be home by tomorrow." Drew looked anxious. "She's going sailing over the weekend. Who'll feed him then?"

Jack knew how much Drew loved his mutt. "I'll look after it," he promised. "Is that all?"

"Another thing." Drew looked rather sheepish. "Can you swing by my hotel? I need you to give someone a message."

Jack could see what was coming. "Who is she?"

"Eva Sanchez."

Jack threw his arms up in defeat. "I told you to stop chasing women at work. Remember last time? You made it out by the skin of your teeth. Listen to me: Mixing business with pleasure is bad!"

"You make it sound like I do it all the time," Drew said.

"Twice in quick succession. Just as bad."

"I like Eva. Just let her know what's happening."

Ingrid stuck her head back into the room. "Delivery for you . . . Drew." She passed him a package and disappeared again. Drew ripped open the wrapping. It was an electronic Sudoku, with a card attached. "Hey handsome," Drew read out loud. "How clumsy of you. That fall just ended a short but oh so sweet relationship. Hospitals aren't my thing, but I am thinking about you and hope that bone of yours heals quickly. Thanks for all the fun times. See you back in New York. Love, Eva. P.S. Hope the Sudoku helps pass the time." Drew stared at the card for a moment. "I guess she's not going to wait for me."

"The type of woman that eats her young, buddy."

"Lucky I'm on morphine or that could hurt." Drew tossed the card into the bin beside the bed. "By the way, have you spoken to Mac?"

"I spoke, he screamed. He's not happy, but they've got someone to replace you."

"Who?"

"Someone new. A woman. Apparently she does a weather report in New York. I haven't heard of her, so it must be with a cable station."

"Do I get a say in this?"

"Yes. They're going to bring her down for a meet and greet when the airport reopens." Jack scanned the contraption that was holding Drew's leg together. "Is there anything else you need me to do for you while I'm here?"

Drew was silent for a moment, and then he laid on his most charming smile. "Jack, buddy . . . just one more thing."

Jack placed his hand on Drew's shoulder. "What is it?"

"Could you deal with my bedpan while you're here? You won't have to worry about me hitting on you."

Chapter Ten

Rowie stood staring up, in front of the USBC building. It loomed before her like a mythical obelisk. The shows created by USBC were an integral part of her cultural heritage, her past. And with any luck this building was the key to her future as well.

She suddenly felt sick.

Rowie adjusted her dress. She'd torn her wardrobe apart searching for the right outfit, eventually settling on an old favorite. It was a jade green Marc Jacobs number that matched her eyes and set off her hair. She looked gorgeous in it.

She joined the throng of people heading through the doors. Everyone was in a hurry. The foyer was filled with screens displaying footage from the network's roster of shows. Ann Mayer, America's leading journalist, was interviewing Ban Ki-moon. Another screen played an episode of the hit series *The Coven*. A third showed Drew Henderson, unaware of what a hurricane had in store for him.

She made her way through security and to the elevator. A good-looking Asian guy pressed the button for her and smiled.

"What floor?" he asked as they got in.

"Fourth."

"Me too. You an intern?"

"No I . . . I might be doing the weather."

The guy smiled and thrust out his hand. "You're Drew's replacement? I'm Shin Higaki. The floor director. We'll be working together."

Rowie shook his hand. "Rowie Shakespeare, nauseated beginner."

"You'll be fine," Shin said.

The doors opened on the main floor of the news center. It was already busy, despite being barely eight A.M.

"News doesn't keep regular office hours. This is the first shift. We'll be taking over for them," Shin explained. "Who were you told to look for?"

"The news director."

"Mac Roberts? First door on the left down that corridor," said Shin. "I'll see you around. Oh, and Rowie?"

Rowie turned. "Yes?"

"Remember to breathe." Shin gave a wave and walked off in the opposite direction. Rowie headed to Mac's office and knocked on the door.

"Enter," came the growl from inside.

Rowie opened the door and noticed Jess seated on a couch.

"Rowie," Jess said, standing to greet her. "This is Mac."

Mac's eyes narrowed as he examined Rowie. She was gorgeous, but in a wholesome way. She certainly didn't look like a whack job. "Good to meet you, Rowie. I've heard great things about you. Take a seat."

Mac was short, stocky, with a mop of gray hair, a goatee and tattoos poking out his rolled-up shirt-sleeves. He looked more like an aging biker than the news director at the nation's top television station.

"So, Rowie, damn good to have you on board."

Rowie smiled. He was as rough as a Brazilian wax job, but she immediately liked him. "Thanks. I'm looking forward to it."

Mac explained a bit about the network and what they expected from Rowie. "Networks have been using gimmicks for years to sell the weather. Admittedly, we've always used trained meteorologists at USBC, but this is only short term, so it should work." Mac glanced at Jess, as if to say, *And if it doesn't, you're to blame.*

Jess jumped right in. "NBC has scouts trawling comedy shows looking for potential weather people. It's the way of the future. Weather needs to be entertaining to be accessible."

Mac nodded. He didn't disagree. Most people had the attention span of a goldfish nowadays. However, using a seasoned stand-up comedian was very different from transmitting a psychic into America's living rooms.

"I'm a bit nervous," Rowie admitted. "This is such an important network and I . . ."

Mac interupted. "Don't think of it in those terms. You're not batting for the whole of USBC. This is the New York station and we're independently run. No pressure . . . well, not much, anyway. Keep it simple and you'll be fine."

Rowie smiled gratefully. "Thanks."

"Honestly, Rowie," offered Jess. "All you need to concentrate on is your spooky-wooky predictions."

Rowie smiled at Jess, but she felt uncomfortable. Jess seemed eager to work with her, yet every kind word, every compliment, had a dark underlying edge.

"Alrighty," said Mac. "I guess we'd better test you

before we go any further. Jess will show you around, and then give you a bit of training on the studio floor. I've had the Chromakey and monitors turned on so you can rehearse. Jess will explain what they are. I'll meet you down there."

Jess led Rowie out of Mac's office and through the news center, pointing to rooms as they passed. "That's the global weather center. Next to it are the extreme weather guys. You don't need to worry about all that. I'll give you a rundown each day, detailing which stories to cover."

"A rundown?"

Jess spoke quickly. "Yes, like there's been twenty inches of snow in Denver and a tornado in Kansas. Briefly touch on what's happening nationally. The major stories. No one gives a shit about nice weather. Stick to that at the start of each segment, then do your little woo-woo thing."

Jess opened a door and motioned for Rowie to follow her. "This is the control room. The director will be in here, not on the floor with you. I'll also be here to keep an eye on how you're doing, along with some audio technicians and graphic operators."

Rowie noticed an attractive woman sitting at a computer in the corner. She had very short blond hair and a tall, lean body. Judging by the way she glared at Jess, the two women had issues.

"Rowie, this is Michelle. She's one of our meteorologists."

Rowie offered her hand and Michelle grudgingly shook it.

"You're Drew's replacement?"

"I hope so. As long as I don't mess up this test."

"Can't you predict if you will?" Michelle smirked before stalking out.

Jess shrugged her off. "Ignore her. Like most of the

female species here, she's having Drew Henderson withdrawals. Come on, let's get you trained."

Jess led Rowie into the studio. It was smaller than it appeared on television. Rowie noticed the news desk.

"Bill and Tina, the anchors, will be there," Jess explained. "They'll introduce you and the three of you will chat for fifteen seconds. Not a millisecond more. The banter will appear spontaneous, but it will be scripted."

Rowie was horrified to hear that. She'd always loved getting her news from Bill Anderson and Tina Eanis. They were an American institution. "Is all their banter scripted?"

"Most of it. Bill and Tina have the combined IQ of a brick. We don't need them commenting on world events while they're on air."

"What are they like?" asked Rowie, not willing to believe Bill and Tina were anything but consummate professionals and darn nice people.

"Utter assholes. And they despise each other. But hey, they're pretty, and America trusts them." Jess pulled Rowie over to a large screen. "This is your area. You'll be here, in front of the greenscreen. Have you ever used one of these before?"

"Never needed one outside Second Site."

"I guess not," said Jess. "Basically, you do the weather in front of this wall. It looks like you're pointing to a map, but you're not. The technical director will take you and superimpose you over the computer-generated weather graphics. Simple, really."

Rowie stared at Jess like she was crazy. "So what do I point to?"

"Nothing. But if you keep your eye on this monitor in front of you, you'll see the graphics there. Now that's not as easy as it seems, because the image is reversed."

Jess jumped in front of the greenscreen and started

pointing. "See when I point to New York but it comes up that I'm pointing to California? Easy."

A guy with coffee-colored skin and a smile that made the Osmonds look in need of floss entered the studio and waved at Jess.

"Hi, Taye," she called. "Come and meet Rowie."

Taye was the director. He was relaxed and cheery, the kind of person who didn't buckle easily. He drilled Rowie in her technique and got her to practice on the Chromakey.

"Remember, the viewers need to think you're talking to them. You've got to look straight into this camera."

Rowie's hands were starting to shake. What had she gotten herself into? "That camera there? Right."

"And do everything backwards," he reminded her.

"That shouldn't be too difficult," Rowie joked, and then doubled over in panic. "I don't feel very well."

"You don't have to be the perfect meteorologist," Jess said, almost kindly. "Drew Henderson has that market covered. You just need to be an amusing distraction. Do what you do outside the shop every morning and you'll be fine."

"Let's test you," said Taye.

Rowie watched him make his way into the tech box and noticed Mac already waiting there.

Jess grabbed her arm and pushed her into position. "Look into the camera in front of you and read the teleprompt." She waited for a cue from Mac and then motioned for Rowie to start.

"Good evening. I'm . . . ah . . ."

Jess rolled her eyes. "The asterisk means 'insert your own name.' Do you think you can manage that?"

"Sorry. I'm a bit nervous."

"Okay . . . start again."

"Good evening. I'm Rowie Shakespeare. Heavy rains battered the Northwest today, causing widespread flooding." Rowie raised her arm and by utter fluke, pointed straight at the Northwest.

"Excellent," whispered Jess.

Rowie cruised her way through the script and managed to point to Cleveland, Cincinnati and the whole of Texas without too much difficulty. Before she knew it, she'd finished. "That wasn't too hard," she said.

"You weren't too bad," said Jess, relieved.

Mac and Taye made their way back into the studio.

"That was great, Rowie. The camera certainly loves you," said Taye.

Mac nodded and continued. "There's one slight hiccup. Drew Henderson has an approval clause in his contract. Unless he's fired, which would obviously never happen, he gets to approve his replacement. And seeing as he's stuck in the hospital . . . the mountain moves to Muhammad."

Rowie looked confused.

"You have to fly to Florida . . . now. To meet Drew," Mac clarified. "If all goes well, then you're on tonight at six."

Jess glanced at her reflection in the camera. "Should we get Drew some flowers . . . from all of us here?"

"I'm not taking flowers and you're not going." Mac challenged Jess with his eyes. He had no idea what had transpired between Jess and Drew, but today wasn't the day for them to reconnect and rehash history. "Ready, Rowie?"

"I . . . yeah . . . sure." A quick trip to Florida to meet America's dreamiest man before making her television debut? Ready? Why wouldn't she be?

Chapter Eleven

Drew was playing Sudoku while Jack gave him the run-down on Rowie. "So if you agree, she'll go on tonight. If not, they'll probably go with John Price."

"And then I'll have to spend months coaxing my viewers back. John has as much appeal as a bowl of tripe."

Jack placed his laptop in front of Drew and showed him Rowie's photo. "She's better-looking than John."

Drew gazed at the photo. She was gorgeous. "Where did she study?"

"Mac didn't say, but apparently she's been doing the weather for years and has quite a following."

"I've never seen her before." Drew was certain he'd remember her if he had. "Where did Mac find her?"

As if on cue, Mac strode into the room. "Freakin' airport is a mess." He glared at Drew, obviously still pissed over the accident. "You in pain?"

"A bit."

"Good." Mac rambled on about what an idiot Drew was, but Drew wasn't listening. His gaze was focused on the woman standing in the doorway. Tiny, beautiful, with creamy skin and flaming hair, real-life Rowie Shakespeare packed an unexpected punch. Drew was horrified to feel himself go hard. He grabbed the tray and positioned it over his crotch.

Her emerald eyes scanned the room, then rested on him. He saw them flicker with sympathy, and then she smiled. It was like someone had lifted the roof and let in the sunshine. Quite simply, she was a knockout. Drew didn't care if she yodeled the weather while she juggled artichokes. There was no way such a creature would ruin his ratings.

Rowie took a moment to compose herself before entering the room. She was coping remarkably well until she actually laid eyes on Drew and felt all her blood heat and then drain from her legs. The guy was way hotter in real life than on TV. Even flat on his back—a position Rowie would love to see him in more often—Drew Henderson exuded a powerful presence. Long, muscular limbs, tanned skin, sea-blue eyes that could stop a woman in her tracks from the other side of a hospital room. She noticed his hands and wondered what they'd feel like running over her bare skin.

She felt transparent and incredibly shy. Thankfully he looked equally surprised to see her, but pulled himself together quickly and gave her a lazy grin.

"Excuse me if I don't get up."

Rowie moved toward his outstretched hand. Their fingers wrapped around each other's. There was a moment of mutual confusion as they both felt a charge of electricity when they touched.

Her green eyes searched deep within his blue ones. Was the recognition mutual? "I'm Rowie. I'm sorry about the accident."

"I shouldn't have been up there." Drew glanced at Mac. "Yes, Mac, I admit it."

Mac's anger visibly dissolved. "Good. And, ah . . . I was going to bring you flowers, but couldn't take the time."

"It's the thought that counts." Drew motioned to Jack. "Rowie, this is Jack, my agent."

Jack grabbed Rowie's hand in a warm shake. "It's so great to meet you. Do you have representation?"

Rowie shook her head, confused, but had to laugh at the man's enthusiasm. "No . . . I . . . I don't even know what that means."

Jack pulled a business card out of his pocket and thrust it at her. "Someone to find you work after this. Call me, we'll talk."

Rowie nodded. She had no idea who Jack was, but instinctively liked him.

Jack stared at Rowie for a moment. She reminded him of someone, but he couldn't think who. "Do you do past-life regressions?"

"My mother does."

"I had a regression once. Interesting stuff."

Drew gave a snort. "No doubt you were royalty, like everyone else who does it."

"Nope. No one famous." Jack grinned and gave Rowie a wink. "Maybe next time."

Drew shifted uncomfortably. "All Swahili to me."

Mac didn't have time for chitchat. "So, Drew, Rowie has been doing the weather for a number of years. Pretty high success rate, but she has a rather unusual way of . . ."

Drew interrupted. "I'm okay if everyone else is okay with it."

"Yes, but you should know that Rowie is a psyc—"

Drew waved away Mac's concerns—whatever they

were—and searched Rowie's eyes. All he needed to know was that she really loved the weather. Was it too much to ask that the person who took his job actually cared about it? Like he did?

Rowie understood, edged closer to the bed and smiled. (Thank God for the well-placed dinner tray.) "I'd love the opportunity, Drew."

Drew was mesmerized. "Then it's yours." Hell, she could have his soul if she asked nicely.

"Your leg will be fixed before you know it," she said. "Until then, I'd love the chance to fill in for you. I really love forecasting the weather. And I'm good . . . at least I usually am. TV is a completely different . . . ah . . . medium. But I'm willing to work hard and learn."

Drew could feel dark storms and blasting sunshine seep through his bones just from talking to her. He also knew she was the right person for the job. Rowie and Drew beamed at each other, their energies playful yet obviously fascinated. And then Drew turned to the others. "She gets my vote. I think she's just perfect."

Three hours later a helicopter dropped Rowie and Mac off on USBC's roof. Jess was waiting for them in Mac's office.

"Drew okay?"

"Fine. The fall may have knocked some sense into him. Main thing is, he liked Rowie."

I bet. "Fabby," said Jess through clenched teeth.

"You'd better get Rowie into wardrobe," Mac said.

Rowie looked down at her dress. "I'm sorry; isn't this suitable?"

"It's great," Mac said. "But it's green. You'll look transparent in front of the greenscreen."

Rowie was regretting ever agreeing to this. "Perhaps

that wouldn't be a bad thing," she said. "I could be the invisible weather woman."

Mac gave her a wink. "They've already tried that one in Cleveland. But a psychic weather woman . . . now that's a first."

Chapter Twelve

Rowie felt frozen with fear. The studio floor was alive with people, and she seemed to be at the center of it all. Her eyes flickered around the room. Everyone else knew exactly what to do, which only made her more nervous. She felt like such an imposter.

A voice boomed over a loudspeaker. "Are you okay, Rowie?"

Rowie looked up at the tech box and noticed Taye giving her a wave. She could see Mac and Jess beside him. She nodded and gave him the thumbs up. What else could she do? Vomit?

Taye settled into his chair. "Three minutes, people."

Mac glanced at Jess. "Tell me this isn't crazy."

Jess looked more confident than she felt. "Just breathe, Mac. It'll be great." She turned and looked at Rowie on the monitor. The little witch was incredibly telegenic. A face like that was hardly going to alienate the viewers. At least she hoped it wouldn't. Her job depended on it.

* * *

"Hurry up, Petey," Lilia urged. "It'll be on in a minute."

Petey sat next to her on the couch, fiddling with the remote control. "It's definitely broken," he announced.

"Just turn it on at the set." Lilia hated these newfangled inventions.

"I think we'll have to. This won't work."

Angel, perched on a cushion on the floor, turned and grabbed the remote from him.

"Gimme that." She flipped the back panel open. "There's no bloody batteries in it."

"I knew that." Petey blushed.

"No wonder it's never worked," Lilia said. She grabbed a couple of batteries from a cabinet drawer and handed them to Petey. "Do you know how to put them in?"

"I think I can work it out," Petey grumbled.

"Perhaps Angel should do it," Lilia suggested. She settled back on the couch and then glanced at Gwendolyn, hunched over a pile of cutlery at the back of the room. "Are you going to watch, Mom?"

Gwendolyn shook her head. "I don't have time. I still need to distribute the silverware."

"Mom, stop it."

"What? It's just a little distraction for her."

Lilia grabbed a cushion and tossed it at Gwendolyn. "You can be a stubborn old woman, you know that?"

"Perhaps. But you'll miss me when I'm gone." Gwendolyn started buffing a fork, but stopped when she realized her husband was glaring at her. "What?"

"You never even liked that silverware," Dorian said.

"Your great-aunt Mildred gave us this for our wedding."

"Would that be the great-aunt Mildred you despised because she opposed our marriage?" Dorian stalked off and joined the others.

"The old cow was wiccaphobic," snapped Gwendolyn, who liked to have the last word.

Angel cut a slab of cheesecake and sauntered over to the eldest Shakespeare. "Were you speaking to me?"

"Nope," Gwendolyn said as she checked her reflection in a spoon.

"Here's some sweet stuff. You seem a bit sour today." Angel placed the cheesecake on the table. "You already have a spoon."

"No, thanks."

"How about some wine? Loosen you up . . . Gwennie."

"Don't call me that," Gwendolyn snapped. "You know I hate it."

"Ditch the Post-its and I'll stick to Gwendolyn."

She ignored Angel's insolence and returned to her silverware. The girl could be quite rude, but Gwendolyn still adored her. Angel was the only person who had ever truly given her cheek. Most people were scared senseless of her, or felt she deserved an almost royal respect. Angel always said what she thought, in that strange accent of hers, and damn the consequences. Gwendolyn liked that. It reminded her . . . of her.

"Come and watch the news," said Angel. "This is really important to Rowie."

"I can see the TV from here."

"Okay, *Gwennnnnnie!* Suit yourself." Angel returned to the others, grabbed some nuts and plunked herself in a recliner.

Petey turned up the volume. "Shh, everyone, it's on."

Jack switched on the television, then propped some pillows behind Drew's head. "Is that better? Can you see the TV?"

"You don't have to baby-sit me, Jack." Drew was

fully aware of how busy Jack was. "You've already done way more than I ever expected."

"Someone's got to take care of you. Eva sure as hell isn't going to. Anyway, I'm on the red-eye back tonight." Jack opened a small, portable cooler and handed Drew a plastic cup. "I got some snacks. There's a little health food shop down the road. Reopened this afternoon. Hospital food is enough to make you sick."

"You're a champion!" Drew took a sip. "Christ! What is it?"

"Wheatgrass juice. It's really good for you," said Jack.

"Couldn't you bring me a beer? What else have you got in there?"

"Spinach salad . . ."

"Please tell me you have some cookies or something."

"There's an organic orange and polenta cake," Jack offered.

Drew rolled his eyes. "That will have to do."

Jack served up a slice of cake on a paper plate, while Drew positioned his head so he could see the TV. He was nervous. What if Rowie were awful?

Or worse, what if she were great? What if she were better than he was?

Rowie could feel her heart pounding in her chest. Oh God, what if she had a heart attack? Was that possible from fear? She'd read somewhere that people who fell from tall buildings were dead before they hit the ground. The fear killed them. She certainly felt like she was free falling, sans parachute.

She saw Bill Anderson strutting toward her, wearing a suit jacket, shirt and tie on top, Bermuda shorts on bottom. He was much smaller than he appeared on TV, and the olive skin and brown hair adored by fans everywhere were obviously fake. It was unnerving, a bit like finding out Santa Claus wasn't real.

"Hey, Rowie, isn't it? Bill Anderson. How are you feeling?"

"Oh you know . . . nauseated."

Bill leaned in and whispered in Rowie's ear, "Quick word of advice. Be careful of Tina. She comes across all apple pie on TV, but believe me, she's a grade-A bitch."

Rowie stepped back, appalled. Jess hadn't been exaggerating. Bill loathed Tina. She could almost smell it on his breath. Or was that whiskey?

Bill gave Rowie a wink and sauntered to the news desk.

Shin walked up to Rowie. "You ready?"

"Yes," Rowie nodded.

Shin readjusted Rowie's mike. "Speak into it for me."

Rowie felt a bit foolish. "Um . . . testing . . . one, two."

"That's great." Shin smiled kindly. "Have fun, and remember to breathe." He turned and scanned the studio. "Places, people."

Rowie took a deep breath and tried to imagine herself surrounded by white light. It was difficult to do, surrounded by a greenscreen and monitors. She noticed Tina Eanis, coiffed to perfection, marching her way. Tina paused for a moment and gave Rowie the once-over before speaking. Rowie suddenly felt like a schoolgirl with muddy clothes and a smudged face.

"I'm Tina . . . obviously. Good luck."

"Thank you."

"And just between us," Tina smirked, "steer clear of Bill Anderson. The guy is a complete sleazebag."

Shin interrupted them. "Thirty seconds, Tina. Hustle."

"No rest for the wicked." Tina made her way to the news desk and sat next to Bill.

Rowie watched to see if they acknowledged each other at all. They didn't. Instead Tina pulled a can of air freshener out from under the desk and sprayed it near Bill. "That's better," she sighed.

Bill Anderson and Tina Eanis appeared onscreen in all their polished glory. They turned and greeted each other: friends, co-workers, and partners. They obviously held each other in high regard.

"I love them," said Angel.

"They look like such kind people," Petey said.

"I bet they're assholes," Lilia chimed in.

Bill stared straight through the camera lens and into the eyes of each individual watching. It was a gift. "Those stories and more, including Hurricane Hilda and a psychic weather woman, in just a moment."

Anticipation filled the room. All eyes were focused on the television. Even the family portraits seemed to turn their gazes.

Gwendolyn counted the dessert spoons again . . . and once more. She couldn't concentrate while the TV was blaring. She resisted for as long as she could, and then decided one little glance wouldn't hurt. One little peek, as they introduced Rowie . . .

She looked beautiful.

Gwendolyn smiled . . . slightly. That's my girl, she thought.

"Ouch!" Something hit her in the side of the head. "OUCH!" And again, square in the chest. Gwendolyn realized Angel was tossing nuts at her. The little minx had caught her.

Angel grinned and gave her a wink. "Sprung . . . Gwennnnnnie!" she mouthed silently.

Gwendolyn poked her tongue out at Angel and returned to the silverware. Obviously they didn't teach manners in Australia.

Rowie desperately needed to go to the bathroom . . . again. But it was too late. Shin gave the final countdown, finishing with a wave of his arm.

"Three, two . . ."

Suddenly the energy around Bill and Tina changed as they sprang to life and became a team.

"More bloodshed in the Middle East with an explosion inside a crowded restaurant today," said Bill, serious, competent and trustworthy.

"And the spotty-beaked woodpecker, close to extinction," said Tina, intelligent, caring and warm.

They turned to each other and, in an Oscar-worthy performance, smiled like long-lost friends.

"Upsetting news, Bill."

"Certainly is, Tina."

Bill returned his attention to the camera. "Those stories and more, including Hurricane Hilda and a psychic weather woman, in just a moment."

USBC's familiar theme filled the room as they crossed to the opening graphics. Tina took the opportunity to scream at Shin.

"Why does *he* get the Middle East, while *I* get a stupid bird that only hippies give a shit about?"

Bill grinned, pleased for an opportunity to push Tina's buttons. "Because you think the Middle East is somewhere around Macy's."

"You're an ass," Tina snarled.

Shin, used to their bickering, dealt with Tina like he would a child. "You know you're better at dealing with animal issues, Tina."

Tina glared at Shin, but kept her mouth shut. He was right. Hadn't she placated the idiots at PETA with that campaign for baby harp seals? They had no idea she slept in a Fendi fur wrap and lived on Canadian salmon.

"Back on in five." Shin counted them back in. "Four, three, two . . ."

Rowie doubled over and tried to calm herself. Just breathe, she thought. She felt a hand on her shoulder and looked up into Shin's smiling eyes.

"I guess it's too late to pull out?" she joked.

"Good luck," he mouthed before slipping away.

Suddenly, Bill and Tina reverted back into best friends mode.

"Hurricane Hilda ripped through Florida yesterday, killing eight people and destroying hundreds of homes. Eva Sanchez reports from the devastated area."

Rowie turned and watched the monitor. Eva Sanchez was polished, articulate and naturally sexy, a sympathetic observer amidst a scene of total devastation. Behind her, the newly homeless searched the rubble for anything they could salvage. There wasn't much. The clip finished, and they cut back to Tina and Bill.

"Heartbreaking," said Tina, stifling a yawn.

"Makes me realize how lucky I am," Bill said. "Of course, Drew Henderson wasn't so lucky. But he's got a lot of support out there. The network was inundated with get-well messages and teddy bears for Drew after footage of his fall was aired last night." Bill turned to Tina. "So, Teen, who've we got to replace Drew?"

Tina beamed. Time to be more upbeat. "Hang on to your crystal balls . . . it's a psychic weather woman. Known here in Manhattan for her eerily accurate predictions, Rowie Shakespeare now intends to take the rest of the state by storm."

Rowie took a deep breath and tried to pull herself together. She was so nervous she felt faint. Beads of sweat broke on her forehead. A makeup woman appeared, wiped them off, then disappeared.

Tina timed the punch line perfectly. "I *predict* everyone will be amazed."

"Great to have you aboard, Rowie," said Bill. "We hear you've been predicting the weather ever since you were a child?"

Rowie was on. She stepped back, startled. It was a shock to see herself on the monitors. That hadn't happened this morning. Adrenaline shot through her body, pumped into her brain. The room spun like a roulette wheel. Whoa, Rowie thought, place your bets. She blinked nervously and tried to focus on the news desk.

Bill and Tina smiled at her and waited for her to answer. She tried to remember what the question was. Was it a question? What was she supposed to say? Her whole body filled with ice and froze. Her mind went blank, and she forgot the scripted banter she'd memorized earlier.

There was a deadly silence and then Bill jumped back in. "I guess as a child you always knew when to put on a warm coat."

Rowie searched Bill's face. She watched as his smile faded. He glanced at Tina. They may have hated each other, but they were definitely on the same team when there was a whiff of failure in the room. She tried to remember what she'd done during the test. Suddenly her brain thawed slightly. It decoded the question.

"Yes . . . um . . . I always told my family if they needed that extra layer." Rowie laughed, but it felt as fake as Tina's boobs.

"And being psychic, do you ever just *know* which numbers to bet on in the lottery?" Bill chuckled.

"I wish, Bill, but my powers don't quite work like that." Rowie bared her teeth. It was meant to be a smile, but would have been mistaken for a sign of aggression in many species.

"So what have you got for us today, Rowie?" asked Tina.

Rowie turned to the camera and tried to remember what she'd practiced. "Good evening."

The cameraman waved his arm at her and Rowie realized she was looking at the wrong camera. She turned to the correct one.

"Good evening. Hurricane Hilda may be over, but the cost of cleanup is expected to exceed twenty billion dollars." Rowie raised her arm and started gesturing at the greenscreen. She felt about as natural as a Muppet. "Nationally today: rain and storms around parts of the Southwest . . ."

She glanced at the monitor and realized she was pointing somewhere around Indiana, rather than the southwest. She turned to the map behind her, but was greeted by a blank greenscreen. She turned back to the monitor and tried again. It had been easier this morning . . . when she wasn't frozen with fear.

"Much of the same in Oregon—Oregon—Ore . . ."

Rowie watched the monitor as she moved her arm around until she finally got it right.

"Oregon! And Washing—oops, there's Washington. To think I aced my geography class at school. So, much of the same for Washington as this trough moves north . . . Oh, that's south. North is . . . this way."

She had it! This wasn't so bad. She could do it. She grinned at the camera and then turned to acknowledge the imaginary map behind her . . . and tripped over her own feet.

"Owww!"

A collective gasp filled the studio . . . and then . . . silence.

No, no, no, no! Rowie lay sprawled across the floor, unsure how she could ever get up and face the camera again. Millions of people had just witnessed the most horrifying, embarrassing moment of her life. The seconds ticked by. The floor was icy cold, but she couldn't bear to leave it. Shame wracked her body as she willed the floor to open up and swallow her.

The control booth was quiet. Everyone looked around at each other in shock. And then . . .

"Oh crap! Why isn't she getting up?" Mac bellowed. "Get up! This is no time for a nap." He watched in horror as Rowie finally peeled herself off the floor and straightened her skirt. "Go to a clip. Go, go!"

"Wait," yelled Jess.

"No way," screamed Mac. "Off, now!"

Jess noticed a change in Rowie. She looked embarrassed, scared, but seemed to be retreating to somewhere she was sure of. She was moving into the same position she'd been in when Jess had first seen her outside The Grove. Jess was determined to go through with this. "Look, she's doing something."

Everyone watched as Rowie lifted her head and her face became serene and otherworldly. Her lips, bow-shaped and pink, curved slightly in a smile that made the *Mona Lisa* appear obvious. Everyone in the tech box fell quiet. The studio floor was still. Countless living rooms across America were hushed. Rowie had cast a spell, and suddenly it didn't matter that she'd messed up. She was just so beautiful to look at.

"What do you want me to do, Mac?" Taye asked.

Mac watched Rowie, mesmerized. "Fine, give her a minute . . . but be ready to pull the plug."

Rowie spoke quietly, calmly, her nerves dissipating into a world she alone could see. "Torrential rain in the Philippines will cause flash floods. A heat wave is closing in on Northern Europe. It will be the hottest summer on record."

"Oh, Christ," Mac moaned, the spell shattered. "World weather? That's a first. Michelle, find out if she's right."

Michelle jumped into action. "I'm on it!"

Taye spoke into Bill and Tina's earpieces. "B and T, if she's wrong we're cutting straight back to you for damage control."

Bill and Tina nodded in the control room TV monitors.

"Parts of Manila are already flooded," said Michelle.

"What about Europe?" asked Mac.

"Temperatures in Germany and Denmark are off the charts."

Mac turned to Jess. "She probably checked this out on the Internet earlier."

"You know she didn't."

Mac and Jess watched as Rowie continued.

"Scattered storms over the tri-state area today. Heavy rain over New York will pass within the hour. Skies will clear, but first . . ." She paused, as though confirming the information she was receiving, and then with absolute certainty: "But first a minor tornado will hit Manhattan."

Mac looked like he was about to have a coronary.

Taye started to laugh, but stopped short when he saw Mac's face. "Mac, have you got your blood-pressure pills?"

Mac ignored Taye and turned to Michelle. "Is it possible?"

Michelle kept her eyes on the computer as she spoke. "The NWS hasn't issued any warnings."

"Does New York have tornadoes?" Jess wasn't ready to dismiss Rowie yet. She couldn't afford to.

Michelle searched for more information. "New York State, yes, but the city . . . ?" Michelle tapped at the computer. "Yes, an F1 in Queens, October '85. Three on Staten Island: 1990, '95 and . . ."

"October 2003, right?" Mac finished for her.

"Right."

Mac's eyes were steely. "Has there ever been a downtown tornado in Manhattan?"

Michelle gave Mac a look that said it all. "No."

"Damn it, Jess. Another good idea." Mac turned and watched Rowie finish. She broke out of her trance and beamed at the camera.

"But don't worry. The tornado will be small and won't cause much damage."

"How freaking fabulous," mumbled Mac.

"I'm Rowie Shakespeare. Bill and Tina, back to you."

Bill and Tina look stunned . . . and then recovered with big smiles.

"And there we have it. Might rethink that vacation in Europe, Bill. You know how you hate the heat."

Bill raised an eyebrow. "More news after the break."

Shin waved them out to a commercial and all hell broke loose. Tina stood and screamed at anyone who would listen.

"That really raised the bar on serious news broadcasting, Dorothy!"

Bill looked shell-shocked. "Who the hell cares if it's raining in Manila?" He turned to Shin. "Where *is* Manila?"

"Get her out of here. *Now!*" thundered Tina. "I refuse to have my reputation sullied by that charlatan."

Shin ran over to Rowie and unhooked her mike. "You'd better come with me." He led her out of the studio. "Don't worry about Tina. She's a bitch to everyone. Are you okay?"

Rowie was shaking. "I don't know. I think so. Was I that bad?"

"Tina will have to eat her words later when your predictions come true."

"You believe me?"

"My grandmother is quite well-known around Tokyo for reading palms."

"So you've been exposed to my sort of weirdness?" Rowie joked.

"Yes. Thankfully. Imagine being scared of it like Tina?" Shin rolled his eyes in mock horror.

"Thank you, Shin," said Rowie, grateful for his support.

"I've got to get back in there. Can you remember how to get to your dressing room?"

Rowie nodded. "I'm sure I left a trail of bread crumbs somewhere."

Shin waved and disappeared back into the studio. Rowie heard footsteps and turned to see Jess marching down the corridor.

"I'm sorry. I was awful, wasn't I?"

Jess stared at Rowie, her eyes cold. "You had your moments. The world weather thing—you just knew all that?"

Rowie nodded. "Of course."

"Surely you don't actually believe a tornado will hit Manhattan?"

"I don't know much about them. I just report what I see."

There was an uncomfortable pause. Finally Rowie spoke. "I see. I'll just get my things."

Drew sat staring at the screen long after Rowie had finished. It was Jack who spoke first.

"I thought she was cute."

"You would," Drew said.

"She looks familiar. Really familiar."

"Probably because you've met her."

"Nah . . . it's not that." Jack gauged his friend's mood. "You okay?"

"Why the hell didn't someone mention the psychic thing?"

"Would you have listened? You were sold the minute you saw her."

Drew lay back on his pillows and fought the urge to scream. "I approved her, Jack . . . without seeing a resume or a tape. I approved her based on shapely legs and a gorgeous smile. Idiot!"

"You wouldn't be the first man to succumb to such charms." Jack chuckled.

Drew felt like he was going out of his mind, stuck in bed, unable to move. His life was falling apart around him and he couldn't do a goddamn thing about it. He was trapped. He had pins drilled into his leg and was attached to a remnant from the Inquisition. He was going crazy with worry, about his boat, his dog, and now that he'd seen Rowie at work, his job.

Drew's work was important to him. Not the TV stuff, the fame and the money, but the actual science of it. He'd spent years trying to make meteorology accessible to the general public. And he'd never once used gimmicks.

Just last week, a teenage boy had approached him outside the network. The kid was a science nut, totally enthralled by the weather. He told Drew he was going to be a meteorologist . . . just like Drew. The kid got it. He understood that Drew was a scientist, not a celebrity. He wasn't at USBC for the perks or the fame. He was there for the weather, and USBC had the best reputation for delivering it properly. Until now. All his hard work was going to be shot down by one gorgeous redhead. He had every right to be upset.

"What am I going to do, Jack?"

Jack glanced at Drew's leg and shrugged. "Not much you can do, Buddy."

Angel turned off the TV, and they sat quietly for a moment.

"Oh dear," said Lilia. "Surely there's something we can do?"

"It's shocking," Petey whispered.

Gwendolyn walked up behind Lilia and placed a hand on her shoulder. She knew how sensitive her daughter could be. "I've told you, when it floods in Asia, there's nothing we can do."

Everyone shook their heads in sympathy and agreed that they would all make a donation to help the flood victims.

Chapter Thirteen

Jess was on her way to Mac's office for an emergency meeting when her cell phone rang. She checked the number and groaned. Drew. She considered letting it go to voice mail, but he'd hunt her down. She knew him well . . . unfortunately.

She answered and tried to sound calm. "You obviously watched the news."

His voice was low and measured. "I thought we didn't use gimmicks at USBC."

Jess paused and moved into an empty corridor. She didn't need any more gossip about her and Drew. "Memo to Drew: Weather forecasting is dull. All networks use gimmicks."

Drew sounded genuinely shocked. "Not us. We take it seriously."

"Don't be naive. Why do you think you're so popular?"

"Because I'm qualified."

"Oh please! The viewers could give a shit about your

credentials, Drew. It's your pretty face that wins the ratings race."

"Why her?"

"Correct me if I'm wrong, but didn't you approve her?"

"No one mentioned the Nostradamus thing."

"So what *did* you base your approval on, Drew?"

Drew decided not to take the bait. He was the first to admit he'd been blindsided by the pretty redhead. "Why didn't you use Eva?"

"Because for some reason, I couldn't get hold of Eva," Jess seethed.

The light bulb went off. "Damn it, Jess. I thought we agreed it wouldn't interfere with our work."

All of a sudden, Jess felt guilty. Would she be treating Drew like this if he hadn't dumped her? If he'd kept his zipper closed with Eva? Probably not. "This has nothing to do with what happened between us," she hissed.

"We've always been friends first, Jess," Drew continued. "And I want to remain friends. I'll do whatever it takes."

Okay, let's start by eloping to Vegas. "What are you suggesting, Drew? Couples therapy?"

"I want us to work well together again," said Drew. "You're a great producer, Jess. It'd be shame if our 'thing' got in the way of your work."

Thing? "Don't flatter yourself," Jess snapped.

Drew was silent for a moment. Everything he said was coming out wrong. He tried a different tack. "Jess, I've worked my butt off to get where I am."

"Haven't we all?" Now Jess was pissed. She was the youngest of seven kids. By the time she'd reached all her milestones, there wasn't a penny left to pay for them. Drew wouldn't know struggle if it bit him on the butt, not compared to her, so how dare he speak down to her like this!

"I'm not saying you haven't, but it's my job and my ratings that are on the line here. A psychic weather woman? Geez, Jess . . . someone could have mentioned that one to me."

"She came highly recommended."

"But messed up anyway. Do you have any idea how it felt, being stuck in this bed, watching her screw up like that?" Drew was being as honest as possible. "I was a goddamn fool to get on that roof. It's just that I love my job. I only want the best. So watching that red-head tonight . . . it hurt more than my leg."

Jess knew now was a good time to tell Drew that he wouldn't have to watch Rowie mess up again . . . but she couldn't say it. She didn't want to admit she'd been wrong. Not yet, and especially not to Drew.

"Ask the doctors to up your morphine and it won't bother you at all," Jess said.

"Come on, Jess, give me a break."

"I thought you had one."

Drew sighed. "Fine, if you could just keep me up to date . . . I'd appreciate it."

Jess hung up and took a moment to pull herself together. Her hands were shaking. She refused to cry . . . she couldn't. Not over him. Not anymore. He had no right treating her like that. It was her job to get a replacement, and that was what she'd done. If he'd refrained from playing chicken with a hurricane, none of this would have happened.

Jess turned off her phone. She didn't want him calling back during the meeting. The way she felt now, she didn't want him calling back ever.

Mac stood in front of the team and tried to contain his anger. This mess wasn't their fault. Well, it was

Jess's fault, but she was huddled at the other end of the table looking sufficiently sheepish. As much as he'd love to throttle her, he'd agreed to the psychic weather woman. An obvious moment of insanity on his part.

Besides, Jess was one of the best producers he'd ever worked with. She'd made some mistakes, but only because she'd taken risks. A lot of young producers didn't nowadays. Everyone was too scared of losing their jobs, or worse, losing money.

Jess had guts. She could be a pain in the ass, but she had an edge he hadn't seen for a long time. Her only weakness was that she obviously had the hots for Drew.

But then, show me a woman who hasn't, Mac thought. "I want Eva Sanchez in place for tomorrow."

Jess perked up. "Fine. But if I can just say, in my defense . . ."

Unbelievable! Didn't the girl ever shut up? Mac cut her off. "If I were you, I'd zip it for a while." Mac looked around the table. "Two options. We can pretend today never happened. Or we can hit all the network talk shows. Turn it into a national debate. 'Psychic prediction—the big con.' "

He waited for a general agreement, but instead everyone looked uncomfortable. Taye played with his pen, and Michelle started coughing. He turned to Shin, who motioned toward the door. Mac realized Rowie was standing behind him, looking embarrassed and hurt.

She mustered as much dignity as she could. "I just wanted to apologize for letting you down."

Everyone murmured that she hadn't, and prayed she'd leave quickly. Michelle turned her attention to some lint on her pants. Taye put down his pen and stared out the window.

"About what I just said . . ." Mac was apologetic. He felt like he'd been caught kicking a kitten.

Rowie stared at him with a mix of understanding and defiance. "Don't worry. I'm used to it."

Mac paused, unsure what else to say. He felt for the girl. She was beautiful and sweet. Obviously a few sandwiches short of a picnic, but that didn't mean he wanted to hurt her.

"Rowie . . ." he started, but was interrupted by Taye.

"Mac?"

"Wait a sec, Taye." Mac smiled at Rowie and prayed he didn't look as patronizing as he felt. "Perhaps we can get you a guest spot on a psychic network infomercial."

"Mac?" Taye tried again.

Mac ignored him. "Have you heard of Brigid and Lugh Dee? Witches, apparently. They have a talk show. We could organize an appearance for you on that."

Rowie felt she'd rather pass a kidney stone. "No, thank you."

"Mac!" Taye yelled.

"What?" Mac turned and found the others staring out the window. "Holy hell!"

He walked across the room, speechless. Michelle, Jess, Shin and Taye joined him at the window.

"It's a tornado," whispered Michelle.

A small but impressive-looking tornado was forming on the other side of the glass. It began to move toward the street. Spinning, dancing, stirring, it propelled itself along Sixth Avenue. People screamed and fled. A bike courier slammed into a wall. The tornado uprooted a tree and hurled it onto the hood of a taxi. Traffic came to a complete standstill as everyone ran from their cars.

All of a sudden the tornado changed course and headed back toward the USBC building. With their noses pressed against the glass, they all watched as it hurtled under them. It took out a whole street corner: a car, some souvenir tables, a—

"Watch out," screamed Mac, as something came flying toward them.

Everyone dived under the table, just as a hotdog stand smashed through the window. Glass exploded everywhere; the hotdog stand tumbled around, and then came to rest on top of the table they were all crouched under.

The room was silent for a moment, apart from the sound of a distant siren. One by one the news team dragged themselves to standing. They noticed Rowie, still in the doorway, a smile on her face.

Everyone stared, dumbstruck. They seemed to be waiting for her to say something, waiting to be reassured.

"Told ya," she said.

Chapter Fourteen

Rowie shut the front door and slipped off her shoes. The Grove was deathly quiet and dark. Strange, she thought. Suddenly a light came on and . . .

"SURPRISE!"

"Ahhhhhhhhhhh," Rowie screamed. "Oh my . . . what the . . . ?"

Lilia, Petey and Angel were huddled together with goofy grins on their faces.

Rowie's heart pounded. "You scared me. What are you doing?"

"Celebrating." Angel laughed as she gave Rowie a hug. "You're a TV star now."

"More like a TV joke. Did you see me fall over?"

"No . . . didn't notice," Petey lied.

"Oh bullshit, Petey," said Angel. "You guffawed like a donkey when she tripped."

"I did not," said Petey, horrified. "You did."

Angel smiled with mock guilt. "Okay, I admit I had a chuckle."

"It was so embarrassing," Rowie groaned.

"Everyone trips," said Lilia.

"Not on national television."

"I think when people trip like that in public it makes them appear more human," Lilia comforted.

Angel agreed. "And you did it with such grace."

Rowie laughed. "Thanks for the support, but it will still take years to get over."

Lilia took Rowie's hand and led her into the kitchen where some snacks and bottles of wine were waiting on the table. They sat and Angel poured Rowie a drink.

"I think you need this."

"To Rowie's new career," Petey began. And then, "Do you still have a job?"

"Yes. There was a tornado on Sixth Avenue a couple of hours ago."

"Of course," Lilia said.

"You saw it on TV?" asked Rowie.

"No, but I knew there'd be one if you predicted it."

Rowie smiled at her mother, grateful for such utter faith. She took a sip of her wine and relaxed back in her chair. She'd made it through the first show—just—and had a lot of people backtracking and apologizing. The network had been inundated with calls and e-mails from viewers who'd loved her. USBC's executive producer had phoned Mac, thrilled that they'd been the network to break the tornado story. Jess told Rowie to unpack her things and leave them in the dressing room.

Even Tina apologized for screaming at her. "My blood sugar levels dropped. . . . Sorry . . ."

Rowie still felt wound up, but she was also excited. She had been handed an amazing opportunity. For years she'd dreamed of an adventurous life, so she fully intended to grab hold. She truly felt her life was on track . . . finally. Now she just needed to meet a man who could kiss her without Cinema's Magic Moments playing in her head, and life would be perfect . . . apart from her moody grandmother, that is. It hurt that Gwendolyn was MIA tonight.

Lilia and Angel were giving Petey a pep talk about his looks.

"You know, Petey, you're not unlike Arthur Miller to look at, and he married Marilyn Monroe," said Angel.

"The way I feel now, I'd settle for someone who looks like Marilyn Manson."

"It's not your physical appearance that's stopping someone from falling in love with you," Lilia insisted. "It's how you feel about your appearance that can be ugly. You get what you expect in life, Petey. If you expect people to find you unattractive, then they will."

"I think you're a bit of a spunk. Especially after I've had a few glasses of wine." Angel winked.

"But look at me."

"I do," Lilia said. "Every day. And I think you are one of the loveliest men I've ever seen."

Petey blushed. "Thank you . . . but loving yourself is easier said than done."

"I know," Lilia agreed. "But you'll get the hang of it."

While the others were speaking, Rowie decided to duck upstairs and see her grandmother. Gwendolyn was propped up in bed, reading the latest edition of *Pagan Monthly*. She raised one finger to her lips. "Shhh, your grandfather is asleep."

"Are you okay, Gran?" Rowie whispered.

"I'm fine. Soldiering on," Gwendolyn replied weakly.

Rowie noticed a bottle of sherry on the dresser. She obviously wasn't too sick for a nightcap. "Did you watch me tonight?"

Gwendolyn pretended to wonder what Rowie was talking about. "Oh, the news? Well, I was so busy . . . Did it go well?"

Rowie looked gutted. "It was okay."

"Lovely. Well, if that's all, I'd better go to sleep. I have a lot of extra work to deal with while you're doing the TV thing." Gwendolyn put the magazine on her bedside table and switched off the lamp.

"Okay." Rowie started to close the door, then stopped. "I love you, Gran."

Gwendolyn squeezed her eyes shut. "And I love you, Rowena." She ignored the urge to reach out to Rowie, and listened as the door clicked shut.

Almost immediately, Dorian opened his eyes. "That was mean."

"Oh, leave me alone," she snapped.

He didn't. He just lay there staring at her.

"You don't understand, Dorian. I was forced into this life . . ." Gwendolyn clapped a hand over her mouth, shocked. "Not forced . . . I don't mean that I ever doubted that this was my path . . . but I had other dreams as well. I wanted to open a shoe shop. But you can't have a psychic shoe shop, can you?"

Dorian was silent. He didn't judge. Gwendolyn was doing that to herself.

"Our work is important, Dorian." Gwendolyn sighed and felt defeated. "Oh lord, I was never this grumpy before you left. Something died inside me that day."

"I came back, didn't I?"

"True. But for how long?" Gwendolyn sat up and turned to Dorian. "I live in constant fear that I'll wake up one day and you'll be gone again."

"That's why you're hanging on so tightly to Rowie. And it's not fair to her."

Gwendolyn rolled over. "Life's not fair. You taught me that."

Rowie played with the stem of her glass and tried to keep up with the conversation. She smiled in all the right places, but she'd hit a slump. Her heart wasn't in it. It was too busy hurting. She didn't understand why her grandmother was so angry with her. She was just about to excuse herself to go to bed when her thoughts drifted to Drew. What if he hated what she had done? And why did it matter to her?

Rowie tossed back her wine—Dutch courage—and walked out to the hallway phone and called the operator.

"Plankaville Medical in Florida, please."

She scrawled down the number, then dialed Drew before she changed her mind.

Drew couldn't sleep, despite being medicated to the eyeballs. He was not the type of guy who relaxed easily. He didn't like lying around doing nothing. He may have worked in television, but he rarely watched it. He was outdoorsy. He liked to surf, hike, ski and play basketball. He was addicted to adrenaline sports and had his pilot's license. He was happiest hitting the road, air or open water. Being attached to something akin to a medieval torture machine was like a slow boat to insanity, and he simply didn't know how to fill the time.

The phone rang and he grabbed it, hoping it was Jess or Mac with more information about the tornado. "Drew Henderson."

It wasn't Jess or Mac, but a soft, melodic voice he recognized immediately.

"Hello, Drew . . . This is Rowie."

Suddenly all the anger he felt toward her dissolved. He was glad she called. He needed answers. "How did you know about the tornado?"

"I don't know. I never question how I know; I just do." She paused for a moment. "It wasn't the most auspicious start to a TV career."

"I'd say being the only person working in weather who predicted a Manhattan tornado was a helluvan auspicious start."

"I mean the . . . the way I fell."

There was a catch in her voice, and he needed to fix it. "You're talking to a guy who fell through a roof on national TV."

Rowie giggled, which made Drew laugh, and suddenly they were both in hysterics.

"So, Rowie, did you enjoy your trip?"

"I did. And listen, Drew, why don't we meet again next fall?" Rowie wiped tears from her eyes. "I was lying there on that floor, wishing it would open up and swallow me."

"The roof I was standing on did." Drew suddenly felt ridiculously happy for someone in his situation. "But I think I win. I'm in traction . . . it gives me the edge."

"Oh all right, you win." There was a comfortable pause. "How are you feeling?"

"Much better." Strangely enough, he was.

"I just wanted to see what you . . . Anyway . . . I'd better go."

No . . . don't. "Oh . . . okay."

"It was good talking to you, Drew."

He liked the way she said his name. "You too, Rowie. Good luck with the show."

Drew placed the phone back on the bedside table and sighed. He was actually tired now. Calm. He squeezed his eyes shut and imagined the gentle rocking of his boat. He could almost hear the slap of the water on the side. Then, just as sleep snatched him away, Drew remembered Rowie's clear green eyes . . . and he wondered what it would be like to gaze into them for all eternity.

Chapter Fifteen

The next few weeks flew by for Rowie. Each new day was a joy. Suddenly she found herself bounding out of bed, raring to get to work. Sometimes she'd stop by the shop on the way, but as Gwendolyn's greetings became colder, Rowie stopped by less.

The whiteboard outside the shop was gathering dust. She'd written an apologetic message on it, asking her regulars to turn on the TV if they wanted to see her weather predictions. She missed her morning neighborhood forecast, but her USBC contract stipulated that she stop while she worked for them.

Day by day, Rowie became more comfortable in front of the camera. She finally got the hang of the Chromakey, and stopped worrying that she was going to make a fool of herself. She was so likable that everyone took time to explain the more technical aspects of meteorology. It wasn't part of her job description, but she was eager to learn all she could about meteorology. Each morning, she pieced together her own predictions using technology rather than intuition. She would sit at a computer and study the models, satellite images, the radar and precipitation. Then she'd put some maps together, based on what she saw, and the other meteorologists would give her a score. She picked it up quickly, but found it more difficult than just "tuning" in to the weather.

She also spent time getting to know her co-workers—and they appreciated that. She especially liked Shin, and often had a drink with him after work. Shin was the only child of a Japanese scientist and an American artist. He'd grown up around Berkeley, so he was an interesting mix of California creativity and Japanese calm. He was great fun, and incredibly good-looking, but he was not for Rowie. She didn't even have to kiss him to know that.

Jess was the one co-worker she couldn't figure out. She was smart, driven, and when it came to work, unrelenting, but she had little patience for most of the women she worked with, including Rowie. To be fair, she helped Rowie in whatever way she could, and worked hard to make the Psychic Weather Woman spot a hit, but she was as warm as an Arctic winter.

Rowie quickly moved from being a nervous outsider to being part of the team. She enjoyed every minute of the job and was determined to completely milk the experience. She spent much more time than necessary at the station, finding long hours at the office preferable to the situation with her grandmother at home.

Rowie wasn't quite sure when things had become so strained with her grandmother. Her childhood memories were filled with laughter and songs and parties. Gwendolyn had swamped her with affection and positive reinforcement. But somewhere along the way, probably when her grandfather had left, Gwendolyn had become angry and manipulative. She was able to turn on the charm when she wanted, but would turn it off just as quickly. She used her charisma as currency, knowing her granddaughter and daughter would barter anything to have the old Gwendolyn around.

Gwendolyn's withdrawal left a gaping hole in Rowie, but Rowie promised herself she'd mend the bridge once her time at USBC was over. She had to. She missed her grandmother. Her sudden and soaring popularity did little to fill the gap, although she was flattered—if slightly scared—by the attention.

Overnight, Rowie found it difficult to walk the street unrecognized. The response was overwhelming. People loved her. The group of fans waiting outside the network grew larger each day. She'd exit the building and they'd stampede toward her, begging for autographs, photographs, information on dead loved ones.

Mac organized a car service to get Rowie to and from work unscathed. But it didn't stop people from approaching her. They called out her name on the street, in the supermarket, while she was in line at Starbucks. Three female fans waited for her to exit a toilet stall at a nightclub. Apart from one woman in Barnes and Noble, who clutched her spiffy new Bible as she yelled passages from Deuteronomy at Rowie, everyone reacted with genuine warmth and affection. She was the classic American success story: the pretty little misfit who'd been minding her own business when she was discovered and propelled into stardom. The very qualities that had always made her an outsider were the very things the public adored.

The network suggested she do some publicity, so Rowie agreed to talk to *Cosmopolitan*, *Marie Claire* and *InStyle*. But first, she arranged an interview with Angel's magazine, *SheStyle*. Angel had interviewed her once before, as part of an exposé on psychics, but she'd never done an exclusive.

"So when did you first realize you were psychic?"

"That's a stupid question. You already know all this," Rowie said.

"Yes, but I have to ask on the record."

Angel interviewed Rowie at The Grove. It was a sticky August afternoon, the air thick with buzzing insects. They lay on banana chairs in the garden with a portable cooler—or esky, as Angel called it—full of beer between them. Angel clutched a packet of Tim Tams, Australia's favorite cookie. They were part of a care package her mother had sent her from home. Rowie reached across to grab one, but Angel slapped her hand away.

"Bugger off. You stick to your Twinkies."

"What did I do?" asked Rowie.

"You gulped the last one down without respecting it."

"I respected it. It was delicious. That's why I ate it so quickly. What did you want me to do? Take it out for dinner first?"

Angel passed over the package. "Okay, one more . . . but savor it, please."

Rowie took a Tim Tam and nibbled it, not daring to wolf it down.

"So where were we?" asked Angel. "That's right, you first realized you were psychic . . . when?"

"Okay." Rowie humored her. "When I was . . . oh I don't know. I've always known."

"What's your earliest weird memory?"

"I remember standing in my crib on my first birthday, surrounded by Shakespeare spirits."

"You mean those witches on the wall?"

"Yes. A bunch of them dropped by to say happy birthday."

Angel looked horrified. "Christ no, how *Macbeth*. That would freak me out."

"I was one," said Rowie. "Things like that don't freak babies out."

"Okay, next question. What were your school years like?"

"Hideous."

"You've got to give me more to work on, Rowie."

Rowie was quiet for a moment. "The other kids thought I was a freak. Their parents were scared of me. The teachers were wary . . . That was probably my fault. I told my second-grade teacher about her divorce before *she* knew about it."

"You'd think she'd be grateful for the tip," said Angel.

"My first kiss was ruined by a vision. Seems David Packer was destined to marry a man. I stupidly told him and he freaked. Made the rest of my school years a living hell."

"Bitch . . . him, not you. So, what else can you tell me?"

"I don't know. Make it up. People are going to believe what they want to believe anyway, no matter what I say."

"What would you like people to know about you?"

"That I'm normal," Rowie said quietly.

"Oh, get over yourself. Why the bloody hell would you want people to think you're normal? What's so great about normal?"

"Well, to start with, people aren't frightened of 'normal' people. I hate it when someone looks at me like my head is about to start spinning around. My gift doesn't define me. I'm just like everyone else. I have the same hopes and desires as everyone else."

"You want to study Tantric sex with Sting?"

Rowie laughed. "You're a maniac. No, I mean I want to meet someone special, fall in love, have a family . . ."

"Germaine Greer will be thrilled to hear that," Angel snorted.

"I haven't finished yet. You interrupted," said Rowie. "Yes, I want a family. But I also want to wake up each day knowing I'm doing something I love. This TV job . . . it's wonderful. I feel passionate about it."

"So you'd like to continue doing the news?"

Rowie paused for a moment. "I'm not sure about news . . . but it's close. Besides, I'm out of a job once Drew returns."

"Ah yes, Handsome Henderson. Called him lately?"

Rowie could feel the heat creep up her cheeks. "I only called him that first night."

"And thought about calling him again every night since."

"But I haven't."

"Then you're a bloody fool. The guy is hot and there's the added benefit of him definitely being there when you call."

"If he wants to talk, he knows how to find me."

"Oh I see . . . playing the old-fashioned card. Not my cuppa, but very hip right now."

Rowie's green eyes flashed at her friend. "This better be off the record."

"Of course. Now for a really important question: How do you feel about that billboard of you in Times Square?"

"I just thank the Goddess for airbrushing," said Rowie with a wink.

Angel laughed. "Somehow I think the Goddess would be against airbrushing."

"Is that all you need? I'm bored talking about myself."

"Yeah, that'll do." Angel grabbed another beer and then lay back on her chair. "Bloody beautiful day."

"Yeah, it is. Bloody beautiful day," Rowie said, as she ignored Angel's glare and shoved a whole Tim Tam in her mouth.

Chapter Sixteen

Time dragged for Drew. He spent most of his days reading, watching DVDs and cursing his rotten luck.

Jack flew down regularly, carrying all sorts of supplies and stories to keep Drew sane. He'd been a pillar of support for Drew. Not only did he visit, but he'd also moved onto Drew's boat to take care of Norm.

"It's easier than me having to drop by the boat twice a day," Jack explained.

Drew felt awful. He knew how busy Jack was. "But moving aboard is . . ."

"Stop stressing," Jack interrupted. "I've always wondered what it's like to live on a boat. And Norm seems pleased to have me there."

"He can go to my father's, Jack. There's no need for you to look after him."

"Absolutely not," said Jack. "The poor mutt is upset enough that you're not around. He needs to be at home."

Drew looked devastated. "Norm's pining for me?"

"Of course he is. You're all he's got, Drew. But he's

okay. We've been watching the new series of *The Coven* together on DVD. Scored it off a friend of mine at USBC."

Drew lay awake all night worrying about his dog. Poor Norm was already the product of a broken home. How much could a canine take? What if he'd been killed? Who would take care of Norm then? And apart from Norm, who would *really* notice if he was gone? Certainly not any of the women he'd dated recently.

Drew suddenly felt very depressed . . . and alone. He knew he had a reputation as a womanizer, but it made him uncomfortable. He knew how to love. He'd proven that once . . . and had his heart stomped on in return.

It had been love at first sight when he met Sarah, a smart, stunning UN interpreter. He had fallen hard and fast, as had she, and within six months they were married. Another six months and she was pregnant . . . and a final six months after that, she was gone . . . to the great suburban wasteland in the sky. . . .

Well, Connecticut actually, but close enough as far as Drew was concerned. Off to Connecticut, with an orthopedic surgeon called Terry—Drew's best buddy since high school.

Should give him a call now, thought Drew. Get a second opinion on this leg.

There had been moments, whole days really, after their betrayal that Drew seriously thought he wouldn't survive. Sarah had ripped his heart out of his chest. He had gone berserk with grief over the end of his marriage. He had reeled over the loss of the unborn child he'd thought was his. And worst of all, the person with whom he'd normally share his pain was the one who had caused it.

Terry's betrayal cut the deepest, and losing him was like losing a limb. Over time Drew's grief had abated. He even came to realize that perhaps he and Sarah weren't that well matched. But there was no denying that the incident had left its mark, and he'd been unable to commit to anyone since.

But then, in his defense, he'd met no one special since the divorce. There had been offers, proposals, friends who knew "just the person," but Drew wasn't willing to settle for second best anymore. He wanted the whole enchilada. He believed he'd love again, and was happy to wait. In the meantime, he was only human.

He'd had flings with some of the women at work. Two actually, despite all reports to the contrary. Eva had been a surprise. She'd asked him out for a drink one night and announced that she'd decided to take his flirting to the next level. She had also made it clear that she had no interest in anything more than very casual sex. "When I decide to get serious about a guy, he's going to be *way* richer than you, Drew."

Within five minutes, they had embarked on a very satisfying four-day affair, cut short by Hurricane Hilda.

Before that there was Jess, who was, in retrospect, a mistake. She'd sold herself as someone with no time for a relationship and no desire for romance. She was looking for, "Casual sex sprinkled with intelligent conversation." It sounded perfect. When a gorgeous, smart, professional woman puts it to you like that, you don't refuse, right?

Wrong!

He'd extracted himself from her clinging clutches as gently as possible. He didn't want to hurt her, or their professional relationship. So far, so good. They were friendly and still worked well together. She wasn't the type to hold a grudge . . . was she?

He wasn't so sure now. Her tone on the phone had been brutal, and she'd refused to take his calls since.

Best to steer clear of co-workers, thought Drew. Especially ones like Rowie. Watching Rowie each night was messing with his head. She was the antithesis of everything Drew believed his job to be. With her gorgeous face and quirky ways, she flitted about in front of the greenscreen, genuinely moved by the calamities the weather caused.

"Oh dear," she'd say apologetically, as if the bad weather were all her fault. "So much rain in Idaho won't be good for the crops."

Then there was the voodoo stuff. She'd stand in that strange little pose, her insanely green eyes focusing somewhere . . . somewhere only a *Star Trek* commander should go. She predicted the weather in an almost monotone voice, breathy and low, and Drew wondered what it would be like to have her whisper in his ear. Wherever her information came from, she never stalled, never questioned it, no matter how crazy it seemed.

And she was never wrong!

Drew liked her immensely. He was strangely drawn to her and found himself dialing her number regularly, although he always hung up before it rang. He knew she was good, in her own wacky way, but he also couldn't help feeling she made a mockery of his years of struggle and study, and of his genuine desire to understand an almost inexplicable science. It was an uncomfortable clash of opposites: science and magic. Kind of like watching Harry Potter do his job. She made Drew feel strangely unsettled.

"You're hot for the girl," Winston, the orderly from the ER, chuckled one night.

Drew rolled his eyes at the Winston. "Yeah, I'm really into weirdness. It's an attractive quality in a woman."

Winston often swung by for a visit. He was an interesting character. Black as night, with regal features and huge, thick hands, he took time to talk to the patients. While the hospital doctors concentrated on the diseases and injuries, Winston concentrated on the patients themselves. He might not know how to cure Mr. Roland in 43B, but he knew that his grandson was a star quarterback, his daughter nagged him about smoking, and his sister was having problems with her car.

Many patients agreed that Winston's ability to listen was the most effective medication available. Drew certainly looked forward to his company. They'd chat, play cards and sometimes watch the news together. Winston made him laugh, with his droll insights into human nature and the often obscure cases he witnessed at the hospital.

"Hot, hot, hot for her," Winston cackled.

"Haven't you got work to do?" said Drew.

"Hey, whatever, I'm just telling you what I see. Every night you lie here mesmerized."

"Like I've got a choice, being in traction and on painkillers and all."

Winston barely paused. "And all day long you're reading those magazine articles about her."

"I don't ask Jack to bring me those," Drew lied. Anyway, it was only smart to be aware of his competition. Rowie's popularity was soaring. Magazine features were lined up, her face was plastered over billboards, TV programs wanted her to guest star . . . Apparently Barbara Walters wanted to interview her.

Drew devoured everything he could get his hands on.

Cosmopolitan urged him to "Come out of the Broom Closet," like Rowie.

Marie Claire assured him that "This Is One Shakespeare You'll Understand."

InStyle encouraged him to "Express Your Inner Psychic," using this season's accessories.

She was everywhere, yet he still didn't know much

about her. She was strangely reticent in interviews. She didn't appear to court the publicity she generated, and never gave away a great deal of personal information.

But one look into those emerald eyes and Drew felt he knew every inch of her soul.

She was obviously a witch.

Ingrid also teased him about Rowie. "Whenever she's on TV, your temperature rises," she said as she removed a thermometer from under his tongue.

"That's your presence, Ingrid, not hers."

Ingrid gave him a friendly slap, and they both laughed. Out of self-preservation, Drew had stopped seriously flirting with her. It was hard to be charming while someone slipped a bedpan under your ass and checked your back for bedsores.

Instead, he'd taken on the role of caring big brother. Ingrid trusted him and told him everything about her chaotic love life. The more she divulged about the men she dated, the more relieved Drew was that he hadn't become one of them.

"Hey, when you go back to New York, do you think you can get her autograph for me?" asked Ingrid.

"I probably won't run into her." Drew watched Rowie flit across the screen. "I'm sure by then her spaceship will have arrived to take her home."

"You could ask her out." Ingrid felt it was her mission to help heal his lonely heart as well as his broken leg. "I bet you'd get along really well."

"Doubt it. We're completely different."

"You know what they say: opposites attract."

"Yes, but they should never date."

Ingrid smiled knowingly. "I just have this gut feeling that you'd like her."

"A gut feeling?" Drew groaned. "Excellent. If I ever break another leg I'll call you to fill in at work for me."

Chapter Seventeen

Rowie stuck her head into Mac's office. "You wanted to see me?"

Mac smiled and waved her in. "Take a seat. I just wanted to see how you're doing."

"Good . . . great. I can't believe I've been here for over a month already."

Mac studied Rowie. "Any plans for afterwards? Any offers?"

"No. But I'm open to them. How about a psychic network infomercial?" Rowie teased.

Mac went red, but laughed. "I was wrong that first day."

"It's okay."

"You've changed my mind about a few things, Rowie," Mac admitted. "You've made a believer out of me."

Rowie nodded. "Good. Then you'll believe me when I tell you that those tests will come back fine."

Mac's mouth dropped open, but remained speechless. He hadn't told a soul.

"Sorry," said Rowie. "That just popped out."

Mac regained his composure. "That's . . . excellent. A huge relief. Thank you."

Rowie stood to leave. "And thank you, Mac. You're a great boss."

Mac walked Rowie to the door, paused for a moment, and then gave her a wink. "Loved the articles. Especially the piece in *SheStyle.* You make for a riveting read, Miss Shakespeare."

Rowie headed down the corridor with a grin from ear to ear. It *was* a great piece. Rowie had picked up a copy on her way to work, and then disappeared into her dressing room to read it. She traced her finger over the promises on the cover.

"Twenty ways to lose ten pounds!"

"Do dermatologists use Botox on themselves?"

"Fake tans for a real summer."

And then this: "An unpredictable friendship: one writer's real-life friendship with the Psychic Weatherwoman."

Rowie hoped Angel hadn't made her sound too weird. It was a big call.

Rowie spread out the article in front of her. She smiled when she saw a series of photos of the two of them, taken in a photo booth at Coney Island. She started reading, feeling confused, and then overwhelmed. She'd expected a more journalistic piece, but instead Angel had written it from her own perspective. She described Rowie as sweet, loyal and funny. She wrote about how "normal" Rowie was, despite her unusual gift. It wasn't an interview; Angel had written an ode to their friendship.

"The day we met was, in retrospect, the best day of my life. I finally found my twin. Despite the differences between us—and there are many spiritual, physical and even cultural ones—Rowie has led me down the joyous path of female friendship."

Even Gwendolyn and Lilia got a glowing mention.

"*They may be eccentric,*" Angel wrote, "*but they are also two of the most moral women you'll ever meet. The history of the Shakespeare clan is littered with tales of prejudice and persecution, yet these women are completely free of these qualities themselves. They welcome everyone into their shop, their homes, their lives, equally and with open arms. I have been blessed, truly blessed, to become a part of their extended family.*"

And this: "*People ask what it's like to be best friends with a psychic. I guess it comes in handy when there's a ghost in the room who wants to talk to me (yes, this has happened). But Rowie doesn't predict my future. I'm not even sure what she sees for me, as I've never asked. I guess if there were something she felt I needed to know, then she'd tell me. Mostly we talk about life, love, guys, work, world events, men, love, sex, books, chocolate, movies . . . guys, guys, guys . . . normal things. Normal conversations for normal friends. I don't concentrate on her psychic gifts. That would be like having a friend who was a dental hygienist and asking her to check my teeth. A friend who was a gynecologist and asking her to . . . well, you get the drift. I'm not drawn to Rowie because she's psychic—although that is an integral and wonderful part of her—but because there's no one I'd rather spend time with. It's this simple: My friend feeds my soul.*"

Rowie wiped the tears from her eyes. She didn't know how she'd ever thank Angel. She'd always felt pathetically grateful that someone as wonderful as Angel wanted to be her friend. The bullying Rowie had suffered at school had left its mark, so it never occurred to her that their friendship was an equal source of joy for Angel. It was the greatest gift a friend had ever given her, and flowers just didn't seem an appropriate response.

There was a knock on the door and Shin stuck his head into the room.

"Hey, Rowie, I was just wondering . . . Oh sweetheart, what's up?"

Rowie blew her nose. "Nothing. Just reading this article that my friend wrote."

"Oh yeah? Where?" Shin strode over to Rowie and took the magazine from her, and gazed at the photo of Angel. "She's . . . wow, drop-dead gorgeous."

Rowie stared at Shin in amazement. Why hadn't she seen it before? How perfect! Angel would be thrilled.

And so much better than flowers.

Chapter Eighteen

"I feel like Nicholson in *The Shining*," Drew said to Jack one Friday. He'd been strung up for five weeks, one day . . . and two hours. But who was counting?

"All work and no play makes Jack a dull boy." Jack laughed. "It's a personal mantra of mine."

"Do you think I should get Doc Hinchey to take this cast off and do more X-rays? What if my leg has healed quicker than expected?"

"Unlikely."

Drew paused for a moment. He felt like a fool . . . but . . . what the hell! "What about that healer you were talking about? Do you think he could fix my leg?"

Jack's eyes lit up, but he kept his voice steady. "We could give it a shot."

Drew tried to look nonchalant. "Yeah . . . whatever. If you want."

Jack kept a straight face. "I'll see what I can organize."

* * *

The following Monday, Jack arrived with an entourage of New Age healers in tow. He looked like the Pied Piper at Woodstock.

One by one he introduced Mel, a tall, bearded Reiki healer; Mitch, a short, stocky reflexologist; Dr. Chan, a qualified GP and acupuncturist; and Delphine, who specialized in chakra clearing, reconnective energy and smelled of ylang-ylang.

Drew nodded politely as they explained their techniques, admitted that they all seemed very qualified, and then asked if he could have a moment alone to speak with Jack. The minute the others closed the door, Drew exploded.

"What the hell are you doing?" he bellowed. "You've just set the whole cast and crew of the Learning Annex on me!"

"You said you wanted to give alternative healing a shot," Jack calmly reminded him.

"I okayed the healer. The one who was on *Oprah*."

"They've all been on *Oprah*, Drew. Oh, apart from Delphine, but she's been on *Dr. Phil.*"

"Get rid of them, Jack."

"Relax, will you? They're here. You might as well try them." Jack bit his lip and tried not to laugh. "Unless you've got something better to do?"

Drew glared daggers at Jack. "Fine. But I refuse to chant or share stories about my childhood."

"That's ruining half the fun," Jack teased. "Kidding! You take yourself way too seriously, my friend. You need to relax."

"Yeah, you'd think a month strapped to this bed would've done the trick!"

Jack opened the door and called the others back in. The group started by forming a circle around Drew's bed and sharing a few "Oms." By the time they were relaxed and centered, Drew was ready to scream.

Everyone decided that four therapies in quick succession would be too much for someone as blocked as Drew, so they split into pairs. Mitch and Dr. Chan would join forces and work on Drew first. Mel and Delphine agreed to go for a walk and return in an hour.

Jack patted Drew's shoulder. "I'll get out of their way."

"Don't leave me alone."

"I won't, you big baby. I'm just going to sit over there," Jack assured him. "You'll be fine."

Drew looked at Jack in amazement. "You're really enjoying this, aren't you?"

Jack grinned. "I haven't had this much fun in ages."

Jack settled into a chair in the corner. Dr. Chan and Mitch began to work. Dr. Chan opened a case filled with acupuncture needles and other tools of torture. Mitch walked to the end of the bed and took Drew's good foot. He traced a finger across the sole.

"Oh, that tickles." Drew giggled, horrifying himself and amusing everyone else.

Suddenly Mitch pressed his thumb hard into the center of Drew's foot. A jolt of pain shot down Drew's arm and seemed to zap out his fingers.

"What the hell was that?" he yelped.

"Blocked energy."

Mitch turned to Dr. Chan and started discussing meridian lines, blockages and various organs. It all sounded extremely scientific, and strangely comforting to a pragmatist like Drew. It was mumbo-jumbo . . . but *scientific* mumbo-jumbo. It couldn't be too weird. It had been practiced in China for a thousand years, so surely they'd perfected it by now. And the Chinese were no dummies; they'd invented everything from gunpowder to the printing press.

Mitch and Dr. Chan consulted each other every step of the way. Every pressure point on Drew's foot complemented a spot where a needle was placed. Before long, Drew resembled a pincushion, and the sour look on his face had disappeared.

He wasn't completely ready to admit he was wrong, but some subtle changes *were* taking place. Firstly, his leg had stopped itching. For the past three or four days, the skin under the plaster had itched continuously. It was driving him crazy. The doctor said there wasn't anything she could do about it until the plaster was removed. Doc Hinchey had obviously never heard of acupuncturology—as Drew decided to call it.

Also, instead of feeling more annoyed as the treatment progressed, Drew felt more relaxed. Really relaxed. He hadn't felt this good since that first shot of morphine.

Mitch and Dr. Chan finished and disappeared just as Mel and Delphine returned. They'd discussed their plan of attack over coffee, and jumped straight into it. For the next hour Mel placed his hands in various positions on Drew's body. There were no weird dances. No Hare Krishna chants. It was all rather . . . normal. Drew was quite disappointed.

"I'm channeling the Reiki energy," Mel explained.

"Yes . . . okay then," Drew mumbled, feeling slightly apprehensive. He wasn't sure what to expect. Perhaps a visit from a choir of angels, or maybe he'd remember life as a surf in Czarist Russia. Instead, he felt calm. A gentle, warm glow seemed to emanate from Mel's hands and permeate through Drew's body, deep into his soul. There was nothing life-altering about the sensation, but it was impossible to dismiss. Mel finally moved on to Drew's damaged leg. He placed his hands on the plaster.

"Unfortunately you can't get to that leg," Drew said.

"Don't worry. The Reiki goes through plaster," Mel assured him.

"Really? That's clever," Drew said, unsure what else to say.

Suddenly an intense heat began pulsating through the plaster. It wasn't painful, but it was obvious.

"It's healing the break," said Mel.

While Mel worked on Drew's leg, Delphine began her treatment. She moved around Drew's body, waving her hands in strange shapes and symbols. Finally, a weirdo, thought Drew. He was pleased that at least one of them was living up to his expectations, and was on the verge of giving Jack a smug look, when Delphine started saying the most unnerving things.

"Your throat chakra, your point of communication, is blocked. You never really told those two how much they hurt you."

Drew noticed Jack grinning at him from the corner.

"Oh dear," Delphine continued. "Your heart chakra is a mess. They really did a hatchet job on you. I'm going to work on it a bit and open it up. That way you'll allow love back into your life."

"I'm too busy for love," Drew joked. "Just leave it closed."

She ignored him and started tracing hieroglyphics into his chest. Drew amused himself by counting the cracks in the ceiling. He noticed his chest felt tingly. He was a bit uncomfortable, actually. He turned his head and pretended to read some of his get-well cards on his side table, but they made him emotional.

Oh God no, he felt like crying!

He pushed Delphine's hands away. "Sorry . . . can you stop doing that?"

She looked at him, straight through him. "I know," was all she said.

She moved away from the bed and had a sip of water. Drew felt edgy, exposed. Mel was still working on his leg, his eyes closed now. For all Drew knew, he was probably asleep, and still charging by the minute.

Delphine returned to the bed and started poking near Drew's groin. "As to be expected. Nothing wrong with your root chakra!"

Drew wished she'd leave his root chakra alone. It had been over four weeks since it had seen any action and it certainly didn't need to be teased by a sixty-year-old woman in a kaftan.

Drew wanted to write these people off as complete weirdos—but they weren't. They were all nice and smart. They made a few well-timed jokes, mostly at their own expense. They were more than willing to find the humor in what they did, and to also listen to and intelligently assuage his doubts. By the end of the session, Drew was wiped. He thanked them for coming, waved them off, and then fell into a deep, dreamless sleep.

He didn't wake for eighteen hours.

Delphine returned every day for the rest of the week. She worked extensively on his leg and drew the occasional symbol on his chest. By Friday she felt her work was done.

"Give it about five days and then demand some new tests," she said.

"As long as the leg has healed enough for me to fly home."

Delphine gave him a sly smile. "I think you'll find it has."

Over the next few days, Drew noticed some changes. He couldn't be sure they had anything to do with Delphine or the other healers, but as a man of science, he couldn't completely discount them either.

He spent a great deal more time than usual on the bedpan, thankful that he'd long since passed the point of embarrassment with Ingrid. He also slept a lot more, something he'd been unable to do since the accident, on account of being so stressed. Best of all, he didn't need any more painkillers. He was uncomfortable popping pills and didn't want to end up doing macramé with other celebrities in rehab.

Whether it was Jack's weird friends, the extra sleep he was getting, or simply because it was time, Drew felt better than he had in ages.

Dr. Hinchey was pleased with his progress and agreed to another round of tests. "Let's not get ahead of ourselves," she said, "but we might be able to transfer you to Mount Sinai in New York."

Later that afternoon, Dr. Hinchey returned with the test results and an ashen face. "I . . . ah . . . sorry it took so long. I had to get some colleagues to take a look."

Drew's heart plummeted. Something was wrong.

The doctor pulled up a chair beside Drew's bed. "It seems . . . your leg has healed . . . exceptionally well—strangely well, considering the extent of the injury. In fact . . . we can't find any evidence of a break at all."

Had he not been attached to his torture rack, Drew would've jumped up and down with joy. "Are you saying I'm fixed?"

Dr. Hinchey shrugged. "I guess. I've never come across a case like this before. It's a . . . and I hate this word . . . but it does seem to be a miracle." She stood, still apparently baffled. "We'll arrange some rehab in Manhattan, but . . . I guess you can go home."

Drew grabbed the doctor by the arm and pulled her in for a hug. "That's the best goddamn news ever!"

"We'll get this contraption off you this afternoon."

"Will it hurt?" Ever the wimp.

"Not much. It can hurt when a tibial traction pin is removed, but it's been on for a while, so it should be quite loose." She smiled at him. "Can someone pick you up in the morning?"

"I'll bribe someone to come down." Drew grinned.

"Okay then." Dr. Hinchey patted Drew's arm. "This has certainly been one for the books."

The following morning, Drew celebrated his pending freedom by hobbling up and down the hospital corridor until Jack arrived. He wasted no time in signing out of Plankaville Medical and, after a teary farewell from Ingrid and Winston, he finally headed home.

Chapter Nineteen

Rowie was struggling to remain professional, but her eyes glistened with tears, and the viewers loved her more for it. All across the tri-state area, people were glued to their sets for one last look at the psychic weatherwoman.

"Not a cloud in the sky, but I predict there'll be rain later. That's it from me. Drew Henderson is back on Monday. Have a great weekend." Rowie stopped, paused a moment, and then smiled. "And thanks. I had fun."

Tina and Bill bade goodnight, and Shin counted them out.

It was over.

Shin appeared and gave Rowie a hug, then removed her mike.

"How do you feel?"

"Okay." Rowie shrugged. "Back to the real world tomorrow."

"I think we should celebrate."

"I'm in," Rowie said. "Any ideas?"

"Apparently Drew is back and everyone is meeting at the Tavern for some drinks. We could go," Shin suggested.

Rowie's heart skipped a beat, but she gave nothing away. "Sounds good." Especially since Drew had invaded her brain day and night since that phone call.

"Excellent. I'll see you at the Tavern."

Rowie took her time saying goodbye to the rest of the crew. Some would see her later for drinks, but others had to stick around for the late news.

"Rowie!" Tina walked up and gave her perfunctory kiss on each cheek. "Goodbye, dear."

"Thanks, Tina. I've enjoyed working with you."

Tina rolled her eyes. It was something Rowie had seen her do countless times. Tina saved all her facial movements for when she was on air. Off camera, she barely moved her face. If someone made a joke, Tina rolled her eyes. If someone was rude, Tina rolled her eyes. If terrorists broke into her home and held a gun to her head, Tina would probably roll her eyes. It was the one facial expression that never left an imprint. Tina took the aging process very seriously. In fact, she took everything seriously, which was why she had no laugh lines around her eyes. Tina's face was living proof that a good dermatologist and complete lack of humor could make a woman over forty look at least fifteen years younger.

"I know things were . . . tense between us at the beginning, but you proved yourself."

"Thanks, Tina." Rowie was touched. Tina rarely gave compliments.

"It's a pity Heartless Henderson has to come back. Next time we'll pray for a bigger hurricane. Anyway, good luck. It's been . . . well, weird really."

The minute Tina left, Bill sauntered up.

"Can't leave without saying goodbye to my favorite redhead."

What a pity, thought Rowie.

"Listen, Rowie, how about you and I go and have a little . . . *drinky* together?"

"That sounds lovely, Bill . . ."

Bill's eyes lit up.

". . . but I already have plans," Rowie finished.

Bill smiled, fifty-thousand-dollars worth of dental work flashing her way. "Some other time then."

"Yes." *Like when pigs fly and women embrace cellulite.*

Rowie returned to her dressing room, removed her TV makeup and replaced it with a touch of mascara and a dab of lip gloss. She threw all her things into a bag and collected her farewell cards and flowers. She intended to drop everything off at home before going to the Tavern.

There was a knock on the door and Jess poked her head into the room.

"Hey, Rowie, glad I caught you. Can you come in for a meeting first thing Monday morning?"

"Sure. Why? Is there a problem?"

"Not at all," said Jess. "Quite the opposite. We might have something else for you."

Rowie couldn't contain her excitement. "Really? More work?"

"Yes. But only Mac and I know, so keep a lid on it for now."

"Of course," said Rowie

"There's drinks at the Tavern if . . ."

"Yes, I've heard," said Rowie. "I'll see you there?"

"Yup."

Jess closed the door and Rowie took one last look around her dressing room. *More work?* She couldn't contain her excitement and did a little jig.

And then she remembered her grandmother and her excitement vanished. Damn her, and her horrible little Post-it notes.

Chapter Twenty

Jess stood at the bar and watched the biggest homecoming since Apollo II returned from the moon. People cheered and clapped and hugged. It was as if Jesus had just walked into an annual Evangelical conference.

Drew looked thinner, his hair needed a trim . . . he was pale. But he was still the most drop-dead gorgeous man Jess had ever seen . . . unfortunately.

She glanced around the bar and wondered if this many people would turn up to welcome her home. Probably not. There would more likely be a celebration if she left. She didn't get it. She worked just as hard, was just as pleasant to everyone, but people never really warmed to her. It was one of the—many—reasons she had adored being with Drew. For once, she had felt accepted.

Let him have his fun, thought Jess. Come Monday, Drew Henderson wouldn't be smiling. Not with the changes she'd just instigated. She paid for her vodka and walked to an empty table at the side of the room. She was never comfortable in social situations. She appeared cool and confident, but she battled low self-esteem. She knew her insecurities were unwarranted. She was smart, articulate, and thanks to a number of scholarships, very well-educated. She'd spent a year in Paris as a student and had been back many times since. It had left its mark on her style, the way she dressed, and the way she carried herself. She was also attractive. Tall, long dark hair, dark eyes, a body honed to perfection at the gym. There was absolutely no need for Jess Walker to lack confidence, but she did. Not that anyone would ever guess it.

She opened her bag, found her compact and quickly glanced into its mirror. Her makeup was fine, although it was difficult to truly tell in the Tavern's dim light.

The Tavern was a rustic old place, complete with the type of original fittings and furniture from the seventies that hadn't even been fashionable the first time around. The place looked tired, but drinks at the Tavern had been a USBC tradition for nearly thirty years.

Drew noticed Jess and limped toward her. "Hey, Jess."

"Is your leg hurting?"

"Nope . . . just a bit weak." He grinned sheepishly. "Still angry with me?"

It took every ounce of willpower not to throw herself into his arms. Instead, she gave him a cool smile. "No. You didn't mean to fall."

Drew looked genuinely apologetic. "Actually, I'm talking about Eva."

What did he want from her? Absolution? "I know."

"I figured that's why you were so harsh on the phone," Drew said.

"I never let my personal feelings get in the way of business," Jess lied, and pushed the meeting she'd just had with Mac to the back of her mind. It was too late to feel guilty. "I think you underestimate my ability to separate the two."

"Okay . . . great. I just want to make sure everything is fine between us."

Everything will be fine once you're mine. "Of course it is."

A cheer went up at the front of the bar and Jess noticed Rowie had entered. Unbelievable! The girl had been at USBC for a nanosecond and was already Miss Congeniality. Jess consoled herself with the fact that she didn't need friends and would one day run the company. She watched as Shin grabbed Rowie and gave her a hug. He said something, and Rowie threw back her head and laughed.

Jess couldn't remember the last time she'd laughed that freely.

Taye grabbed Rowie's arm and she twisted around to speak to him . . . and fell over her own feet. Jess shook her head in amazement. The witch even fell flat on her face with style. But then, she'd obviously had an awful lot of practice.

"Graceful little thing." Drew's eyes were riveted on Rowie. "Cute, though."

Alarm bells began to ring in Jess's head. "Don't even think about it."

"Just making an innocent observation." Drew sipped his beer and watched as Michelle gave Rowie a friendly hug. Wow, that was a first. Michelle was usually allergic to other women, especially pretty ones. Ms. Shakespeare didn't waste time making friends. "Is she single?"

Jess didn't like the direction this conversation was taking. "Has that ever stopped you before?"

Drew turned to Jess, anger bristling under his cool exterior. "I only hit on unattached women. You know that."

Jess did know it. He'd shared that with her in no uncertain terms. She knew it was an old wound, not completely healed. His Achilles heel, so to speak. She fired an arrow into it. "Is your ex still with your friend?"

Drew ignored Jess. "Call Rowie over."

"You didn't answer my question."

"You didn't answer mine."

Jess caved. "Yes, she's single. Why?"

"It's just a question, Jess."

"Fine." Jess stared at Rowie. She looked incredible. She'd obviously gone home and changed into something more comfortable. She was wearing jeans and a funky, flowing green top, her flaming hair loose around her shoulders. Jess suddenly felt uncomfortable in her gray suit that had seemed so right when she saw it at Barneys. Compared to Rowie, she felt stiff and dull. Of course Drew found Rowie attractive. She was beautiful, mysterious . . . unexplored territory. Drew was a regular Lewis and Clark when it came to women.

Jess glanced at Drew. He seemed mesmerized by Rowie. She wanted to scream and rage at him for not looking at her like that. Even when Drew had been pursuing her, he had never looked at her with such obvious admiration. Such fascination. Jess was certain he'd been interested in her simply because she was the one woman at work who didn't fawn all over him.

They'd shared some great times. It had been the most intense three months of her life. For the first time ever, she'd been swept away by a man. She wasn't quite sure why he'd ended it and had been devastated when he did. His excuse was they weren't really compatible . . . but what did compatibility have to do with love?

And she did love him.

Okay, she'd gotten a little clingy toward the end, but she couldn't understand why he wouldn't go public with their relationship. She wanted him to meet her friends, her family . . . her therapist. She wanted to tell the whole world about Drew Henderson.

He wouldn't even let her meet his dog.

To be fair, he had ended things gently and behaved respectfully since. Well, apart from boinking Eva Sanchez right under her nose, but she'd heard Eva had initiated that. And, according to the office grapevine, it *was* just sex.

No, Drew had been quite considerate of her feelings—which surely meant something—until this moment. He was watching Rowie like a five-year-old glued to the Disney Channel. And it was like a knife in Jess's gut.

It amazed Jess that Drew was so blind. Didn't he see how compatible they were? He could upgrade from the weather (yes, yes, he loved the weather . . . but it wasn't really the top of the media food chain) and have his own show. She'd produce it. They could be the golden couple of the media world. They were obviously meant to be together. It was crystal clear to Jess. If only she could make him see. If only there was a way to . . .

Holy shit! Why hadn't she thought of it earlier?

Jess stared at Rowie and remembered what she'd said when they first met.

"When I kiss someone I see their whole future in my head . . . like a movie."

Jess smiled to herself. How convenient! Rowie could kiss Drew and tell him exactly who he was meant to be with. Perfect! It was a surefire way to get her relationship with Drew back on track. She knew they were meant to be together. He just needed a nudge in the right direction. She knew a prediction from a psychic wasn't the most rational way to reel Drew back in, but hell, she was clutching at straws here. And Rowie certainly had Jess questioning her own skepticism. In the past six weeks, Rowie had made some outrageous predictions, and they'd all come true. Her track record was faultless. She may be weird, but she was also *always* right.

Jess quickly formulated her plan. First, she needed Drew and Rowie to kiss. The thought hurt, but it wouldn't be too difficult to set up. Judging by the way he was drooling, Drew was already planning it himself.

Rowie might need more manipulating. But it was just one kiss . . . and she'd made it perfectly clear that she didn't go back for seconds if the guy wasn't meant for her. She'd said it herself: "*I'm waiting for a man I can't read.*"

Jess could picture it. Rowie and Drew would kiss—okay, she didn't want to picture that bit—and then Rowie would pull away and, in a gentle, but firm voice say: "Why, Drew, you're in love with Jess." For some reason she even had a southern accent when she said it. And then Drew would step back . . . reeling. "By God, you're right. I've been such a fool."

Jess gave Rowie a cheery wave, called her over and turned back to Drew. "Try not to scare her. She's a bit—naïve. Innocent. She's led a sheltered life. She told me it takes her weeks before she'll even kiss a man."

"I bet I could change that," Drew said, only half joking.

Bingo! "You're on."

Drew frowned. "What?"

"It's a bet. One hundred dollars."

"You're betting I can't kiss her?"

"Yup. One kiss. Tonight," Jess challenged.

"No thanks," Drew said. "I'm not a betting man."

"You're forgetting, I've seen you in action in Atlantic City," Jess said.

Drew watched Rowie as she made her way toward them.

"So, how about it?" Jess asked.

"Not interested," Drew said. "She's . . . not my type."

Jess burst out laughing. "Oh bullshit! She's female, she has a pulse . . . what more do you usually ask for?"

Drew ignored the dig. "The psychic thing is a bit of a turnoff."

"You don't have to marry her." Let's just make that point clear, thought Jess. "It's cool. You wouldn't be able to do it. It's a tough call."

"Of course I could."

He was on the hook. Now all she had to do was reel him in. "Sure you could . . . But from what she's told me, there's no way . . ."

"One kiss? Okay, why not? You're on. You're a wild woman, Jessie girl."

Jess took that as a compliment. "You'd better believe it."

Rowie arrived, like a breath of fresh air in the musty bar. She gave Jess's arm a quick squeeze hello and then turned to Drew. "It's great to see you out of bed." An embarrassed heat crept across her cheeks. "I mean . . . out of the hospital . . ."

"Thanks for filling in for me." Drew quickly scrutinized her. She was even prettier than he remembered . . . if that was possible.

"I had such a great time." Rowie beamed. "I'd love to keep your job."

Drew raised his eyebrows at Jess. "Sounds like I've got some competition."

Jess smirked. He didn't know the half of it. "Sounds like it." She slugged back her drink. "I'm going to the bar."

Rowie watched Jess walk off and then turned back to Drew. "How's your leg?"

"Good as new. Just weak from lack of use." He gave a little hop to prove his point, but grimaced in pain. "Been aching a bit today."

"It's predicting rain."

Drew shook his head in disbelief. He'd seen the forecast. "It won't rain tonight."

"Want to bet?"

Drew stalled. He didn't know whether to feel guilty or excited at the prospect of winning Jess's wager. "I'm not really a betting man."

"I bet it's great to be home."

"Hell yeah . . . although there's a lot of maintenance to catch up on. I live on a boat," Drew explained.

"Really?" Rowie was impressed. On TV he seemed more of a Tribeca loft kind of guy. "I didn't realize people could live on boats in Manhattan."

"It's rare. There's another boat basin not far from me, near Riverside Park. There are quite a few permanent boaters there. The marina where I live is privately owned and quite small. There are twelve of us on six boats, living aboard year round. Over the summer there are seasonal boaters who come and go, a lot of regulars we've gotten to know over the years, a handful of newcomers each season. It's a world of its own down there. I'm so grateful to be a part of it."

"It sounds amazing," Rowie said. "What are the boats like? Are they houseboats?"

"They're all different. The marina owner and his wife live on a converted shrimp trawler. The way they've decked it out is amazing. Most of the others live on motor yachts . . . although I'm a bit of a sailboat snob. I believe if it doesn't have a sail then it's not a proper yacht."

Rowie didn't know a great deal about boats, but was enjoying the conversation . . . and the excited gleam in his eyes. He obviously loved his lifestyle. "So you live on a yacht . . . one with sails."

"I sure do. She's a beauty too. An Alpha . . . that's the builder. I bought her in New Zealand."

"Wow! Why?"

"It just worked out that way. I decided to take three months off and travel before I started with USBC. I went to Auckland for the America's Cup, and while I was there I looked at a couple of boats that were for sale. The Kiwis build great yachts, and because of the exchange rate they're a lot cheaper than over here." Drew grinned. "It was love at first sight. I just knew I had to have her. So I bought her, had a few things altered, canceled my flights, and sailed her back home."

The surprises didn't stop coming. The guy was amazing. Rowie was riveted. "By yourself?"

"No, I had my father with me. He's an old sailor too. It wasn't long after my mother died, so it did us a world of good." Drew looked wistful for a moment. "It was an amazing trip. We sailed across the Pacific, through the Panama Canal and up the East Coast to New York."

Rowie was dumbfounded. She had no idea what to say, so she just stared at him. He picked his beer off the table, fumbling slightly.

"God, I'm sorry. I must be boring you." He looked genuinely embarrassed.

"On the contrary. I'm impressed," Rowie assured him. "I feel completely ordinary by comparison."

"Yeah . . . completely ordinary," Drew chuckled. "Gorgeous redheaded psychics are a dime a dozen."

"They are in my family." Rowie laughed.

"So, are you actually related to *the* Shakespeare?"

"I'm descended from his great aunt. It's a matriarchal line. The women pass on the family name."

"And the men?"

"What about them?"

"What do the men pass on?"

Rowie grinned mischievously. "Genes."

"Ouch." Drew laughed.

"We also need them to take out the garbage," Rowie teased.

"Cute! What if your future husband really wants you to take his name?"

"Oh please! Do guys like that still exist?"

Drew smiled. She was quite delightful. "Obviously not in your world. Have you ever lived up to your name and written a play?"

Rowie cocked an eyebrow. "Ever lived up to yours and sketched a picture?"

"Huh?"

Rowie groaned. "Oh, Drew, pick up the pace."

Chapter Twenty-one

Jess leaned against the bar and watched as Rowie and Drew got along like a house on fire. It was annoying, but she'd cope. As long as her plan worked and no one—namely her—got burned.

"He'll never change."

Jess jumped at the sound of Eva Sanchez's syrup-smooth voice. "Eva! I haven't seen you for ages. How was Florida?" Her smile was as fake as a Canal Street watch.

Eva gave a sexy shrug. She didn't care what Jess thought of her. "Hot and wild. And I'm not just talking about Hurricane Hilda."

They both watched Drew for a moment, Eva in amused silence, Jess in abject misery.

"You still like him, huh?" Eva's sympathy was genuine. Unlike Jess, she'd thankfully escaped the Henderson love bug, although he'd been great fun and incredible in the sack.

Jess nodded. Whether it was Eva's concern, or the

three vodkas she'd had, Jess felt like sharing. "We were good together."

Eva laughed at the joke . . . but stopped when she realized Jess was serious. "Hell, if you want him that much, fight for him."

"I am." Jess's mouth set in a determined line. "By the end of tonight he'll want me back. He's just got to kiss her first."

"She must be a really bad kisser." Eva chuckled.

"Rowie's psychic," Jess explained. "One kiss and she'll see his future . . . and me in it."

"What if you're not?"

Jess looked genuinely astounded. "But I am."

"If you're so psychic, what do you need her for?"

They watched as Rowie said something to Drew, then headed to the bathroom. His eyes followed her like a boy who'd just lost his puppy.

"Wow, he never looked at me like that," said Eva.

"I've got to powder my nose," said Jess.

Eva grabbed Jess's arm. "You know the difference between us, Jess?"

Three bra sizes and a full set of acrylic nails? "Enlighten me, Eva."

"I never wanted more than he could give."

Jess stalked off to the bathroom, more determined than ever to win Drew back, just to prove Eva wrong. Rowie was washing her hands when she entered and gave Jess a smile. Jess was once again reminded how genuinely nice she was. She didn't want to go shopping with her, or have pedicures together, but Jess liked Rowie. Hiring her had worked out well, and she wasn't a threat—on any level. It was a perfect combination.

"Hey, Rowie, having fun?"

"Sure am. You?"

"Fabby. Drew seems to be holding up well."

"His leg healed quickly," Rowie agreed. "Surprisingly so, actually."

"Dreadful that he had to go through this so soon after that other disaster." Jess shook her head, and then pretended to realize, "Oh, of course, you wouldn't know." She lowered her voice slightly. "A bit over a year ago, he was married, his wife was pregnant, life was grand. Then she ran off with his best friend. Turns out the baby wasn't Drew's."

As planned, Rowie was appalled. "That's awful."

Jess had Rowie hooked. Now she reeled her in. "It took him ages to get over."

"It would. What a betrayal."

"Trust *is* an issue." Jess checked her appearance in the mirror. Not bad. She took a comb out of her bag and tidied her hair. "He'd like to meet someone else, but . . . he's scared."

"Naturally," Rowie sympathized.

"I don't think he wants to get involved unless she's The One. But how can you tell?"

They fell silent, both pondering the enormity of Drew's heartbreak.

"Oh my God." Jess paused for dramatic flair. "You could kiss him."

Rowie was thrown. "What?"

"You told me you see a movie reel of someone's life when you kiss him."

"Yes, but . . ."

"You could get a description of who he's meant to be with," Jess enthused. "And then he could keep an eye out for her."

"I can't just walk up to him and kiss him." As much as I'd like to, thought Rowie.

"So flirt with him a bit first. Then whack one on him as you say good night."

"I don't want to lead him on."

Jess cocked her head to one side. "He's a big boy, Rowie. He's not going to be hurt over one kiss."

Rowie was uncomfortable with where this conversation was heading. "I really couldn't."

"Why not? It's not like he's Quasimodo."

"True." No, actually, he was leg-meltingly hot, thought Rowie.

"Think of it as . . . charity work."

"Can I declare it on my taxes?" Rowie joked.

Jess was determined now. "I'm serious. You'll be doing a good man a great favor. What if he already knows the woman he's meant to be with?"

Rowie stared at Jess and couldn't help being swept along by her enthusiasm. It was actually starting to sound like a good idea. The woman could sell the Brooklyn Bridge.

"One kiss, Rowie."

Rowie caved. Jess had a point. Drew was a nice person, and if she could help him move on, then she should do it. "Okay. I'll see."

Jess looked elated. "Thank you!"

"I'm not promising." Rowie laid down the conditions. "And I'm not kissing him if he has bad breath."

"Deal," Jess grinned.

Jess pushed her way through the crowd, back to Drew. The bar was packed now, and Drew was—surprise, surprise—surrounded by women.

"I'm going home, Drew," she shouted in his ear. "Remember, no cheating. Got to be on the lips and more than ten seconds."

"I know how to kiss."

Jess blushed, then glared at the women around Drew. "Better ditch the fan club."

"Yes, ma'am."

Jess slipped her hand into the side of her purse,

pulled out some breath mints and handed them to Drew. “Just in case.”

Drew watched Jess leave and then quickly checked his breath in his hand.

Rowie reapplied her lip gloss and checked her teeth. She couldn’t believe she’d agreed to kiss Drew. Jess could be very persuasive. And strange. One minute she was indifferent toward her colleagues, and the next she was trying to solve their relationship problems.

Rowie tried to pick up why, but couldn’t. Jess seemed genuine. Perhaps she was a cool character, who stepped up to the plate when needed. And Rowie understood that. One of the great benefits of her gift was helping others find their soul mates.

Rowie zipped her bag shut and headed for the door. Drew was gorgeous . . . and nice. One kiss really shouldn’t be a problem.

Chapter Twenty-two

Around midnight Rowie said her goodbyes to everyone on the sidewalk outside the Tavern. Shin flagged a couple of cabs and they all piled in.

"You need a ride, Rowie?" called Taye.

"No thanks. I'll walk. It's not far." Rowie waved as the cabs drove off, and then noticed Drew waiting for her.

He smiled, almost shyly. "We didn't get to finish our conversation."

That's because clones from the Playboy Mansion surrounded you all night, thought Rowie. "Some other time."

She'd spent the evening talking to Shin and Taye, while Drew was busy with his harem of fans. She was somewhat relieved, as the night progressed, that she wouldn't have to go through with Jess's plan.

"It was nice to meet you, Rowie."

Or perhaps she would. "You too, Drew." Oh Goddess, he was handsome.

They smiled at each other, countless unspoken words thickening the space between them.

"Did I hear you say you were walking home?" asked Drew.

"Yes. I live just around the corner."

"Then I'll walk with you. Protect you from muggers."

"What about your leg?"

Drew slapped his thigh. "Right as rain."

Suddenly, as if by magic, it began to rain. Warm sprinkles paved the way for a deluge.

Drew looked shocked. "What the . . . ?"

"Told you." Rowie laughed.

"I don't have an umbrella." Drew looked genuinely alarmed.

Rowie started walking off. "You're in the wrong business if a little rain bothers you, Drew," she called over her shoulder.

Drew went after her. They walked for a while in an unusually comfortable silence. Drew noticed that Rowie's face was lifted slightly skyward. The warm shower soaked them both, but she didn't seem the slightest bit bothered by it.

What an unusual creature, thought Drew. She looked beautiful drenched, and he was almost sorry when the rain stopped as suddenly as it began.

Rowie stared upwards, as though looking for answers. "Short and sweet."

"I'm not sure where you get your information, but you're quite good," Drew grudgingly admitted.

"You've got a fairly high success rate yourself."

"I'd never have foreseen that tornado. How'd you do it?"

"I don't know."

"How can you not know?" It was an alien concept to a man who always demanded answers.

"I've never analyzed my gift that much," Rowie confessed. "It is what it is."

Drew also had a confession to make. "You're different from what I expected, Rowie."

"What did you expect?"

"A broomstick and a pointy hat."

Rowie laughed loudly. "Only during a full moon."

"So this gift of yours . . . can you read my mind?" Drew asked. If so, then some of the thoughts he was having about her needed to be censored.

Rowie placed a finger on her forehead. "Yes. You're thinking about food, football and sex. In that order," she said dramatically.

"Wow, you *are* psychic," Drew raved, mock-impressed.

They grinned at each other, acknowledging how much they were enjoying each other's company.

"How long have you been predicting the weather?" asked Drew.

"My whole life. What about you?"

"My dad was a pilot and he used to take me up in his plane. Get to see all sorts of weather up there."

"I know," said Rowie. "The few times I've flown—I just loved it. The sky filled me. Sounds weird, I know."

"Not at all. I get a similar feeling."

They turned onto Rowie's street and Drew noticed the billboard. "He'll be back" had been plastered across his face.

"Scary." Drew whistled.

"I'm under you."

Drew looked flustered. "Excuse me?"

"This is my house," Rowie explained.

"You're subjected to that billboard on a daily basis?"

Rowie shrugged. "My grandmother and mother both think you're handsome."

"I'm strangely flattered." Drew looked up at The

Grove. It was quite a sight, and not unlike Rowie herself: extraordinary, elegant, and slightly unnerving. "So they both live here as well?"

Rowie laughed at the look on his face. "It's not that bad. It's a huge house and they're . . . unusual."

"What do they do?"

Rowie pointed to Second Site. "That's our shop."

"Easy commute."

A shadow crossed Rowie's face. "Yes, very convenient. We're in the most exciting city in the world, and my life revolves around these two buildings."

Drew found Rowie's flash of unhappiness alluring. He wanted to know what troubled her. More than that, he wanted to fix it. "What do you want to do?"

"Can I have your job?" Rowie teased.

"I knew you couldn't be trusted."

They walked up the steps and Rowie searched her bag for her key.

"The Grove. Sounds witchy," said Drew, reading the brass plate attached to the front door.

"That was the point."

"Right. Sorry, I'm a bit slow tonight."

They smiled shyly at each other.

Rowie found her key. "Thanks for walking me home."

"Any time." Drew stared at the damp ringlets around her face. His eyes grazed the curve of her neck, and drifted upwards until they locked eyes. "Good night," he said, unable to leave.

Rowie didn't say a word, but her breath quickened. The air between them was as thick and sweet as honey. Their energies danced, and zapped, and nipped at each other.

"I should . . . go in."

Drew instinctively stepped between Rowie and the door. "Wait . . ."

His hands closed around her as he pulled her to him. His mouth crushed down on hers. She kept her arms frozen at her sides. Her eyes remained open, waiting . . . waiting . . . *waiting* . . .

Finally, she pulled back, shocked. She grabbed the handrail for support. Something was wrong. Really . . . wrong.

She didn't see anything.

Drew looked equally stunned by the kiss. He waited for her to say something, but was mortified when she did.

"Nothing," she whispered.

How could she feel nothing when he'd felt so much? He pulled her in again and kissed her softly, tenderly, determined to counter her reaction.

Rowie let her bag slip from her hand, and she wrapped her arms around his neck. She melted into his embrace, dissolved into his kiss. Darkness and light and every color in between exploded in her head. She waited for the images to start, but nothing played, not even a preview.

Drew pulled away, ruffled, strangely disturbed by the power of the kiss. His voice cracked slightly. "Better?"

Rowie's eyes were glazed. "Nothing," she gasped, and grabbed his collar and pulled him in again. She kissed him with a primal force as something snapped and unleashed inside her. She felt a tsunami of desire rush through her body. She jerked backwards, incredulous. "Damn, I—!"

But before she could speak, Drew dragged her straight back in for one wham-bam-helluva kiss. Rowie's sixth sense was shoved aside, and taste and smell and touch took over. Her senses were assaulted, a hunger awakened.

It was the most blissful moment of her life.

Finally, they both pulled away, wiped out by the kiss, the emotion . . . the strange familiarity.

Drew was breathless . . . and quite confused. "That?"

Rowie nodded, her eyes searching his. "Perfect." She picked up her bag and key, and tried to open the front door. Her hands were shaking so it took a while. "Anyway, lovely to meet you," said Rowie.

"Yes. You, too," Drew agreed. "Good night." He started to walk off, unsure of what else to do. He was flustered. He felt like a teenager after his first kiss . . . only this kiss was better and he felt more awkward. If only his brain would work. He didn't want to leave her like this. He swung back around. "I'd like to show you something. Are you free tomorrow?"

Rowie realized she'd been holding her breath. "Sure. What time?"

"Nine?"

"I'm a vegetarian."

Drew frowned as he tried to decipher the meaning behind this information. Rowie decided to translate.

"Just in case you're taking me to a . . . burger joint . . . or something. . . ."

Drew was still baffled. "For breakfast?"

"What?"

"I'll pick you up at nine A.M."

The confusion broke the ice and they both laughed.

"A.M.! Oh . . . okay."

Drew was finding it difficult to leave.

Rowie made the move for him. "Good night," she said and then disappeared into The Grove.

Drew made his way across the road and hailed a cab. This was definitely new emotional territory. The kiss had been awesome, wonderful and slightly frightening. He didn't even know a kiss could be like that. It was like he'd been playing in the minor leagues his whole life, even during his marriage, and suddenly he'd stepped into the majors. And if baseball analogies were the order of the day, then that kiss with Rowie was a home run.

He smiled to himself and stared out the cab window. His thoughts drifted to Rowie and her amazing eyes; her laugh, and the way it cut through the air like sunshine. He felt a stirring in the pit of his gut, and lower, as he thought of how his fingers had run through her hair, bunching it, clutching it. And her lips, pink, soft, sweet. He couldn't wait to see her tomorrow.

It was only then that he remembered the bet with Jess, and the memory of Rowie's sweet taste soured in his mouth.

Rowie closed the front door and made it to the foot of the stairs before her legs buckled. It had happened! Her mother and grandmother had always promised it would.

Blissful nothingness!

Suddenly, she was overwhelmed by the implications. It was all very well to dream about your One True Love, but knowing him was a whole new ball game. What now?

Her skin tingled as she thought about the kiss. It was enough to warm her on a thousand winter nights. And then she realized . . . what on earth was she going to tell Jess?

Chapter Twenty-three

Rowie's bedroom was light, airy and sparse, with big pieces of wooden furniture and white linens. The curtains always fluttered in the breeze, even when the large windows were closed.

Rowie loved her room. While the other rooms were a clutter of antique furniture and ornate ornaments, gilded framed photos and candelabras, her room was Zen-like in its appearance. Usually. This morning it was a mess of clothes, makeup and jewelry. It had taken two hours, and a not-so-minor breakdown, to settle on an outfit: Gap cargo pants and a top from Chelsea-Girl. They were going to breakfast. It was bound to be casual. Besides, she was a casual kind of girl when it came to clothes. Casual, with a splash of vintage.

She turned to the mirror and gave herself a three-and-a-half star rating. Now if only her butterflies would stop, although why they were called butterflies was beyond her. This was more like the hippos from *Fantasia* skating around in her stomach.

The doorbell rang and Rowie ràn out of her room and hung over the banister at the top of the stairs. "I'll get it!" she yelled. She rushed down the stairs and grabbed her bag. Gwendolyn and Lilia were in the living room, watching a rerun of *Touched by an Angel*.

"Bye," Rowie called as she ducked past the door.

"Can't we meet him?" called Gwendolyn.

Rowie reversed and stuck her head into the room. "No!"

"I look at that billboard every morning and think to myself, 'One day, before I die, I'll meet my favorite weatherman.'."

Rowie glared at Gwendolyn. The grand manipulator was in fine form this morning. "I thought Al Roker was better."

"Don't be ridiculous," said Gwendolyn, aghast.

The doorbell rang again and Rowie gave in.

"Oh all right. But please, act normal."

"Define *normal,*" said Lilia.

Gwendolyn waved her hand around, as though shooing away a pesky fly. "Why you'd want a man who likes normal is beyond me."

Rowie walked off, oblivious to the mischievous grin her mother and grandmother shared.

"Hi!" said Rowie as she opened the front door.

"Hi yourself." Drew was wearing jeans and a T-shirt and looked like he'd walked straight off a billboard. Considering how much time Rowie had spent staring at the billboard across the road, he really was like a dream come true.

"Are you ready?" he asked.

"This is so embarrassing," Rowie said, "but my grandmother would love to meet you."

Drew looked strangely thrilled at the prospect. "The one who thinks I'm handsome? Sure, no problem."

"You don't have to."

"I'd love to."

"It's not a big deal."

Drew raised an eyebrow. "I'd be honored, Rowie."

Rowie nodded and led him into the living room. Her heart sank when she realized the TV was now off, and Gwendolyn and Lilia were sitting opposite each other at a table with a crystal ball between them.

"Looks like the Mets have a shot this year, Lilia," said Gwendolyn.

Rowie glanced at Drew, expecting to see his eyes bulging in horror, but instead he was smiling.

"Mom, Gran, this is Drew."

"Morning, ladies." Drew sounded like a bingo coordinator at a nursing home.

Gwendolyn and Lilia both looked up and feigned surprise at having a visitor.

Gwendolyn stood and, channeling Queen Muck on Meet The Peasants Day, swept across the room and gave Drew a warm hug. "Drew the weatherman. How lovely to meet you," she gushed. Then acting surprised, "You're much shorter than you look on TV."

"Nice shoes, though." Lilia didn't miss a trick.

Gwendolyn squeezed Drew's hand. "We've missed you on the news."

"Rowie's done a great job filling in for me."

"Has she?" Gwendolyn seemed pleased to hear it. "I didn't really get to watch her. I've been so busy holding the business together." She ignored Rowie's death-stare and beamed at Drew.

Drew looked around the room. "What an amazing house." He noticed the portraits on the wall, replete with Post-it notes.

"A few of our ancestors," Gwendolyn explained. "That's Granny Elke," she said, pointing to the portrait closest to Drew. "She was stoned to death in 1603."

Drew took a step toward it and studied the beautiful

woman dressed in Tudor garb. "The painting must be very old."

"Oh no, Elke sat for it last year." Gwendolyn tried not to smile. She wanted to test the boy's mettle.

Drew looked confused, and a bit unnerved, but regrouped quickly and turned his attention to some of the other paintings. "They're gorgeous women."

"They'll be pleased you said so."

He noticed a row of four urns on the mantelpiece and, before Rowie could stop him, walked over to them. "Interesting urns."

"We should leave," said Rowie.

Lilia giggled softly. "Ashes to ashes, dust to dust."

"That's our mantel of marital mortality," Gwendolyn explained. She walked over to the mantel and tapped the first urn.

"This is my first husband, Ed. We weren't married long when he died. Tragic." She moved to the third urn. "Number three is Tedious Tom. Fortunately Tom choked on a fish bone before he bored me to death. He's so much more interesting now." Gwendolyn paused and then tenderly ran her fingers over the second urn. Her whole demeanor softened. "And this is my One True Love. I still can't believe he's dead."

"You must miss him," said Drew, gently.

Gwendolyn shrugged and smiled bravely. "He drops by when he can."

"On that note," Rowie interrupted, "let's go."

Drew ignored Rowie and pointed to the final urn. "And this?"

"That's mine," said Lilia.

"Poor boy was killed in Vietnam."

Drew frowned. "That's dreadful." He turned to Rowie, his eyes searching and compassionate. "Can you remember him?"

"No, he was killed before I was born."

"War is so senseless," said Drew. "You must feel ripped off, losing your father like that."

Rowie cringed visibly, while Gwendolyn and Lilia burst out laughing.

"That's not Rowie's father," said Lilia. "He's not up there yet, but he was the great love of my life."

Drew looked relieved . . . and slightly confused.

"We should go," Rowie whispered

Drew nodded, but wasn't finished with the history lesson yet. "Where's your father now?"

Rowie felt flushed. She shuffled uncomfortably. "I don't know. I've never met him."

This piqued Drew's interest more. He turned back to Lilia. "How long were you together?"

Gwendolyn grinned at Rowie. She liked the boy. "Inquisitive young man, isn't he?"

Lilia was delighted to share all the details. "We had one night. Time's not important."

"You think? I'd love the last two minutes back," snapped Rowie.

"Where did you meet?"

"Mom," Rowie interrupted. "I don't think Drew needs to hear . . ."

But Lilia was on a roll. "We met under the light of a full moon, by the fires of Beltane. I didn't see his face. We wore masks. But he had blue eyes and a tattoo of a mermaid on his shoulder."

"Who was he?" asked Drew, riveted.

Lilia simply shrugged. "He didn't say." She turned and smiled at her daughter, ignoring Rowie's glare. "He just gave me the greatest gift."

Drew looked like a child being introduced to tales about Narnia. "What an amazing story."

"Really heartwarming," said Rowie, feeling defeated. "Not much help to me at school when I was asked to tell the class about my father."

Lilia surveyed the mantel. "We must start making room for Rowie's urns."

Drew gave Rowie a wink. "That mantel is enough to make me think twice about dating you."

"Any man scared of that mantel isn't strong enough for Rowie anyway," announced Gwendolyn.

"Can we leave now?" Rowie begged, half expecting him to refuse. *Sorry, Rowie . . . now that I've met your family, I need to run a mile.*

Instead he smiled, bade a charming goodbye to Gwendolyn and Lilia, and followed Rowie out the door.

Rowie breathed a sigh of relief once they'd escaped. "I'm so sorry. They're completely insane."

"I loved them," he enthused. "Weird, but wonderful. I'm from a long line of accountants. Our family dinners should be bottled and used as a cure for insomnia."

Rowie laughed gratefully. "Sounds perfectly lovely."

Drew stopped at a Prius and opened the door for Rowie.

"This is yours?" she asked, impressed. "You drive a hybrid?"

"Do I look more like a Hummer kind of guy?"

Rowie laughed. "Less and less as I get to know you."

"I think we have enough oil guzzlers around without me adding to it. Hop in." Drew walked around to the driver's side and got in. "Are you free all day?"

"Yes. Why?"

"It's a surprise . . . and a bit of a drive."

Chapter Twenty-four

"We're going to a place near *Tarrytown,*" Drew explained, as they hit the West Side Highway north, toward Westchester.

Rowie nodded, not caring if they were going to the moon. She was just happy to be with him.

"So, tell me more about your family," said Drew. "Any sisters?"

Rowie cracked up. "Oh yes, I'm one of triplets, and we love pleasing men."

Drew thumped the steering wheel in amusement. "Excellent!"

"Sorry to disappoint, but I'm an only child."

Drew had yet to find anything disappointing about Rowie Shakespeare. He glanced at her as she slipped off her right shoe and curled her foot under her left leg. The simple gesture was highly erotic and Drew had to concentrate to stay on the road.

"I'm also an only child," Drew revealed. "But I have lots of cousins."

"I've got two. Calypso and Nell. Actually, they're

second cousins, but we're close. They lives in London so I don't get to see them very often."

"Are they like you?" Drew asked.

"You mean . . . *touched?*" Rowie offered.

"Yeah, little witches?" Drew teased.

"Yep. Red hair, weird visions . . . typical Shakespeare women. Calypso is very wild and free, while Nell is more conservative . . . shy." Rowie's face softened. "I adore them."

Drew's voice dropped slightly. "Listen, Rowie . . . I'm sorry if I brought up a painful subject back at The Grove. About your father and all."

"It's not painful," Rowie said honestly. "I never knew him, and there have only been a couple of times in my life when I've ever missed him. I just hate it when Mom starts going on about the night I was conceived. It's embarrassing."

"I was conceived in the back of the car after a bottle of cheap wine. I think your conception was more romantic."

"At least there were no naked Pagans dancing around your parents," Rowie grumbled.

"Nope." Drew chuckled. "You beat me there." He pulled off the main road and onto a country lane. "We're here." A minute later he turned into a small airfield and parked the car.

"Still wondering?" asked Drew.

"I take it we're not going to the movies."

"Come on, I'll show you."

They both got out of the car and headed toward the hangar. Inside, Rowie noticed a large man dressed in overalls working on one of the planes. He gave a wave and walked over to them.

"Drew! It's been a while." He grabbed Drew's hand and shook it vigorously.

"I broke my leg, so I had to lie low," Drew explained.

The guy nodded. "Yeah, I saw that on the news. You're a regular stuntman."

Drew laughed. "Joe, this is Rowie."

Joe gave a gap-toothed grin. "Nice to meet you, Rowie. Thinking of taking a spin?"

"Am I going up in a plane?" Rowie was starting to feel nervous.

"I'm trying to surprise her," Drew said to Joe. "Are you free for a tow?"

Joe was delighted to be in on the secret. "Sure am. What do you want?"

"The usual. Three thousand feet."

"I'll get the Pawnee ready." Joe walked off, wiping his hands on an oily rag.

"What was that in English?" asked Rowie.

Drew gave Rowie a mysterious smile. "Patience, grasshopper, patience."

Thirty minutes later, Rowie and Drew were standing on the tarmac, next to a glider. Drew was excited, but Rowie didn't share his enthusiasm. She stared at it with the same wary expression one would a rabies shot.

"What is it?" she asked.

"A glider."

"How does it work?"

"Joe's plane tows us up to three thousand feet. I pull a release knob and then we're on our own. You game?"

Rowie sounded slightly panicked. "It hasn't got an engine?"

"Nope, no engine."

Rowie wasn't sure. "You know how to fly this . . . dirigible . . . thingy?"

"I have a license."

Rowie snorted . . . and was then mortified that she had. "My mother has a driver's license but you couldn't pay me to get in a car with her."

Drew took Rowie's hand in his. "Do you trust me?"

Rowie considered him for a long moment. She could feel the warmth of his hand seeping through the rest of her body, calming her. Did she trust him?

"Yes. I do."

Drew checked the glider, then walked over to Joe's plane. The two men spoke for a moment. Joe disappeared inside the plane, and Drew returned to Rowie. He helped her into the glider and buckled her harness, then seated himself in the front.

Rowie watched as he flipped a series of switches. She shoved her hands under her legs to stop them from shaking. *What was she doing?* And then she heard a little voice inside her answer: living! For years she'd been dreaming of love and adventure, of breaking free. And here it was, with Drew. She was standing on the threshold; all she had to do was leap.

"You ready?" Drew yelled.

It was now or never. Rowie leapt. "You bet! Bring it on."

Joe's plane started to move. The glider lurched forward and followed the Pawnee up the runway. Rowie felt the force pushing her back into the seat. Faster, faster, even faster, until the nose tipped up and the ground sank below them and they took off.

Drew punched a fist in the air. "Yeah baby!"

Rowie forgot all her fears and allowed herself to fly. "Holy woo-hoooooooo!"

Before long the tow plane gave a wave of its wings.

"That's it," Drew yelled. "We're on our own."

He pulled the release knob and Joe's plane disappeared from view. They were alone, soaring through the sky. The wind outside was noisy, but without the sound of an engine there was the illusion of silence.

Rowie looked up at the endless blue, then peered at

the world below. She felt safe, untouchable, alone with Drew in their small flying capsule.

"What do you think of the sky from this angle, Rowie?"

Rowie pressed her fingers and nose against the window. She was in awe. "Oh Drew, it's just magical."

It was all over way too soon. Drew brought them in to land, smoothly, expertly, and once the glider was at a standstill, he lifted Rowie onto the tarmac. She threw her arms around him and held him tight, the adrenaline still pumping through her veins.

"That was incredible, Drew. Thank you."

Drew squeezed his eyes shut and returned the embrace. "Any time."

Strangely enough, he really meant it.

Chapter Twenty-five

Rowie and Drew left the airport and headed down the road to a large field. Drew parked and got a picnic basket and blanket out of the trunk.

"I thought you might need a drink after that," he teased. "And you'll be pleased to see I've provided only vegetarian fare."

Rowie grinned and threw herself down on the rug. "I thank you on behalf of the animal world."

"Is that why you're vegetarian? Because you love animals?"

"That's part of it," said Rowie. "But also the environment."

"I know what you mean," said Drew. "It has an impact. As a meteorologist, it's blatantly obvious how much damage we've done to the planet. Over sixty percent of natural disasters can be attributed to global warming now."

Rowie lathered some hummus over a chunk of bread. "And it will only get worse, unless we do something."

"Immediately," Drew agreed. "Or we won't have

much of a planet to leave our children." He looked momentarily mortified. "I mean 'our children' in the generic sense. I'm not hinting at you to bear my offspring . . . I mean who knows . . . anything really . . . I should shut up now, shouldn't I?"

Rowie gave him a mysterious smile. "It's okay, Drew. I know what you mean."

After lunch, and some much safer topics of conversation, they lay side by side on a picnic blanket and stared at the clouds.

"I think we flew through that one," said Rowie. "It looks like a moose."

"Looks like a stratocumulus to me."

Rowie gave him a friendly slap. "How imaginative of you."

"Just stating a fact."

"You're very big on facts. Don't you ever go with your intuition? Your feelings?"

Drew grinned. "Only if they can be backed up with facts."

"Do you believe in destiny?"

"Nope. I believe you make your own luck. Forge your own path."

Rowie pushed for more information. "What about love? Haven't you ever been in love?"

"Yes. Once. I was married. She got pregnant . . . by my best buddy, as it turns out."

"That must have been very difficult for you," said Rowie quietly.

"I was completely governed by my feelings, so it was weird territory for me. I didn't deal with it very well. It rocked me . . . I just didn't see it coming." Drew chuckled. "I'm not psychic like you." He sat up. "I don't deny that you seem to have a . . . gift. I mean . . . I'm not sure I believe in psychic phenomena, but you're doing a good job of converting me." He paused for a moment and ran his fingers through his hair. "It's just that it makes me nervous. It's not something I can explain. Science is a sure thing."

Rowie couldn't help but roll her eyes slightly. "Every scientific fact started as a great mystery."

"Perhaps. But it never benefited us until we understood it."

"Oh Drew, magic and mystery have done more for mankind than facts and figures ever could."

Drew would not be swayed. "It was the great scientific minds who changed this world. From Galileo . . ."

"Who was tried for heresy," Rowie interrupted.

". . . And Pythagoras," Drew continued.

"Pythagoras was a Pagan. A mystic."

"Really?" Drew looked unconvinced. "Next you'll be telling me that Einstein was a Buddhist."

Rowie grinned and scored another point. "No . . . but he *was* a vegetarian." She reached out and took Drew's hand. "These men understood that science and divinity go hand in hand. Look around. The weather hasn't always been about computers. With nature you can gauge things differently."

Drew reached over and gently plucked a blade of grass from Rowie's hair. "Okay Nature Girl, what's your forecast for the rest of the day?"

Rowie lifted her face to the sky. Her gaze started to shift, but she looked strained. Something was wrong. She was blocked.

She tried again, squinting her eyes and really giving it her all. Same thing. She couldn't understand. This had never happened before. She shook her head, disconcerted—frightened even—but quickly pulled herself together. She glanced at Drew, avoiding his curious stare, and moved closer to him.

"You know what?" Rowie leaned toward him, her

tongue lightly flickering across his ear. "I can think of a much more enjoyable way to spend our time together."

Drew couldn't agree more. He rolled her back onto the blanket. "You've cast quite a spell on me, Miss Shakespeare," he whispered.

Within five seconds of his lips hitting hers, Rowie forgot all about how the sky had just failed her.

Chapter Twenty-six

Rowie stood on the marina and stared at the boats. Drew hadn't been kidding when he described it as a world unto itself. Each boat was completely different, but fit perfectly as part of a bigger picture. It was as though they all belonged there together. The din of the city was muted, and apart from the occasional creak and slap of water against a hull, the boat basin was quiet.

Drew ushered Rowie along the wharf, giving her a rundown of each boat they passed. "That huge monstrosity belongs to Dell and Kris. They live there with their six-year-old twins. Amazing people. Made a fortune in real estate but decided not to live in any of it. This pretty little sloop is Henry Hunter's boat. He's a single father. He lives there with his son Nick."

"Isn't he a writer?" asked Rowie.

"Yep, mysteries. They're not bad. The *New York Times* called them beach books and Henry phoned them and said they were actually boat books. See that little motor cruiser, called *I Presume*? That's Frank Livingston. He's ninety-eight years old . . . amazing. Oh, and this one belongs to Dawn and Pascal. They run a lesbian workshop at the Seminar Center."

They reached the end of the wharf and Drew stopped. "This is her," he whispered with a reverence usually reserved for newborn babies and Christian Saints.

Rowie read the name on the side. "*Aspasia.*"

"She was . . ."

". . . Pericles' lover. She was one of the most beautiful and powerful women in ancient Greece." Rowie finished. "It's a wonderful name for a boat."

Drew jumped on, reached out his hand and helped Rowie board. He pointed out a couple of things on deck and then guided her to the bow. They watched as the sun set across the Hudson.

When all that remained were a few streaks of orange, Drew led Rowie to the hatch and down a small set of stairs. He flicked on the lights, and Rowie gave a cry of surprise as a large scruffy dog pounced on her.

"Norm, get down," Drew yelled.

"So you're the famous Norm? It's nice to meet you." Rowie exclaimed, immediately winning brownie points from both Drew and Norm.

Norm was placated and tottered off, and Rowie was able to have a good look at the inside of *Aspasia*. Drew was right to be so proud of her. The boat was classy and completely unique.

"This is the main saloon," said Drew.

The room was all deep wood and muted colors. The furniture was built-in, yet still smart and comfortable. There was a large table surrounded by dark navy upholstered seats on one side, and a small round sofa that overlooked an entertainment system on the other. The floor was wood, as were most of the fittings, including a couple of bookcases filled with books.

"Don't the books fall off the shelves in rough weather?" asked Rowie.

"Everything is built to stay put," Drew explained. "Come and I'll show you the galley."

The galley had granite countertops and stainless steel appliances. It was narrow, but designed to utilize the space well.

"There's not much room, but I can still cook up a mean lasagna here."

"This is amazing," said Rowie. "I had no idea boats could be so beautiful. Apart from those huge ones owned by people like Aristotle Onassis. My Gran always says yachts are for Eurotrash. She's obviously wrong . . . again."

"There are a lot of people who own boats for show, but the majority of boat owners just love the lifestyle. I've grown up around sailboats. My father has always been a bit of an action man. It was his way of rebelling from his rather dull family. I grew up flying and sailing. I love the water, the ocean. I hate being caged in. It just makes sense for me to live here."

Rowie stared at the curve of Drew's chin and the slight shadow of beard. She could feel herself being pulled into a vortex of fascination. She was interested in everything about him. His home suited him perfectly. It gave her a sense of who he really was. The simplicity of it put Rowie at ease. There was something so honest and refreshing about Drew Henderson and the world he inhabited that Rowie couldn't help but trust him.

"Come through here." Drew took Rowie's hand and led her through the cabin, past a tiny enclave with a radio and computer, and to the other end of the boat. He opened a door and pulled her into a bedroom. "My bedroom," he announced. "What do you think?"

What could she think? The room was lovely. It had a

large wooden bed on a raised platform, with deep drawers beneath. Behind the bed head were wooden panels. One wall was a wardrobe. Opposite was a door that led to a shower stall. The decor was a mix of wood, navy and white fabrics. It was the kind of bedroom that was relaxing and inviting. Perhaps too inviting.

"So you like my boat?" Drew looked like an eager child.

"I love it."

The air was thick with tension. Rowie could hear Drew breathing next to her. She pretended to be interested in the doorframe. She was unsure of what to say or do next. They were in his bedroom, which may have seemed convenient for some, but for Rowie it felt terrifying. It was the same room where he had probably ravished countless women. Drew was the type of guy who ravished.

She turned and headed back into the main cabin area and looked at the framed photos attached along the shelves. There were photos of Drew camping with friends, on his boat, standing in front of what looked like Angkor Wat, with a man she presumed was his father.

"You've traveled a lot."

"Forty-two countries and counting."

"You make me feel like a complete homebody," said Rowie. "Although I guess that's what I am. I like to be near my family, close to home."

Drew waved his arm around at his boat. "Me too, now. Which is why I love my boat. I get to travel without leaving home."

She stared out the window. The sky was dark. She imagined what it would be like out in the middle of the ocean where the starlit sky petered off until it merged with the ocean, heaven and earth indistinguishable in the darkness of night. Drew walked up behind her. She could feel his breath on her neck, his energy permeating hers.

"New York isn't famous for its starry skies."

"You still get a sense of it." She moved away from him and sat on the couch. The carefree magic of the airfield had been replaced by something far more momentous in the privacy of Drew's boat.

He sat down next to her, reached out and gently stroked her cheek. "I really enjoyed today."

Rowie's heart began to pound. "So did I." She paused, uncomfortable, and then blurted out, "I bet this boat comes in handy when you're seducing women." Oh God! She couldn't believe she'd said such a stupid thing.

Drew looked amused. "The last woman to see my boat was my wife."

Rowie nodded, too afraid to open her embarrassing mouth again.

"And she hated it. So no, you're not treading in well-worn footsteps."

Rowie had no idea whether he was lying or not. It was the first time *ever* that she really couldn't read someone. She had to decide for herself, without any psychic assistance, whether Drew was to be trusted. Normally she *knew*. Now she simply hoped.

It was crazy, but she felt so nervous. The kiss on the steps at The Grove had been mind-blowing. Rolling around in the field had nearly driven her insane with desire. But this was different. Being on his boat was the express train to sex, and it scared the hell out of her. What if she didn't live up to his expectations? Or worse, what if he didn't live up to hers?

Drew's eyes burned into her. She felt incredibly shy, so she searched the room for something to focus on, something to comment on, anything to break the tension.

"Is that a golf trophy?"

Drew grabbed Rowie and pulled her close. They were inches apart and she could feel his breath on her face. And then, gently, he moved forward, closing the gap between them as his mouth landed on hers. His kisses liquefied her body, her brain. His lips tasted fantastic. Rowie moaned and slipped into the same state of bliss she had experienced outside The Grove. Time disappeared as they kissed and touched and stroked each other's face and neck.

Finally, he pulled away. His eyes were almost predatory as they searched hers. "Will you come to bed with me?"

Rowie nodded, her normally cautious character submerged under overwhelming desire. Drew scooped her up and carried her into the bedroom. It was very *Gone with the Wind* . . . until he knocked her head on the door.

"Ouch! Owww."

"Never like it is in the movies, is it?" He laughed as he tossed her on the bed and crawled on top of her. They stared into each other's eyes, their breathing shallow and rapid. And then, unable to wait a moment longer, they tore at each other's clothes, and finally, skin on skin, dissolved into each other. Her hand slid across his chest, down his stomach, until . . . she smiled. He really was perfect. She stroked him and Drew groaned. He was rock hard and felt like he was about to detonate.

Time vanished into each kiss, each caress, their breath, the heat, their energies rising. His fingers slid inside her and his mouth lowered onto her nipple. Rowie was grinding herself against him and begging for more. She grabbed at him, demanding he enter her.

And when he did, finally, she held his shoulders, using them to keep herself anchored to the bed, to reality, scared she would lose herself in the emptiness inside her head. She had never been so present with a man. They rocked together, until Rowie was unable to tell whether the fluid motion was from the boat or the connection they had. The rhythm got faster, more heated, and more urgent. They devoured each other with their eyes, their mouths, their hands.

"Oh Drew, oh, yes . . ."

He gathered her into his arms just as the shock wave jolted through his body, pumping, draining his very being into her. She tumbled over the abyss, joining him in one long, intense explosion, staring fiercely into his eyes, calling out his name as she slowly melted into a heap.

They lay melded together for some time, the silence adding to their momentous feelings and fears. Both were fully aware of where they were headed, yet frightened of the implications. Finally Drew spoke, trying to lighten the mood.

"I certainly never predicted that while I was stuck in traction and watching you on the news." Drew wrapped his arms around her and smiled. He could feel a gentle tingling sensation in his chest, and silently thanked Delphine and her wacky hieroglyphics. For the first time in his life, he truly wanted the woman in his arms to stay there.

Chapter Twenty-seven

When Rowie woke on Sunday, the bed was rocking even more than it had the previous night, yet there was no sign of Drew. As she climbed out of bed, the boat lurched to one side and sent her flying across the room.

"Shit!"

She felt panic rising, but knew that even if the boat was sinking, the wharf was only a dog paddle away. She quickly dressed and made her way on deck, only to discover all nearby land missing. A quick scan of the boat and her surroundings revealed that *Aspasia* wasn't sinking; she was sailing, with an ecstatic-looking Drew at the helm.

Rowie—carefully—made her way to sit beside him.

"Morning, sleepyhead," called Drew. "Figured I'd take you out for a spin."

"I thought we were sinking," Rowie said, relieved.

"Not much chance of that. Although there are life vests under these seats and the ones in the cabin."

"That's comforting. I see Norm already has his on. Does he know something I don't?" Rowie ruffled Norm's head. He was slumped at Drew's feet, wearing a doggie vest.

"Norm has land legs. He's fallen overboard a couple of times. I figure it's better to be safe than sorry."

Rowie took in the view. The Hudson looked glorious from this angle, sitting onboard *Aspasia* with her magnificent sails flying. There were boats of all shapes and sizes around them. She could see the Statue of Liberty in the distance. The water was dark and *Aspasia* soared across it with all the grace and might one would expect from the famed woman she was named after.

"Is there anything I can do?" asked Rowie. "Man the jib, hoist the mast . . . squeeze oranges to ward off scurvy?"

Drew threw back his head and laughed. Rowie felt faint just watching him. The guy was freaking gorgeous, a resident of Mount Olympus come to life.

Drew pointed to a tray of pastries. "You can relax and have some breakfast."

"This looks delicious," said Rowie, suddenly ravenous.

"So do you." Drew felt the same, but not for the food.

Rowie grabbed a croissant and smothered it with butter and jam, unaware of Drew's admiring stare. He adored it when women ate with gusto.

Around lunchtime they anchored in a small cove and jumped off the side of the yacht, screaming and laughing as they hit the icy water. Rowie, clad in some of Drew's boxer shorts and a tank top, felt completely liberated. The water was refreshing, as was her behavior. She felt like a 'fifties haus-frau who had suddenly woken up in the pages of the *Kama Sutra*.

Back on board, Drew slipped Rowie's wet shirt over her head and gently laid her down on the deck. She didn't even question the convenient appearance of a condom. It was better to remember the moment as *From Here to Eternity* than "From Here to Maternity."

They drank each other in, kissing and stroking themselves into a frenzy. Rowie pushed Drew onto his back and climbed on top of him, her wetness almost burning his skin. He grabbed her, pulled her forward and kissed her fiercely just as she positioned herself so he could enter her. He thrust inside her and they both groaned, their lips pressed together. Rowie began to move. She arched back and rode him, faster, faster, faster, until Drew was begging her for more. He grabbed her hips and pushed her down, down, but still he wanted to fill her further. He wanted to be completely swallowed by her. She felt the energy rise. She felt him peak. She felt him shoot throbbing waves of pleasure through her body until in one frenzied moment she came. Hard, long, loud, the sheer bliss of it spurring Drew on, his entire body shuddering as he yelled out her name.

Rowie collapsed in a heap on top of him. "I really like sailing." She laughed.

They eventually sailed back to the boat basin and spent the evening relaxing on deck. Rowie felt happier than she could ever remember. Drew occasionally fed her something, or nibbled at her neck, or slipped his hand up her shirt, but on the whole they talked. And talked and talked.

"Where did you live before you bought *Aspasia?*" asked Rowie.

"I had an apartment."

"I can't imagine you living on land."

"I can't imagine it anymore either," Drew agreed. "I grew up in a house, but my father sailed regularly. I've always been around boats."

"Does your father still sail?"

"More than ever since my mom died. She wasn't a

great fan of sailing. She got seasick. She fully encouraged us, though. Dad has a small sloop called *Seanessa*, which he virtually lives on now."

"I bet he misses your mom."

Drew's eyes misted over. "Yeah . . . we both do."

Rowie stroked his arm. "She's still around."

"Rowie, this psychic thing . . . well . . . what does it mean? Can you read my mind, or my future? What should I expect from this talent of yours?"

"I thought you weren't sold on the idea of psychic phenomena," she said.

Drew looked sheepish. "Well, if I were to change my mind . . ."

Rowie poured a coffee and tried to look nonchalant. "I can't read you."

"What do you mean?"

"Normally, if I wanted, I would be able to pick up all sorts of information about someone. With you . . . I don't get anything. Nothing. Zip."

"Why do you think that is?"

Rowie stared deep into his eyes and, for the first time ever, was baffled about what the future held. She was both frightened and excited by the mystery of it, but she couldn't tell him that. She couldn't tell him that she had always known the man she would spend her life with would be an enigma. She couldn't let him know that after only two nights she felt he might be that man, and that it was her inability to be sure that made her so.

"No idea." Rowie shrugged. "Maybe you're just a mysterious guy."

Drew was fascinated. "So do you see dead people?"

"You make it sound like *The Sixth Sense*. Yes, I see dead people, but 'dead' is a very deceiving term. I see spirits and energies. Energy never dies; it just changes form."

Drew looked out across the river, lost in his own thoughts and memories. "I think I saw my mother . . . the night she died."

"I'm sure you did," Rowie said gently. "Perhaps she wanted you to know she was fine, and still with you."

"It probably had more to do with the bottle of vodka I drank," Drew scoffed.

"Perhaps," Rowie said. "But everyone has intuitive abilities. You are a very sensitive man. I don't need to be psychic to see that. I'm sure it was your mother."

"As you've already seen, I don't like things I can't explain."

"I don't try to explain things," said Rowie simply. "I just accept them."

Norm ambled up and pushed himself between them. Drew and Rowie laughed and gave him an affectionate pat. Norm flopped down and placed his head on Drew's lap and promptly began to snore.

Rowie smiled regretfully at Drew. "I should go home."

"I don't think you should ever go home."

"Don't tempt me . . ."

He ran his fingers through her hair. "I'll drive you."

Rowie grabbed her bag and they headed for his car. Tearing herself off *Aspasia* was the hardest thing she'd ever done.

Chapter Twenty-eight

They were both quiet on their way back to The Grove. Neither wanted the weekend to end. Drew parked and walked Rowie to the front door, and memories of their first kiss flooded back. Had it really been only two days ago?

Rowie stood one step higher than Drew and wrapped her arms around his neck. She pressed her body against his as they kissed, a rerun of the first night, only this time more urgent. There was no mystery now, just a fierce need to be naked and joined together.

"Will you come in?" Rowie tried to keep the pleading out of her voice.

Drew was tempted. "Isn't it weird, with your . . . ?"

"It's nearly midnight. They're probably in bed."

Drew pushed a lock of Rowie's hair back behind her ear. He couldn't stop touching her. "What if they're not? What if they see me?"

"Knowing them, they'd give you some tips and wish you luck." Rowie laughed.

God, he was tempted! "I'd hate to offend them."

"In case you haven't noticed, they're not your average parents. They think sex should be fully embraced."

"Then I'd hate to let them down." Drew grinned.

Rowie led Drew inside and up the stairs. It was dark and the house was deathly quiet. The normal Manhattan sounds barely penetrated the walls. Drew crept behind Rowie, hardly breathing. He didn't want to run into anyone, no matter how liberal they were. A floorboard creaked and he froze.

"Shhhhh!"

"Don't be so uptight." Rowie giggled. "It's really not a problem." She bounded up the stairs, singing as she landed on each step. "Do-re-mi-fa-so-la-ti-do!"

Drew almost had a coronary. "Please be quiet! I seriously don't want to see your grandmother right now." He felt the stare of the portraits that lined the wall. A long row of dead redheads glared as he passed by. Rowie's mother and grandmother might have been quite open-minded, but these women were definitely judging him. "I feel like a schoolboy," he whispered.

Rowie tossed him a seductive smirk over her shoulder. "You definitely don't look like one." She stopped and opened a door. "This is my room."

Rowie's bedroom had been transformed into a mystical harem of color and lit candles. Shadows danced across the walls, and vanilla scent hung in the air. Someone had been expecting them and had prepared the boudoir.

"Who lit the candles?" asked Drew.

Rowie took Drew's hand. "The spirits."

Drew glanced around nervously. *I don't believe in ghosts . . . I don't believe in . . .* "Are they . . . watching?"

"They're always watching."

Drew regained his composure and pulled Rowie into his arms. "Then you'd better tell them to cover their eyes."

Drew lay on his side and watched Rowie sleep. Her face was incredible. Her lips had a naturally pink pigment, so it always looked like she was wearing lip gloss. He presumed it was a physical quirk that most women would sell their souls for. Her eyelashes were long and thick and darker at the roots than the tips. She had a freckle near her left ear. Actually, there was one near her right ear as well.

Rowie stirred slightly.

"Good morning," he whispered.

She was silent for a moment, then slowly opened one green eye, and then the other. She gave him a lazy, contented smile. "More like great morning. Have you slept?"

"Nope. Just lay here all night staring at you."

"I hope I didn't snore."

"No, but you did drool once or twice."

Rowie playfully hit him. "I did not!"

"You sleep like an angel." Drew touched Rowie's hair. "I love your hair. It's so . . ."

Rowie rolled her eyes. "Red?"

Drew jumped to her follicles' defense. "Some of the world's greatest beauties have been redheads. Rita Hayworth, Jane Digby, Boudicca . . ."

"Raggedy Ann."

"She's a doll!" He kissed her lightly on the head. "And how about Jessica Rabbit? Wowzer!"

"Now you worry me."

Drew lifted her hair off her face. "I bet the boys at school loved you."

"Ah, no . . . they called me bloodnut and tampon

head." Rowie giggled. The memory of it didn't seem so painful anymore.

"I want to know everything about you."

"There's not much to know," said Rowie. "I'm not that exciting. I've certainly never sailed up the Panama Canal."

Drew traced a finger around her breast. "Perhaps you will one day." His finger slid down to her stomach. "So any weird traits I should know about . . . apart from the psychic thing? Any major flaws?"

Rowie exhaled. No point dying while trying to impress him. She had to breathe. "You're playing with one of mine, although a few sit-ups would probably remedy it."

"You have a weird perception of what a flaw is. I think your body is magnificent."

Magnificent! Between his compliments and his sensuous stroke she was turning into putty in his hands . . . oh no . . . tongue!

Drew began to lick around her navel and down her thighs.

"Oh no, Drew I . . ."

"Shhhhhhh."

He grabbed the tops of her legs, thrust them apart, then buried his face in her. Rowie wanted to die, wanted to protest . . . wanted to shower first. She wasn't ready to expose herself like this. But the persistent licking and hot waves of pleasure soon had her groaning and succumbing, until her whole body shuddered and she collapsed into a sighing heap.

"That was incredible," she purred. "If you ever lose your job you could take that up professionally."

"So what were we talking about before?"

"I can't remember. My brain melted somewhere between 'stop' and 'don't stop.' "

"I remember. You were going to tell me about yourself."

Rowie nuzzled in beside him. "I'd rather have a nap."

"Why don't you do that," said Drew. "I've got to love you and leave you anyway. I need to drop home before work."

"I'll see you there," said Rowie.

Drew looked surprised. "At the network? Why's that?"

Rowie remembered how Jess had asked her to keep a lid on Monday's meeting. Did Drew count? She'd better not say anything, and then they could celebrate together later. "I've got to . . . tie up some loose ends. No biggie."

"Great. Let's have lunch." Drew kissed Rowie. "What a weekend!"

"I know," Rowie agreed. She felt like she could ride high on it forever.

Drew jumped out of bed, pulled on his pants, and then stalled. "Will your scary mother and grandmother be downstairs?"

"No," Rowie assured him, deadpan. "They go to Mass every morning."

"Really?"

Rowie grinned mischievously. "Of course."

Chapter Twenty-nine

Drew retraced his way back along the hall and past the disapproving portraits. He glanced sideways at one stern-looking woman, and nearly fell over when the portrait grinned and winked at him. Drew shook his head and continued down the stairs. He was obviously seeing things. He hadn't gotten much sleep. . . . Best not to dwell on it . . .

He reached the kitchen door and paused. He could hear Gwendolyn and Lilia chatting over breakfast. He knew it was rude, but he really couldn't summon the courage to face them, so he crept past. He'd almost made it to the front door when Gwendolyn's voice rang out behind him.

"Leaving without saying goodbye?"

Damn! Drew swung back around with a forced smile. "Not at all. Just checking for my shoes. Yep, there they are."

"Did you have a nice night?"

Drew's face flooded with embarrassment. He wasn't sure how to answer.

It was okay.

Translation: Your granddaughter didn't live up to expectations.

Lovely, thank you.

Translation: Your granddaughter was a bit of a dud.

Great!

Translation: Your granddaughter went off like a firecracker.

He couldn't win. He settled for a nod.

There was an uncomfortable pause while they stared at each other—Drew apologetically and Gwendolyn with a glimmer of amusement in her eyes.

"Well, I'm off," Drew said.

"Not before you eat breakfast, you're not."

Drew knew Gwendolyn wasn't going to take no for an answer, so he followed her back into the kitchen. Lilia was at the table, sipping tea.

"Skipping church this morning?" Drew asked.

Lilia gave him a sly grin. "We've been skipping it since Salem."

Gwendolyn marched over to the stove and doled out some breakfast for Drew. "Take a seat, Drew. Scrambled tofu?"

Scrambled what? Drew pulled up a chair opposite Lilia. "Sounds . . . delicious!" *For a toothless octogenarian hippie.*

He stared at Lilia. She was wearing a simple pale blue dress and her hair was pulled back in a chignon. Her makeup was minimal—she didn't need any—and she wore tiny earrings with stones the color of dewdrops. She was a stunning woman.

"You look very nice," Drew said.

Lilia smiled at him from under her endless eyelashes. "Thank you, Drew."

"What a charmer." Gwendolyn chuckled.

"I have a date," Lilia explained. "For brunch."

As if on cue, the doorbell rang.

"That will be him. Bye." Lilia patted down her dress and raced from the room.

"Poor wretch." Gwendolyn sighed.

Drew looked at Gwendolyn in surprise. "She seemed excited."

"I'm talking about him, not her. No one can live up to Rowie's father. Just watch."

They both stared at the door. Sure enough, a minute later, Lilia floated back in . . . alone. She was holding a bunch of flowers, which she immediately dumped in the trash.

"I had to cancel," she announced. "Carnations."

Gwendolyn nodded in understanding. "When will they ever learn?" She placed a plate of scrambled tofu in front of Drew. He looked less than enthusiastic, but smiled bravely.

"Excellent!"

"Would you like some salt?" Gwendolyn's voice was almost challenging.

"No thanks." *Just a bucket.* "Are you all vegetarians?"

"We don't eat anything with a face," Gwendolyn said.

"Or oysters," Lilia added. "They may not have a face, but they still have feelings."

"I'm kind of a veggie," Drew admitted. "I only eat fish."

Gwendolyn looked at him in amazement. "Since when does fish grow in a garden?"

"Okay, so I'm more veg-aquarian than vegetarian." Drew ginned sheepishly. He stared at the plate of tofu and bravely raised his fork. "Bon appétit."

Rowie entered the kitchen just in time to see Drew gag. "What are you doing here? You'll be late for work. Go!"

Drew jumped to his feet—too quickly—and waved

goodbye to Lilia and Gwendolyn. "I've got to race. Sorry . . . I was really enjoying . . . Thanks anyway."

"Next time," Gwendolyn said with a wink.

"I look forward to it." It's right up there with my first prostate examination, thought Drew. "Thanks for rescuing me," he whispered to Rowie once they were safely out of earshot.

"It's okay. It's an acquired taste. Even Gran hates it."

"But she . . ."

Rowie patted his arm and tried not to laugh. "She was just testing you, Drew."

"If I'd known that was a test, I would've studied."

Rowie led Drew out onto the footpath in front of Second Site. He paused and stared at the display in the window. The front of the shop had been turned into a magical underwater scene.

"Mermaids?"

"Yes . . . my mother is working with mermaid energy at the moment."

"What are they?" asked Drew.

"Sirens."

"And that . . . thing . . . creature?"

"He's a Selkie. Used to be quite common in Ireland and Scotland."

"What do you mean, *quite common*? They don't . . . don't really exist . . . do they?" Suddenly Drew wasn't so sure of anything anymore. Perhaps some things defied explanation. Around Rowie, anything seemed possible.

Rowie paused for a moment. Now probably wasn't the time to mention the family rumor about Kate Shakespeare and her Selkie lover. She settled for a simple, "Some people believe they exist."

Drew decided to change the subject. "Will you go back to work at the shop?"

Rowie looked like she'd rather live on Lean Cuisines

for the rest of her life. "I'm hoping something else will come up and I won't have to," she admitted.

Drew flagged a cab and then wrapped his arms around her. "I bet the offers start flooding in." He kissed her. "I'll see you later."

Rowie stared into Drew's eyes and smiled. "Most definitely." She watched as the cab sped off and a patrol car pulled up in its place.

"I should have you arrested."

Rowie laughed and walked over to the car. "Officer Washington, Officer O'Hare. How are you both?"

"We miss your weather reports 'round here."

"Get real, Justice. You always lost money on my predictions."

"True, but at least I always had an umbrella when I needed one. When will you be back?"

"I'm not sure," said Rowie. "I hope soon."

They both seemed happy enough with that and gave her a wave as they drove off.

"Rowie!"

Rowie spun around and saw Sunny racing toward her.

"She's home. . . . You were right, she came home," he cried.

Rowie threw her arms around him. "Oh Sunny, that's such a relief. Is she okay?"

"She's fine. Rather . . . how do you say? Contrite? I don't think she'll cause us trouble anymore." Sunny beamed. "I've got to open the shop, but thank you."

Rowie gave Sunny a wave and raced inside. She had to get ready for the meeting at the network. It had barely crossed her mind all weekend (wonder why), but now she was excited. She was just at the foot of the stairs when Gwendolyn called out from the kitchen.

"Did you kiss him?"

Rowie grinned and reversed into the kitchen. Gwendolyn and Lilia were both seated at the table, searching her for clues.

"Mom! Look at her aura," Lilia exclaimed. "She did more than kiss him."

"Obviously things move faster than in my day." Gwendolyn smirked. "So what does the future hold for Handsome Henderson?"

Rowie paused. This was it. Once she admitted it, there would be no going back. "I didn't see anything."

There was a beat filled with nothing but hope. "Blissful nothingness?" Gwendolyn asked quietly.

Rowie nodded.

"You're sure?"

"Certain."

All three women stared at each other for a moment, stunned. And then the joy kicked in and Lilia and Gwendolyn rushed to hug Rowie.

"I knew it," Gwendolyn squealed. "And such excellent genes."

Lilia clapped her hands over and over as tears coursed down her cheeks. "It's finally happened. It's fabulous, isn't it?"

"Brilliant," Rowie agreed. "Better than I ever imagined."

"And what a gene pool." Gwendolyn seemed fixated.

"Thanks for lighting the candles, Mom."

"I had a feeling you'd need them."

Rowie looked at her mother and grandmother. Their happiness was so genuine. "Do you like him?"

"He's gorgeous," Gwendolyn said. "Not at all thrown by us, which was good to see. And very inquisitive, which is another excellent quality. What did you think, Lilia?"

Lilia gazed into her daughter's eyes. "He has a lovely energy. He's a very good man."

"Was it worth the wait?"

"Every frustrating minute, Gran." Rowie sighed.

What a great day," Gwendolyn declared. "You've met your OTL. You've experienced blissful nothingness. *And* you'll be back at the shop today. Life is definitely back on track."

Rowie's heart dropped into her gut. Why did her grandmother always make her feel so guilty? "Yes . . . about that. I have a meeting at the network this morning. There might be some more work for me there."

It took a moment for this to register on Gwendolyn's face. "But Drew's back. You promised!"

Suddenly Rowie felt defensive. She was a grown woman. She didn't have to explain herself to anyone. "I might have to break that promise," she snapped. "And you'll have to live with that."

"No, I won't, because soon I won't be living at all." Gwendolyn raged from the room, stomped all the way up the stairs and slammed her bedroom door shut.

"You're a manipulative old woman!" Rowie screamed in frustration.

"True," said Lilia gently. "But what if she's right?"

Rowie slumped onto a chair, defeated. "She'll never understand, will she?"

"Probably not. But that doesn't mean you should give in to her."

"I don't know how much longer I can fight her like this," Rowie admitted.

Lilia stroked her daughter's head. "You open the shop, and I'll deal with Mom."

Rowie nodded. "Try to make her understand."

Lilia gave a soft chuckle. "I'll give it a shot . . . but I'm not a miracle worker, sweetie."

Chapter Thirty

An hour alone in Second Site was exactly what Rowie needed. She could feel her spirits—no pun intended—lifting. She dusted a bit, browsed through some of the new stock and served a handful of customers. But mostly she thought about the meeting at USBC, and wondered what they were going to offer. Whatever it was, she fully intended to grab hold of it with both hands. As much as she loved the shop, she couldn't come back permanently.

Her thoughts were interrupted when the door jangled and Georgette, the client that Rowie suspected had breast cancer, walked in.

Georgette looked pale and nervous. "Excuse me . . . do you remember me?"

"Of course," said Rowie. "How are you?"

"Not good. You were right."

"Oh . . . I'm sorry."

"Don't be. You may have saved me." Georgette paused, but only for a moment. "I had a mastectomy."

Rowie's eyes immediately flickered to Georgette's

chest, and she hated herself for doing so. "Are you okay?"

"I'm getting there. It's been a month, so . . . you know"

Rowie didn't know. How could she understand what this young woman was going through? Georgette seemed to appreciate her predicament, so she got straight to the point.

"I came here to ask . . . is there life after death?"

It was not an uncommon question at Second Site.

"What do you think?" asked Rowie.

"I don't. I've never really thought about it. When my mother died I decided that if there was a God, then he wasn't a good God. My view of eternal life has always been colored by my anger. I've never envisioned my mother in some misty realm playing the harp."

Rowie smiled. "That's because no such realm exists. No god, not even your harsh one, would ever subject us to eternal boredom."

Georgette's lips twitched slightly, as though she were about to smile. She didn't, but her voice seemed calmer. "You've seen proof of eternal life, haven't you?"

"Every day," said Rowie simply.

"How can you be sure?"

"Well, either it exists, or I'm completely stark raving mad. And if that were the case, then I would rather live in my world of madness than a world where such possibilities don't exist. When we die we go home. It's as simple as that, Georgette."

"Are you afraid of death?" Georgette obviously was.

Rowie nodded. "Sure I am. I'm only human. I'm not afraid of dying, just the manner in which I die, leaving loved ones behind, stuff like that. But being dead? That's just a word for being truly alive again, returning to our normal state."

"My father isn't dealing with this at all. I need to know, so I can prepare him . . . Am I going to die?"

Rowie looked at Georgette, her pale face so full of fear. "We're all going to die. I do believe you have incredible strength . . . enough to fight this."

Georgette stared deep into Rowie's eyes. "You think I'll live?"

"I . . ." I don't want to answer these questions, thought Rowie. "I . . ."

The door signaled another customer. Saved by the bell.

"Wow, Rowie, look what I just found floating outside the shop." Petey came bounding into the room holding a red helium balloon. "It must be a sign of some sort . . . Oh . . . Sorry to interrupt . . ."

There was an uncomfortable pause. Georgette stared at Petey for what seemed like an eternity. She glanced at the balloon, then at Rowie, a look of confusion in her eyes as she tried to recall something. Rowie froze as a sense of impending doom clutched her gut. She remembered her prediction for Georgette. Judging by the look on her face, so did Georgette.

"A red balloon," Georgette whispered. And then a smile spread across her face, large, welcoming and bright. It was the first time Rowie had seen her smile.

Rowie realized what was about to take place. Every instinct she had told her to push Georgette out the door. Instead, she politely introduced her to Petey and watched as their eyes locked and held.

She witnessed the click.

Petey was immediately smitten and offered Georgette the balloon.

"I haven't had a balloon in years." Georgette giggled. "Can you tie it to my wrist for me?"

Petey did as she asked, occasionally glancing up at her. Then they stared at each other again and smiled, as two friends do when they meet again after spending a long time apart.

Rowie placed the palm of her hand against her forehead and tried to stop the visions. She silently willed Petey to leave before it was too late. Normally she reveled in uniting destined lovers, but right now her heart was in her throat, and she wanted to scream at them to stop. But her voice failed her and she watched her friend choose the path in the road that would lead him to complete devastation.

"Where did you two meet?" asked Petey, oblivious to his fate.

"I came to see Rowie for a reading a couple of months ago," Georgette explained.

"And what did Ms. Shakespeare predict for you?" asked Petey, throwing Rowie a wink.

Don't wink at me, you naive fool, thought Rowie. Run!

"Breast cancer," Georgette said simply. "Turns out she was right."

Petey looked like he'd been kicked in the gut, aware on some level of what it meant for him.

Rowie threw him a line. "Lots of women survive breast cancer, Georgette."

"Most of the time, I believe I'll beat it. But then, occasionally, I can feel it inside me and I know it's not only the breast."

"That's just your fears," Rowie assured her.

"No . . . I can't explain it. It's like lava from a volcano. Very slow, very hot, seeping through me. It's there. Or at least, it will be."

Rowie glanced sideways at Petey, who looked crestfallen. She tried to sound positive. "Then you'll beat that too."

Georgette nodded. "I'll certainly try."

"For every illness there's always a percentage of people who do very well, who beat it. You just have to choose to be part of that group," Rowie said.

Georgette thought about that for a moment. "Yes, that's true."

Petey disappeared behind one of the shelves and Rowie prayed she'd hear the door jangle soon after. Instead, he returned with a copy of a book called *101 Things to Do Before You Die*.

"I don't believe you'll die. But, just in case you do, there are a couple of things you should experience first." Petey opened the book to a random page and read, "Number 47: Watch the sun set from the Empire State Building." Petey looked thrilled at the prospect of being able to help. "There's one you can do right away. Tonight. I'll come with you. What do you think?"

Georgette didn't need to think. "Okay . . . yes . . . YES! I'd love that." She thought Petey was the most magnificent man she'd ever met.

They both grinned at Rowie, as though they were beginning the most fabulous adventure and she'd be thrilled for them.

Rowie forced a smile. "The Empire State . . . great," was all she could manage.

Petey offered Georgette his arm and suggested they go for coffee. He looked proud, handsome even, as he grinned at Rowie over his shoulder.

"Enjoy your coffee. . . ." Rowie pulled herself together. It wasn't her place to interfere with Petey's destiny. And besides, Georgette may very well live. Love was the greatest healer.

Georgette would agree wholeheartedly. She left Second Site sure she would beat all of the odds stacked against her. She had something to live for now.

Chapter Thirty-one

Drew danced into Mac's office like a character from a 'fifties musical. Well not quite, but that's how it looked to Jess, who was in the office alone and already seated near the window.

"Mac said he needed to see me."

Jess nodded. "He'll be here in a minute. Take a seat." She watched as Drew collapsed into a chair with a huge grin on his face. What the hell was he so happy about? "Did I win?"

Drew looked confused. "Win?"

"The bet!" *You clown.* "Did you kiss her?

Drew plummeted to earth with a thud. "Oh, that. I . . . Yeah, I kissed her."

Jess didn't know whether to be thrilled or devastated. But at least her plan had worked. "Congratulations. You were right. I'll give you the money later."

Drew looked mortified at the prospect. "Don't worry about it."

"A bet's a bet."

"It's only a hundred bucks."

Jess stared at him for a moment. And then horror clawed at her gut as she realized, "You like her."

Drew shrugged and tried to downplay his feelings. "I guess I do." He gave Jess an apologetic half smile. He didn't want to hurt her, but he also didn't want to lie. "She's different from what I expected, Jess. She's . . . surprising."

The door flung open and Mac entered, with Rowie following three steps behind.

Jess's mouth pursed tightly as she glared at Drew. "Surprise!"

It certainly was. Rowie looked surprised to see Drew, and he looked really surprised to see Rowie, but then they both smiled in shy delight.

"Hi, Drew."

"Hi, Rowie."

Hi, Drew, hi, Rowie . . . Good night, John-Boy . . . how freakin' Waltons. Jess wanted to hurl all over them. She watched Rowie sit near Drew. Not right next to him, but it may as well have been on his lap, the energy between them was so obvious. Jess realized they'd done more than kiss. Way more! So much for Rowie not wasting time with someone else's man. Still, she knew how persuasive Drew could be. The women at USBC didn't call him *Quick-Drew McGrew, the fastest pistol at the network* for nothing. Actually that's what she'd called him and then spread the word, but it had caught on quickly.

As long as Rowie had the prediction ready, then she'd be big enough to forgive them. If her year in Paris taught her anything, it was that men will stray and women will look the other way. The French have so much class when it comes to infidelity, thought Jess.

Mac looked uncomfortable, but decided to get straight to the point. "I won't drag this out. We have decided to keep Rowie in the prime-time spot for now."

Rowie and Drew looked equally floored. "What?"

"Effective immediately," Mac added.

Drew looked devastated. "You can't."

Mac cringed. He hated this part of the job. "We can."

"Her ratings are phenomenal, Drew," Jess explained. "We've never seen anything like it."

Drew was reeling. "What . . . better than mine?"

"Yup."

Rowie finally found her voice. "But this is Drew's job."

"He still has a job," said Mac. "He'll be replacing Marc Price."

Drew looked like he'd been told he had to wear spandex for the rest of his life. "I'm being demoted to late-night?"

"It's a solid spot," said Mac.

Rowie placed a hand on her chest. This was turning out to be an awful day. First her grandmother, then Petey and Georgette, now this. She felt strange . . . like she couldn't breathe properly. This wasn't what she had expected, or wanted. Was it? "This isn't right. Drew is a trained meteorologist. I'm just a . . ." She searched for the right word.

"Gimmick?" Drew offered.

Rowie glared at him. "Not quite the word I was looking for."

Mac looked surprised. "Are you saying you don't want the job, Rowie?"

"No—yes, it's just . . ."

Jess felt now was the perfect time to stick the boot into Doris and Rock. "You seemed very interested when we spoke about this on Friday, Rowie."

Drew turned to Rowie, betrayal etched on his face. "You knew about this? On Friday?"

"I didn't realize . . ."

"This is the 'loose ends' you needed to tie up? God, I'm a fool. You even admitted you wanted my job."

"I was joking."

"Obviously."

Mac had no idea what was going on between Rowie and Drew, but they were starting to annoy him. "We need a decision now, Rowie. Do you want it or not?"

"Of course I do," said Rowie, weakly. "But not this way."

Drew shook his head in disgust. "No? How about I gift-wrap it for you?"

Rowie stared at him, begging him to understand. "Drew, I . . ."

But it was obvious from the contempt in his voice that it was too late. "Don't speak. I don't want to waste one more second on you." Drew stormed out and slammed the door.

Jess could barely conceal her delight. "That went well."

"Excuse me," Rowie mumbled, as she rushed out after Drew. She caught up with him near the elevators and grabbed his arm. "Drew, please, I'm sorry. You've got to believe me. I didn't know."

Drew looked at her in mock surprise. "A psychic who didn't know?"

"What about what happened on the weekend?" She was pleading with him to stop, so they could work this out. "What about us?"

Drew pushed her hand away. "Let me see. I predict . . . we're over."

Rowie watched helplessly as Drew stepped into the elevator and the doors closed between them.

Chapter Thirty-two

Bill and Tina were in fine form, their dislike for each other obvious to everyone but the millions of viewers who adored them.

"The Japanese build great cars," said Bill, referring to a Toyota SUV on the monitor behind them. "I wouldn't mind owning a hybrid myself."

Tina fluttered her eyelashes innocently. "Are you allowed to drive after that little D.U.I incident?"

Bill gave a loud, fake laugh. "And how about this weather? Chilly for this time of year. Has fall arrived early, Rowie?"

Rowie jumped when she heard her name. She'd been deep in depressed thought. "I . . . ah . . . . the weather?"

Tina rolled her eyes (as usual). "Yes, Rowie, the weather. When you're ready."

Rowie gave a nod and turned to the Chromakey. "The temperature has certainly dropped in parts of the state, but it won't last." Her eyes filled with tears. "Nothing good ever lasts . . ."

* * *

Drew quietly slipped into the studio. He felt like a fool, but he had to see Rowie in action. What made her so popular? Yes, she had . . . a certain . . . what would you call it? Presence? Star quality? He'd seen her night after night on television, but really needed to see her working live to put his finger on it.

Oh, who was he kidding? He simply needed to see her. And he knew exactly why she was so popular, why everyone had fallen in love with her. He knew exactly why he had.

Which made her betrayal all the more hurtful.

She was in the middle of the national rundown and her attention was focused on the map. From where he stood, Drew could see the curve of creamy neck he'd been kissing a few hours earlier. Something stirred in his gut . . . and lower. He banished the thought and reminded himself that she had just screwed him over. How that hurt . . . probably Delphine's goddamn hieroglyphics burning into his chest.

Rowie was dressed in a slim-fitting pink dress. So much for redheads never wearing pink. She looked born to carry off the color. Her hair was up in a ponytail that swung suggestively as she turned from monitor to map. Her voice was steady, smooth and warm. And that face!

He watched as she smiled and joked, yet she wasn't as bubbly as usual. She seemed sad. Good, Drew thought. He hoped her guilty conscience was ripping her apart.

Drew felt completely betrayed by Rowie, yet on some masochistic level, he missed her already. He felt torn between wanting to be with her and wanting to destroy her.

"I'm told more hot days are just around the corner. Let's check."

He watched as she moved into her psychic prediction

pose. Her body relaxed and her chin lifted and those magnificent green eyes began to cloud over. But just as the veil began to lift, she noticed Drew and stopped. Her gaze locked with his, and for just a moment they both almost smiled. Almost. Then his face hardened and hers fell, and she broke the stare and returned to her report.

Only nothing happened.

Her body seemed tense. She shuffled slightly and tried to concentrate again. But something was bothering her and she looked close to tears. Mortified, she turned to the camera.

"The line seems to be busy," she joked weakly. "I'll just dial again."

She returned to her pose, but remained silent. Still nothing.

"I think I just went to voice mail." Her voice was wobbly. Her eyes searched the studio for Drew. Her panic almost softened his resolve, but then he remembered how she'd lied to him, and turned his back on her and left the studio.

Rowie, defeated and humiliated, gazed into the camera. "I think the cold is here to stay."

Rowie didn't have to be psychic to know who was hammering on her dressing room door. "Come in, Jess."

"Oh great. Now it works!" yelled Jess as she stormed in. "What the hell just happened?"

"I don't know."

"Where were your little voices?"

"I don't hear voices."

Jess put her hands on her boyish hips and glared at Rowie. "Whatever! You're the 'psychic' weather woman. Not the 'stand there like an idiot' weather woman."

"Thanks for clarifying."

"Does this happen a lot?"

"It's a first. Don't worry. I'll be fine," Rowie said.

Jess calmed slightly. "Okay, you've had a lot going on, stealing Drew's job and everything."

"I didn't—"

"You're here, aren't you? I wouldn't lose any sleep over it, though. He'll probably quit and go to another network. Did you see anything?"

It was hard keeping up with Jess. "When?"

"When you kissed him. In the spooky movie reel. What did you see?"

Oh that! "Nothing."

"No work stuff? What about his love life?" Jess gave Rowie a strange smile. "See anyone familiar starring?"

"I didn't see anything, Jess."

Jess's eyes narrowed slightly. "Are you telling me you've lost your psychic powers?" If so, Mac was going to have a coronary. He'd been reluctant to replace Drew with Rowie, despite her ratings. He didn't think they'd last. Jess knew he was right, but talked him into giving Rowie a shot. She'd sold it to him as a great business move, but deep down, Jess knew it was personal. And it was eating away at her. Rowie's spot *had* to work, so she could justify to herself what she'd done.

Rowie started wiping off her makeup. She just wanted to go home. "No. They work fine when he's not around."

"Then why didn't they work just now?"

"Drew was in the studio."

"Let me get this straight," Jess muttered through tightly clenched teeth. "When Drew's near you . . . when you kissed him . . . nothing? No weird visions?"

"No."

"Nothing?"

"Nothing."

Jess stared at Rowie in utter disbelief. "You don't expect me to believe he's The One? The one you can't read?"

Rowie shrugged. What could she say?

Jess glared at Rowie for a moment, and then spoke in a carefully measured voice. "I see. And if there was a movie . . . when you kissed him . . . You'd tell me, wouldn't you?"

"Right now, more than anything, I wish I had seen something. But I didn't."

Jess nodded. "Right. Well, I guess we solved the problem of who Drew is meant to be with."

"Free will still rules us, Jess. Even if we are meant to be together, it doesn't mean we will be. Especially now."

"Who knows what the future holds?" Jess mumbled, and then with an almost manic laugh, she stalked from the room. "Obviously not you anymore."

Chapter Thirty-three

Jess stacked her empty vodka glasses neatly on the bar in front of her. She waved the bartender away each time he went to clear them. She needed to keep an eye on how much alcohol it took to forget Drew Henderson . . . just for future reference. She had a feeling it would take more than one night, or one bottle, to exorcise the bastard from her system.

Eva's perfume wafted up beside her, followed by Eva herself. Great, thought Jess, all the bars in Manhattan and I run into another ex of Drew's . . . although it would probably be a rare bar where I wouldn't.

"Drinking alone?" Eva's voice was as spicy as the fragrance she wore.

Jess barely glanced sideways. "Yup. You?"

Eva scanned the bar. "I'm meeting someone."

"Girls like you never drink alone."

"Lower your standards and you won't either." Eva chuckled.

Jess gave Eva an almost friendly smile. She admired the fact that Eva didn't give a shit what anyone thought. It was something Jess herself aspired to. "Is that an insult to me, or an insight into you?"

"Your psychic movie plan didn't work?"

"Apparently I wasn't even an extra." Jess emptied another glass. "Good ole Rowie gazumped me."

"So what now?" asked Eva.

"I'm taking control of destiny, Eva."

Eva glanced at the pile of empty glasses. "Good for you."

A short man in an expensive suit entered and waved at Eva from across the room.

"There's my date."

Jess squinted across the room. "Cute."

Eva gave a warm, throaty laugh. "Honey, you've had way too much to drink."

Angel and Rowie were drinking at another bar across town.

Angel scanned the room. "What's your friend's name again?"

"Shin." Rowie played with her straw. "So how's work?"

"Who gives a shit about work?" Angel leaned across the table. "More importantly, this Shin . . . is he cute?"

"Yes. I think you'll like him." Rowie's eye's filled with tears. "I've had such a crap day."

Angel took Rowie's hand. "Stop worrying about what happened. It's over."

Rowie frowned. "Do you mean with Drew or my job?"

"From the sounds of things, both," said Angel. Seeing the look on Rowie's face, she quickly added, "I'm joking. Drew will come 'round. Just give him time. As for the psychic thing, it's never happened before and it won't ever happen again. It's like writer's block . . . not that I've ever had it myself. But if I did have a dose . . . I'd know it wasn't permanent."

"Yeah? So tell me, how *is* your novel going?"

"Cheap shot, Rowena," said Angel. "Actually, I think the elephant you have in the shop is possessed."

"Who? Ganesha?"

Angel nodded. "He's Hindu-haunted, honey. Came to me in my dreams a few nights ago."

"Really? What did he say?" asked Rowie, as though a visit from a Hindu god was a perfectly normal occurrence.

"He handed me a gold fountain pen and said, 'Use it wisely. Write from your heart; everything will follow.' "

"Oh, how wonderful." Rowie sighed.

"Why is a rep from Montblanc in the form of a talking elephant *wonderful?*" Angel asked.

"He was telling you to stop procrastinating and write that novel you're always raving about. He's guiding you and telling you it will be a success," Rowie explained.

"You think so?" Although skeptical, Angel wasn't completely closed-minded. The New Age may be a pile of dog droppings, but she would trust Rowie and her wacky insights with her life.

"You've been talking about this novel ever since I met you. Write it! What are you waiting for?"

"I've been collecting life experiences," explained Angel. "'How vain it is to sit down and write when you have not stood up to live.' "

"Thoreau! And didn't Tolstoy say, 'If you want to be a writer, then write'?"

"How can you write about life if you haven't experienced it?"

"How much experience do you need, Angel?"

"There are things I haven't done yet." Angel tried to think of something. "I haven't been sky-diving or drunk vodka in Russia with a poet. I hear med students at NYU pay fifty dollars an hour for women to be practice vaginas."

"Darling, your vagina has had enough practice." Rowie laughed. "You realize this novel will be a bestseller?"

"You're just saying that because you're my best friend. It's the law."

"I see it, Angel. I know I never let you know what I see in store for you, but today I'm breaking the rules. You don't take a visit from Ganesha lightly."

Angel looked uncomfortable. "Great, you're on the elephant's side. What if it wasn't Ganesha? What if it was Dumbo playing a joke? I'm not the perfect candidate for a visitation from a god. I'm messy, I swear too bloody much . . . The last time I gave to charity was when I shagged my ex."

"The gods, from any religion, Hindu, Tibetan or Ancient Greek, are simply our inner archetypes; aspects of Divinity within ourselves. Divinity knows what you're capable of, even if this sexy mess you mistake as your real self doesn't. It was that higher part of yourself that came to you in your dream."

"As an elephant?" Angel joked. "Then I don't think it was a sign to write but one to quit the cheesecake habit."

Rowie smiled and knew that, despite the jokes, Angel was listening. "Ganesha symbolizes the writer. You work it out."

"You know Rowie, you really talk the talk . . . but do you walk the walk?"

"No. While the lives of others are oh so clear, mine is but a muddy puddle." She laughed.

"Well Miss Muddy Puddle, is that hunk of manhood over there your friend?"

Rowie turned and noticed Shin standing by the door, scanning the room. "Sure is." She gave him a wave and he made his way over to them.

"Bloody hell . . . he's lovely," Angel whispered.

Shin arrived, gave both Rowie and Angel a kiss on the cheek, and then ordered a fresh round of drinks. Rowie could tell he was trying to be cool, but was completely bowled over by Angel.

The attraction was mutual. After an awkward start, alcohol, the great social lubricator, kicked in and the two were soon chatting away like old friends—old friends who desperately wanted to get naked together. Rowie's spirits lifted. Her intuition about her two friends had been spot on. Her gift still worked. It really only failed her when Drew was around, so as long as she stayed away from him, everything would be fine. And staying away from Drew wouldn't be a problem, now that he despised the ground she walked on.

Silent tears spilled into her vodka.

Shin noticed and put his arm around her. "Hey, are you still upset about today?"

Rowie nodded and downed her vodka and tears.

"You were there, Shin," Angel said. "Do you think Rowie made a complete fool of herself?"

Shin shook his head. "Not at all. It actually looked like she wasn't well. By the time I left work, there were dozens of e-mails telling her to take echinacea."

"See, it was noticeable." Rowie groaned.

"But it wasn't a big deal," said Shin. "And I'm sure it won't happen again."

"And what about Drew?" Rowie wiped her eyes. "We spent the most amazing weekend together, and it ends like this. He thinks I knew I was getting his job."

"He'll get over it," Shin promised. "He's not the type to hold a grudge."

"Really?" Rowie was clutching at straws.

"Really," Shin assured her. "I bet he'll call."

Angel nodded enthusiastically. "Definitely. He'll call."

* * *

Later, after leaving Shin and Angel together at the bar, Rowie curled up on the couch in front of the TV. There was only one way to deal with her heartache: chick flicks.

First up, *Bridget Jones's Diary*. For the next few hours she barely moved from the couch. She vacuumed down a bucket of Ben & Jerry's and a couple of Toblerones, and then stretched out on the floor and prayed her gut wouldn't explode. After Bridget, she watched *How to Lose a Guy in Ten Days*. Ten days? Hell, she could do it in three!

And every half hour—okay, every ten minutes—she checked that the phone was still working. It was. He had no excuse for not calling. He would call.

Rowie fell asleep waiting.

Chapter Thirty-four

Drew was tempted to call Rowie. Every half hour—okay, every ten minutes—he picked up the phone, but he never dialed. Why should he call her? She should be calling him. If she apologized and gave him his job back, he'd be willing to forgive her. Hell, if she just called, he'd seriously consider it.

He was halfway through a bottle of Jack Daniel's when the phone finally rang. He let it ring three times—he didn't want her to think he was waiting by the phone—and answered it in a relaxed, carefree voice—he didn't want her to know how desperate he was.

"Ye . . . llo." *Great, answer the phone with a primary color.*

"Drew . . . it's Jess."

Drew's heart sank . . . plummeted a thousand feet. Rowie wasn't going to call. "What do you want, Jess?"

"I need to talk to you."

"Fine. I'll see you at work."

Jess wasn't going to take no for an answer. "I'm standing outside the gates. Let me in."

Drew walked up the hatch and onto the deck. He could see Jess standing behind the security fence. Freaking fabulous! Just what he needed. He let her in and then, without a word between them, led her back to the boat and offered her a seat on deck.

"I don't get to see inside?" she asked.

"I only invite friends inside."

If looks could kill. "I thought we were friends."

Drew shook his head in amazement. "You completely screwed me over at work. Is that how friends treat each other? Perhaps you'd like to sink my boat, or run over my grandmother as well."

"You're taking this personally, Drew."

"Of course I am," he said. "It's personal. It's my job, my life. You pulled the rug out from under me and didn't even have the decency to warn me."

"I would have, but you were busy all weekend," Jess hissed.

Norm ambled up and plopped himself at Drew's feet. He sensed trouble brewing and decided to be on hand in case he was needed.

"Is that your dog?" Jess asked.

"No, it's my goat," Drew snapped. "What are you doing here, Jess?"

"I know how you can get your job back," Jess said quietly.

"Really?"

"Yes, really."

"What about your precious ratings?"

"It wasn't my call."

"Bullshit."

"I didn't say it wasn't my idea," Jess admitted. "Her ratings *are* better than yours, Drew. It was a business decision."

Who was he to argue, thought Drew. Dumping Jess had largely been a business decision as well. "If her ratings are better, why do you want me back?"

Jess went quiet and stared out at the water. Finally she shrugged. "I want her out. Watching her mess up today scared me. She's a gimmick, so I think your style is better in the long term." Jess paused for a moment. "Mostly, I just want things to be like they used to be."

"Before or after we slept together?"

Jess looked Drew straight in the eye. "During."

Drew was tempted, for a moment. She was beautiful; he was drunk . . . she was there. It was like dial-a-bonk, delivered straight to his door. But then she flicked her brown hair over her shoulder and he realized he might never settle for anything but a redhead ever again.

"As much as I'd like to, I think we'd both regret it when we sobered up," he said.

Jess nodded. It had been worth a shot, and she was too drunk to feel embarrassed.

"I really enjoyed what we had, Jess. I don't regret it at all." Drew chuckled quietly. "Well, perhaps I did for a moment or two today." He looked her square in the eye. "But it wasn't right, long-term."

Jess shuffled uncomfortably. As drunk as she was, this conversation was getting way too Dr. Phil. She decided to change the topic. "Totally. I agree. Let's forget about that and concentrate on how you can get your job back."

Chapter Thirty-five

Gwendolyn straightened her skirt, gave her hair a quick pat, and then pressed the doorbell. She noticed her reflection in the ornate brass knocker in the door. Someone had recently polished it. William Walters was obviously a man who took time to maintain his home properly.

She could hear footsteps approaching the door and had an intuitive flash of the man who was about to open it: tall, smart, and quite irritated. He regretted agreeing to meet *this Shakespeare woman*. Gwendolyn smiled. She'd soon change his mind.

She'd heard of William's plight through Petey, who felt Georgette's father needed some counseling. Georgette had been living with William again since her mastectomy. They both pretended she was there so her father could help her while she underwent chemotherapy, but really, Georgette had moved home to help him.

William Walters was devastated. He couldn't bear the thought of losing two beloved women to the same disease. He had stumbled into fatherhood late in life.

He'd been forty-five when he met Isabel, a much younger woman whose love and energy knew no bounds. He was glad he'd waited. They had shared eighteen magical years before cancer stole her away, but even then, he felt blessed to have experienced such a marriage, such a woman.

And he still had Georgette.

Each time William saw his daughter, dressed in her simple conservative clothes with subtle tones, he felt proud and counted his blessings. To be faced with the possibility of losing her was more than he could bear. He couldn't go through it again.

It had been ten years since Isabel had died and the darkness of her demise had lifted. William still missed her, but her breastless corpse was not how he remembered her anymore. It was the wave she gave him from her bike while wearing a bright yellow sundress. Or her subtle smile as she looked into his eyes and handed him their daughter for the first time. It was the slightly crooked way her feet pointed, the wave in her hair that annoyed her so, how she sang while she baked. These were the memories he had of his wife, and he hated himself for staring hungrily at his daughter's every move in an attempt to make a catalog of memories he could draw on later, in case she died.

Georgette understood what her father was going through, which was why she'd moved back home. She tried to talk to him about the possibility of life after death. She tried to discuss the idea of an afterlife that wasn't limited to heaven and hell. But whether it was the deeply ingrained teachings of his Catholic-school days, or the prospect of believing in a tempting idea that would one day prove itself untrue, he rejected the concept completely.

Until the day he met Gwendolyn Shakespeare.

William opened the door and looked surprised to see

an attractive redhead wearing a neat wool suit and shiny shoes. He'd been expecting one of those overdone Gypsy women from the Lower East Side, not this rather conservative *lady*.

"You must be William." Her voice was low, her enunciation crisp. Her green eyes penetrated straight through his stoical veneer. "I'm Gwendolyn. Petey asked me to drop by and chat with you about Georgette's cancer."

William felt a weight lift off his shoulders. Finally, someone had said the word: *cancer*. His friends and family meant well, but skirting around the issue with words such as illness, predicament, or worst of all, tragedy, was not helping him one iota. He realized he needed to talk about the *cancer*. About death. And suddenly he wanted to talk about it with this woman.

He led her into the dining room where a pot of tea was waiting. Gwendolyn nodded her approval. The man was well mannered and prepared. She reached into her bag and pulled out a cake she'd baked that morning.

"Banana cake," she offered.

William visibly relaxed. While he was all for equality for women, there was something comforting about a woman who baked. "My favorite."

Gwendolyn sat, while William went to the sideboard and took out some plates and a knife. Then they both took a moment to savor the cake.

"Delicious," said William. "Very moist."

"The secret is organic bananas," said Gwendolyn.

"Is that so?" Fascinating stuff.

Gwendolyn removed a couple of crumbs from her skirt and placed them back on the plate. "Tell me, William, what are you going to do if Georgette dies?"

William looked horrified. "I . . . I can't bear to think . . . do you think she will?"

Gwendolyn leaned across the table and patted his hand. Even the biggest skeptic would be open to a psychic prediction if there's a chance it would produce hope. "She's a very strong woman and they caught it early."

They talked for hours, discussing love, loss and the possibility of life after death. He offered countless reasons as to why it was unthinkable, and she briskly deflected them with intelligent but firm answers as she sipped her Earl Grey.

"The odds are against you, William. The majority of the world believes in reincarnation."

"Not the Christian world."

"Actually, reincarnation was removed from the Bible. Such a pity, it ruined a perfectly lovely belief system. More tea?" Gwendolyn poured William another cup. "So you're a mathematics professor?"

"Yes . . . a bit dull, I know." He felt positively bumbling around this gorgeous force of nature. "But I find numbers fascinating."

"Oh, so do I," Gwendolyn enthused. "Numerology is a passion. Pythagoras . . . what a man."

"I'm sure he was."

"Believe me, he was." Gwendolyn chuckled, with a wink.

William thought Gwendolyn was the most fascinating person he'd ever met. He liked her immediately and invited her back the following day. And then the next. He thoroughly enjoyed her company and began to trust her and her unusual ideas. She'd revealed insights about his past that were too detailed, too exact, too private for her to have known through any source other than the psychic talents she was purported to have. Her charm, humor, spirit, and refinement won him over, for no woman who held herself in such a way could ever be considered anything but in full control of her mental faculties, no matter how peculiar they might be.

"Even scientists admit that matter can't be destroyed, William."

William nibbled on a biscuit. Lord, the woman could bake! "If I set fire to this newspaper, it will be destroyed."

"No it won't; it will just change form. It'll become ash."

"So we are nothing but energy that changes form?"

Gwendolyn nodded and handed him a slice of cake.

William thought about this for a moment. "Gwendolyn, if you're right, then everything I've ever believed will be wrong."

"No, William, it too will just change form."

"What if you're wrong?"

Gwendolyn brushed some crumbs from the table. "If I'm wrong, then I'm from a long line of women who should have been on medication, William."

Four days later, William agreed to an experiment, to see if his late wife could be contacted. He had no idea that she'd been hanging around since Gwendolyn's initial visit, possessively at first, but eventually grateful that someone was finally knocking some sense into her oblivious husband. Isabel had been trying in vain to contact him for years. She made the bedroom lights flicker regularly, and from there graduated to ghostly tapping on the walls. But rather than realize he was having a metaphysical experience, William had had the house rewired and hired someone to check the roof for squirrels.

Gwendolyn put a great deal of thought into the best way to contact Isabel. William needed to be gently eased into the experience. She decided against the Ouija board, for it often drew in negative energies. She chose a more conservative route for her friend. She made tea, served it in Isabel's best china—much to the watchful spirit's approval—and set an extra place at the table.

It was very civilized and not at all creepy. Gwendolyn, William and Georgette all ate cake, drank tea and chatted about dear dead Isabel, during which Gwendolyn called upon her own energies to help Isabel make an impact.

Gwendolyn could see Isabel's translucent form sitting in her chair. She stared lovingly at her husband and daughter who were unaware of her presence, until the teacup in the fourth place setting began to elevate, as though being lifted by some invisible hand. Then slowly, and ever so gently, the cup was placed back on its saucer.

William sat with his mouth agape, his eyes frantically searching the room for a sign of his dead wife. No one moved. No one spoke. Then without warning, a framed family photo, taken years before the disease that was destroying them ever reared its ugly head, lifted off the sideboard and leisurely drifted over to the table and settled in front of William. He felt someone's hand on his shoulder, like a light, comforting suggestion, a whisper of the past, and perhaps the future now that he'd been shown a different way. The hairs on the back of his neck stood on end, and his heart ached and soared at the same time. He knew it was Isabel. He never doubted it for a moment. He could sense her, he could smell her musky scent. Every atom of his being could feel his wife.

Gwendolyn tilted her head as though listening to someone. "Isabel wants you to know, both of you, that when your time comes, she'll be waiting. But while you have life, you must live it."

Both William and Georgette nodded and cried and clutched each other's hands.

"She says she's here if you need her, although she's taking opera lessons, so sometimes you might have to call loudly."

William laughed and sobbed simultaneously as he spoke. "She always wanted to be an opera singer. She had a beautiful voice." His eyes scanned the room, searching, searching . . . "Isabel, you hear me, you had . . . you have a beautiful voice. I miss your voice, love . . ."

Suddenly a ghostly aria rang out through the room. It was brief, but clear and enchanting, each note perfect, echoing as it faded away.

It was then that Gwendolyn broke down as well, for although she mixed within the realms each day, she was only human and such wondrous displays from the world of spirit reminded her of the true majesty of the universe.

Georgette lost all fear of death that afternoon. The experience confirmed all the new and unfamiliar beliefs she was forming regarding death and life and love, the three being so utterly intertwined. She left her father's home that night to be with Petey. It was all she wanted now. And William was happy to let her go. *While you have life, you must live it.* That meant both of them.

Chapter Thirty-six

Petey and Angel were sprawled out on Rowie's bed, watching as Rowie paced up and down the room.

"Five days ago, everything was perfect. I'd finished my contract on a high. There was a promise of more work. Drew and I were falling . . . we were getting to know each other. . . ."

"Really bloody well," Angel added.

"For the first time ever, my life seemed to be on track." Rowie turned to her friends, hoping they had some answers. "How can everything go from perfect to crap so quickly?"

"It sounds like you and Drew really clicked," said Petey. "I'm sure he'll come around, once he gets over his anger."

"Yeah, but would I want him back after what he's done?" Rowie snapped.

"Back up a bit." Angel sat up. She needed to get this straight. "What exactly *has* he done? You still haven't told us why he's responsible for all your problems at work."

Rowie sat on the edge of the bed and collected her thoughts. "Basically, my psychic powers don't work around him."

"So these meltdowns are caused by him?"

"Yes. By him being around me."

"From what your grandmother tells me, your grandfather blocked her clairvoyance as well," Petey said.

"That's right," Rowie said. "And even the one night my parents shared . . . one reason my mother knows so little about my father is because her powers didn't work while they were together."

"Isn't that a bit inconvenient?" said Angel. "To spend your life with someone who short-circuits your gift?"

"It eventually sorts itself out. It's temporary, when we Shakespeare women first fall in love."

"Did you tell Drew about this?" asked Angel.

"Hell no! But he seems to realize the effect he has on me. He's turned up in the studio every day this week."

"Do you really think he's doing this on purpose?" Petey hoped Drew and Rowie worked things out. He wanted everyone to be happy, like he was.

"On Monday, no. I don't think he was trying to sabotage me then. But he must have realized why I had the meltdown on air, because he's been back every day since, deliberately distracting me."

"How?" asked Angel.

"On Tuesday he suddenly appeared again, with a big stupid smile on his face. He kept waving at me, like a complete spaz. I just crashed and burned. Once again—no weather."

"Are you sure he was waving?" asked Petey. "Perhaps there was a fly . . ."

"He was waving," Rowie snapped. "Then Wednesday . . ."

"I saw Wednesday," Angel admitted. "What was he doing to make you cry?"

Rowie visibly cringed at the memory. "It was so embarrassing."

Petey tried to placate her. "It wasn't so bad."

"Yes, it was," Angel blurted, and then gave Rowie's arm a comforting pat. "Sorry, darl, but I'm not going to lie to you . . . it *was* awful."

"He was leaning against one of the monitors, reading a newspaper," Rowie explained. "And completely ignoring me."

"What an ass," Angel muttered.

"But fortunately there was that tornado in Kansas, so you had *something* to report on." Petey was a glass-half-full kind of guy.

"Absolutely," Angel agreed. "That was such a big story, it made up for the meltdown."

"Did he speak to you at all after the show?" asked Petey.

Rowie shook her head. "He sent an intern over to me with the paper and a message. 'There's a three-day weather report on page D7 . . . just in case you need it.' "

Angel and Petey shook their heads in disbelief.

"But today was the worst," Rowie moaned. "He wasn't there, but I was still nervous. I got through most of the report . . . talked about the forest fires in California. I started to relax. I seriously thought I'd be able to tune in, uninterrupted. I began . . . everything seemed okay . . . my powers worked and I could clearly see a storm . . . but before I could find out where . . . I heard a cough."

"And that broke your concentration?" Angel asked.

"Yes . . . it wouldn't normally. But I was already on edge," Rowie explained. "So I glanced to the side of the studio, and there he was, leaning against the wall, flirting with the gorgeous slut of an intern . . . punching her number into his cell phone."

"Bastard!" hissed Angel. "Have him banned from the studio."

"I didn't want to go down that path because then everyone will know why." Rowie put her face in her hands and groaned. "I'll be seen as another Henderson conquest."

"Shin said everyone has a fair idea anyway," Angel offered.

Rowie raised an eyebrow at her friend. "You two seem to talk a lot."

"No, sweetie, there's not much talking going on." Angel smirked.

Rowie threw herself down on the bed. "You're so lucky! Both of you have found someone special. I thought I had. I even thought he was the one. How pathetic is that?"

"I don't think it's pathetic. I think it's romantic," sighed Petey, who constantly got PMS with the girls: Pre-Menstrual Sympathy. "What if he *is* the one?"

"You think we really only have one?" Angel looked horrified at the thought.

"Depends on what you mapped out for yourself prior to incarnating," Rowie explained. "Some people have several; I only have one."

"Just one? Out of all the men on the planet, there's just one? What if he's a Bedouin camel driver? How do you know you'll find him, Rowie?"

Rowie's green eyes bored into Angel's blue ones. "Faith, Angel. I have faith."

"You don't think our desire for a soul mate comes from a steady diet of Hollywood films and sappy romance novels?"

"No. There's no smoke without fire. True love exists and they capitalize on that. The only damage they do is they make us believe it's easy. It isn't. It takes work, even with the right person. Especially with the right person. Hollywood also leads you to believe that everyone only has one true love. Again not necessarily true. I met one woman who had eighteen. But us Shakespeare women, we're swans. We mate for life."

"So do tortoises," said Petey.

"Yeah well, they can't split up. Imagine them trying to work out who keeps the house," Angel joked.

"I have to keep the condo, dear, I'm wearing it." Petey chuckled.

"As much as I'm loving Shin right now, I guess I have loads." Angel laughed.

"No, you get married twice. I also see the number two for Petey . . . oh shit, sorry, guys." Rowie apologized, realizing she'd stepped into territory she normally shied away from.

Petey grinned. "Two, eh? Well I'm happy with just one . . ."

Rowie squeezed Petey's hand. "How is Georgette?"

"She's good. The chemo is knocking her around a bit, but she's a trooper."

"Gran seems to be hanging out with her father a lot," said Rowie.

"William thinks she's wonderful. They're having some sort of séance today. Gwendolyn is definitely making him open up to some new ideas. Georgie is thrilled." Petey looked deep into Rowie's eyes. "I would never have consciously chosen this love for myself. But now that it's here, I intend to embrace it. Perhaps you need to do the same with Drew."

"Yes, if he turns up in the studio tomorrow, to sabotage me . . . I'll give him a hug."

"He thinks you sabotaged him," Angel reminded

her. “One of you needs to swallow your pride and stick out the olive branch.”

Rowie’s green eyes flashed and her redheaded stubborn streak flared. They made quite a combination. “Sure, I agree . . . but it ain’t going to be me.”

Chapter Thirty-seven

Rowie's eyes flitted around the studio. She was just about to launch into her prediction for the next day, and so far there was no sign of Drew. For the first time all week she felt relaxed and in tune. She turned her attention to the monitor and concentrated on the national weather.

"The downpour resulted in a flash flood. Fortunately there were no reported injuries, apart from a Jersey cow who lost her footing." Rowie pointed to California. "And more bad news for Californian firefighters, with the searing temperatures here to stay."

A quick scan of the studio. Still no Drew. Rowie beamed at the camera. "I know I owe you an apology. I've been about as reliable as a Manhattan pay phone recently. Difference is, I've never had problems getting connected before. I'm hoping everything is okay tonight. Let's give it a go."

Rowie moved into position. Her chin tilted upward. A pinprick of energy settled on her forehead and began to expand. The heat spread and she felt the connection, felt the power rise, sucking her backwards into the place where she found her facts. The fog descended, the veil lifted . . . It worked . . . *She was there!* Images flashed before her.

"The fires aren't over in California yet. There will be four more days of burning. I see big flames . . . many houses destroyed. Take heed and there'll be no lost lives. The heat wave extends . . . I'm getting Hawaii . . . heat, heat . . . a heat wave. Expect Hawaii to be hot . . ."

Something moved beside her. Damn it! It was him, she could feel it. She paused for a moment and then tried to reconnect. "Hawaii is . . ."

It was no good. She broke concentration and glanced sideways at Drew, who was standing a couple of feet away, wearing a loud Hawaiian shirt.

"Hawaii is handsome!" *What!* Rowie slapped a hand across her mouth. That had just come out. She began to panic. Fear clawed at her stomach. Why was he doing this to her? Why? And then she knew, without a doubt, that she didn't have the strength to fight him. All her energy had gone into trying to stop herself from loving him.

She regrouped and stared straight at the camera. You win, Drew, she thought. You win. "Hawaii is overrated. It's hot and completely unappealing at this time of year. Back to you, Bill and Tina."

Bill looked like he was about to explode. "Is that it? What about New York?"

Rowie shrugged. "Oh Lord . . . I don't know. Your guess is as good as mine. Let's see? September first . . . it'll probably be sunny all day tomorrow."

Tina gave a big fake smile. "Great! No weather . . . again. Is there anything you do know, Rowie?"

Rowie glared at Tina. "I know you two are made for each other."

Bill and Tina burst out laughing.

"Good one, Rowie," Bill snorted. "You can't predict the weather, but you can come up with that?"

"I've known since the first day I met you both," Rowie said. "You're destined to be together."

Tina rolled her eyes. "Why that's . . ." She turned and caught Bill's eye. "Ridiculous, isn't it, Bill?"

Bill nodded, yet seemed unable to break Tina's gaze. "Preposterous . . . Tina."

Rowie gave a careless shrug. She didn't care what they thought anymore. "You'll be married within a month."

Bill pretended to be horrified, but he was obviously thrilled. He tried to regain control of the situation, but kept glancing at Tina like an infatuated schoolboy. "Okay! That's all from us here at the *rather crazy* newsroom. Good night."

Tina looked like she was about to swoon. "Night . . . Bill."

Eleven million viewers across the tri-state area watched in amusement as Bill grabbed Tina and gave her a passionate kiss in time with the closing music.

We're the first, we're the best, we're a cut above the rest. Nobody delivers quite like us. . . . USBC news.

"Guys!" hissed Shin. "Not on air, you mutants."

But Tina and Bill were completely oblivious to the commotion they were causing. They'd finally found each other.

Shin appeared next to Rowie and removed her mike. "I don't know how Drew got in here. I tried to keep him out."

"It's okay, Shin. It's not your fault."

"Rowie!" Jess was marching furiously toward her, but stopped short when Rowie raised her hand.

"Stop! Don't say anything." Rowie stormed out of the studio and caught sight of a loud Hawaiian shirt strolling up the corridor. She sprinted up behind Drew and yanked on the shirt.

"Happy now?" she yelled.

Drew spun around and faced her. They stared off for a moment and then Rowie shook her head. He wasn't worth it.

"You look like a dick in that shirt," she said.

She started to walk away, but Drew grabbed her arm and pulled her toward him. Their faces were inches apart and the electricity between them was palpable. His eyes bored into hers. She was almost glad he was holding her so tightly because all of a sudden her legs felt rather weak. For a moment she thought he was going to kiss her. For a moment, she desperately wanted him to.

"Happy? Happy?" Drew hissed. "Rowie, I'm . . . I'm . . ."

Their eyes locked. Drew softened slightly. "Rowie, I'm . . ."

Silence descended, so Rowie finished the sentence for him. "An asshole?" She shook free from Drew's grip and stalked off.

Jess sidled up to Drew, a look of triumph on her face. "Congratulations! You got what you wanted."

Drew looked anything but thrilled. "Yeah. Be careful what you wish for."

Jess entered Rowie's dressing room and found Rowie frantically throwing her things into a bag.

"I'm saving you the hassle of firing me," Rowie explained.

"It's no hassle," Jess said. At least she was honest. "You said your powers would be fine."

"I was wrong. Predicting things isn't my forte this week."

"Drew knew. That's why he kept turning up in the studio."

Rowie stopped and stared at Jess. "Did you tell him?"

Jess pretended to be offended, but was as transparent as glass. "No! God no, he worked it out himself. He's ruthless like that."

Rowie realized how blind she'd been. "You're in love with him."

"As if!" Jess sighed and looked defeated. "Okay, yes. Took you a while."

"I obviously have a block where Drew's concerned."

"So do I," Jess admitted.

"What a shame you're not meant for each other. You're similar types. You both trample on others to get what you want." Rowie picked up her bags and headed for the door. "Good luck, Jess. And goodbye."

Chapter Thirty-eight

Gwendolyn and Lilia were chatting over tea when Rowie arrived home. Lilia had been baking, and the whole house smelled of fresh bread. Rowie slipped off her shoes and followed her nose to the kitchen.

"Lovely woman. Obviously has faerie blood," Lilia said.

"Don't meet many of them nowadays," said Gwendolyn.

It took them a moment to notice Rowie standing in the doorway and a few seconds more to register the devastation on her face.

"Rowena, what happened?" Gwendolyn's voice filled with worry.

"Drew, he . . ." Rowie couldn't explain what he'd done. "It's over. Everything is over. I lost my job."

Lilia rushed over to her daughter. "There, there, it's okay."

Rowie's tears began to flow. "It's not okay. I finally had a life of my own, and now it's gone."

Gwendolyn grabbed some tissues off the counter and

handed them to her granddaughter. "You've always had a life."

"Not my own."

Gwendolyn looked incredulous. "If not yours, then whose was it?"

"I was born into this."

"Of course you were born into it," Gwendolyn snapped. "Everyone is born into his or her life. None of us drop out of the sky, or sprout up in a flowerbed. One doesn't just turn around nearly thirty years into her life and go, 'Oops, I think I got the wrong life . . . I'd better return it and get a refund.' What do you plan to do? Toddle off to the big returns desk in the sky and swap this one for another? If that were possible, don't you think I'd have longer legs? Or a husband I can touch?"

Rowie grabbed a tissue and blew her nose. "What's the use of fighting? This is it for me. I'm back, and I bet you're thrilled."

Gwendolyn took a deep breath. This wasn't going to be easy, but it was time they knew. "I don't need you back. I've decided to sell Second Site."

It was as though all the air had been sucked from the room.

Lilia shook her head. Surely she'd heard her mother wrong. "Sell? I don't understand . . . sell."

Rowie glared at her grandmother. She wanted to throttle her. "What? You can't."

"I can. I'm the official owner, and it's my decision." Gwendolyn was serious. For once, she wasn't playing games. She had made her decision, and both Rowie and Lilia knew it.

Rowie's head was spinning. "But . . . but . . ."

"But, but what, Rowena? You suddenly feel some attachment to the shop?"

"Of course I do."

Gwendolyn rolled her eyes. "You've shown so much loyalty to it."

"You have no right to treat me like this. Just because I want something else in life doesn't mean I don't love the shop." Rowie turned to her mother. "Mom, say something."

Lilia's face was etched with betrayal. "I'm sorry, Rowie."

"For what?"

Anger surged through Lilia like lava through a volcano. She pointed at her mother, and Gwendolyn lurched backwards, as though lightning had poured forth from her daughter's fingertip. "For raising you around such a manipulative old banshee," she roared. "How dare you do this to me, Mother? How dare you?" Lilia burst into tears and ran wailing from the room.

"Now look what you've done," Rowie screamed, as she raced after her mother.

Lilia was sprawled dramatically across the couch, sobbing into a cushion that had *Where There's a Witch There's a Way* stitched across one side.

Rowie wrapped her arms around her mother. "We'll be okay, Mom."

Lilia lifted her head, her green eyes clouded with grief, her face already blotchy from crying. "You will be. You don't want to be there. But I do. That shop is my life. I'm fifty-one . . . three . . . ish. I can read tea leaves and tarot cards and speak to the dead. Who the hell will employ me?"

"You're a brilliant woman, Mom. Someone will see that."

Lilia laughed hysterically. "Oh yes . . . so many jobs for psychics out there. I can imagine the reference: extensive herbal knowledge, can astral travel for work. What good will all that be on my Subway application?"

Now Rowie was confused. "Subway?"

Lilia sat up, hysteria rising again. "Yes, Subway. It will be the only place I can get a job. I can be a Psychic Sandwich Artist and predict everyone's orders."

With one mournful sob, Lilia disappeared through the door and up the stairs, her tiny heels clattering all the way to her room.

Rowie turned to the portrait beside her. "I envy you, Sylvie. Orphaned at twelve. Free to enjoy . . . the Inquisition. It had to be a hell of a lot less dramatic than this."

For a moment, it looked like Sylvie was about to nod.

Chapter Thirty-nine

Lilia paused outside Hirsch Shocoladen and, for the third day in a row, gazed at the window display while she made her choice. She was still reeling and couldn't believe how her mother had betrayed her. The past four days had been a haze of anger and grief. Lilia was madder than ever before. Normally she retreated into her dreams and remained quite numb. But this time she was Vesuvius. She felt a ferocious anger boiling her blood. She filled with panic when she considered life without the shop. But mostly, she simply . . . felt. And she hadn't felt anything for such a long time.

Her eyes flickered across the rows of Austrian chocolates: the Altmann & Kuehne gift boxes filled with liliput sweets or marzipan fruits. The chocolates bearing images of Austria's regal past: Emperor Franz Joseph I truffles, Sissi-Kugeln and Mozartkugeln. And of course the trays of gourmet truffles, handmade by Herr Hirsch himself.

She made her choice and entered the shop, breathing in the scent of chocolate and spice.

"Ahhh . . . Madam Shakespeare! Name the man who has hurt you and I vill cut off his head." Hans Hirsch's voice boomed through the shop, his Viennese accent as sweet as the confections he sold.

Lilia laughed. "I'm afraid I can't blame a man for my daily appearances, just a chocolate addiction." And my evil mother, thought Lilia.

"Vell, at least you are addicted to fine *shocolade*. Hirsch, not Hershey's. You are a lady with fine taste."

"And expensive taste, Hans." Lilia pointed to half a dozen truffles and Hans wrapped them for her.

"So no broken heart?"

Lilia shook her head. "No, I'm just a pig."

"But such a pretty one." Hans leaned across the counter. "So vat if you vent on a date vith me?"

Lilia moved toward him with a sly smile. "That's so tempting, Hans, but you're eighty years old and happily married."

Hans threw his arms up in mock defeat. "Oh vell, it vas vorth a try."

Lilia passed him a box of Mozartkugeln. "I'll also have these. I can't resist."

"You vill get fat and never find a boyfriend."

"I wouldn't know what to do with a boyfriend, it's been so long." Lilia chuckled.

"It's like riding a bike. You never forget."

"Ah, see, I never learned how to ride a bike." Lilia paid for her chocolates and blew Hans a kiss as she left. She unwrapped a truffle and popped it in her mouth, moaning as the taste registered. She adored fine European chocolate. Was chocolate a substitute for sex? Maybe. But then she'd only ever had one sexual experience that even came close to a good dark chocolate truffle.

Her face flushed as she thought of that night, so long ago. The bonfire and flame throwers had lit the field with an enchanted glow. The drums beat a rhythm that didn't waver. Everyone danced, free and wild. Some were naked. Some not. And then Lilia saw him, through the flames. She knew he was watching her, even though his mask concealed his face. She had stood frozen as he moved toward her; slow, graceful steps, honoring the Horned God he represented.

He stood before her, naked from the waist up, his body glistening with sweat from dancing near the flames.

"Who are you, May Queen?"

"Yours," she whispered.

He led her into the woods. The wood folk whispered their approval as they passed. They found a small clearing and he laid her down on the soft grass.

"Take off your mask," he urged.

But she couldn't. She was honoring something much larger than the sum of them.

Lilia gave herself to the stag, mind, body and soul. It was an urgent, almost ferocious merging of soul mates, and they both knew it.

He whispered in her ear, "I have been here before, but when or how I cannot tell. I know the grass beyond the door. The sweet keen smell. The sighing sound, the lights around the shore. You have been mine before . . ."

Later, as the full moon lit them from directly above, they made sweet tender love, this time conceiving a child, a merry-be-got.

Lilia extracted herself from his sleeping embrace just as morning threatened to break. She washed her face with the morning dew, but quickly replaced her mask in case he woke. She was tempted to remove his mask, to gaze upon the face of this man, but she didn't. She couldn't disrespect the Beltane gods. If they were meant to be together, they would be.

She lightly touched the tattoo on his arm, committing it to memory. It was a copy of the John William Waterhouse painting *A Mermaid*. Strangely enough, it looked like Lilia. She gently kissed it . . . and then she left, ignoring the cries of a faerie urging her not to.

That had been nearly thirty years ago. She'd waited, trusting that he'd return . . . but he hadn't. She felt duped by destiny.

She thought about the men she'd dated over the years. She'd lost count of the kind, perfectly agreeable men who had asked her out, only for her to cancel at the last minute. She suddenly felt guilty for rejecting Warren simply because his sideburns were too long, and Les because he looked too nervous, and Harry because his fingernails were dirty. He was a horticulturist after all. And did it really matter that most men were quite unimaginative when it came to buying flowers?

Lilia still couldn't help thinking it did.

She'd managed a six-month relationship with Geoffrey. But his respectful, somewhat fumbling strokes in the privacy of a bedroom could never compare to urgent clawing under a full moon. And an on-and-off affair with Sam only made her yearn to be alone.

It felt unfair that nearly thirty years had passed, yet the memory of that night still made her go weak at the knees. She popped another truffle into her mouth and sighed, though not for the taste of the marzipan.

Lilia shoved the rest of the chocolates into her bag. This was ridiculous. It was time she admitted she'd been wrong, about him, about that night. He'd been sent into her life so she could conceive Rowie. That was it, the only connection, and it was time to move on and forget about the Horned God.

The shop was for sale. She'd have time to devote herself to a relationship now. Lilia suddenly felt quite free. She was only fifty-four . . . ish, and looked a lot younger. She was in her prime. If she were receptive and put her desire for love out there, then the Universe would provide. She was determined to prove that she had not missed her chance for love.

She stopped and realized she was standing outside Lola's Lingerie. It was a sign! She entered the store, stalling slightly at the sight of so much revealing lace.

A young, impossibly slim yet busty woman approached her. "Can I help you with something?"

Yes, I'd like your breasts and legs, thought Lilia. "I'm looking for something . . . sexy." She scanned the shop. "But not cheap. Age appropriate," she added.

The woman nodded and took a royal blue silk slip off a rack. "My mother is in her forties too . . . and she recently bought this."

Forties! Goddess bless the child. "I'll take it," said Lilia. "And I'd also like some lacy underwear."

Later that night, Lilia tucked her pretty purchases away in her drawer. You just never knew . . . Well that wasn't true. She did know. And she was ready now.

Chapter Forty

Jess and Mac sat side by side, eyes glued to the television in Mac's office. They were watching a montage of Bill and Tina shots. A series of images flew by: Bill teasing Tina about her new haircut. It had been malicious at the time, but translated into lighthearted fun on film. And there was Tina giving Bill's arm a comforting squeeze after his drunk-driving offense had been made public. There was no mention of her outing him. And of course that first kiss.

Cyndi Lauper sang their song: "And I'll see your true colors shining through . . ." It was a moving tribute to the love Bill and Tina shared, and it would close the six o'clock news today, the eve of their wedding.

Jess flicked off the TV and turned to Mac, who was surreptitiously wiping a tear from his eye. "Oh come on, Mac . . . Jesus."

"It reeled me in, Jess. It actually made me forget what assholes they are."

Jess grinned. "I'll take that as a compliment. So we'll run with it?"

"Definitely," said Mac. "This is the biggest wedding since Brad and Jen."

"And as doomed," said Jess.

"Two weeks ago they despised each other. Tomorrow they exchange vows at their new home in the Hamptons. Call me cynical, but I hope they've both got ironclad prenups."

"I just pray they don't breed." Jess looked at Mac in horror and they both cracked up. "Rowie was right. She predicted this."

"Great to hear she predicted something," Mac said.

Jess surprised herself by jumping to Rowie's defense. "That's a bit unfair. Her predictions were faultless up until the day Drew got back."

"Weren't you the one who said, 'we need to fire her ass immediately'?"

"Yes," Jess admitted. "And you were right when you said we should keep Drew in primetime. The numbers have barely dropped since he returned."

"He's good at what he does, Jess." Mac softened. "And so was Rowie for a while there. I never really believed in psychic phenomena before I met her. I just wish I knew what went wrong."

"Let's just say . . . she was too nice to fight fire with fire." Jess stood and headed for the door. "I'll let Taye know that we'll be using the montage."

"Before you go, Jess . . ." Mac scratched his head. "I don't mean to pry, but . . . everything okay with you?"

"Sure. Why?"

"You seem rather . . . sedate lately."

Jess looked horrified. "If my work hasn't been . . ."

"No, your work is fine," Mac assured her. "Better than it's been in months."

"That's good to know."

"It's just that you don't seem really . . . happy."

Jess stalled for a moment, tempted to pour her heart

out, but instead she settled for a wry smile. "Who ever is, Mac?"

Later, as she watched Drew deliver the weather, Jess thought about what Mac had said. She wasn't happy, but then she never really had been. Even when she'd been with Drew, certain life couldn't get any better, she was still too scared, too insecure to be *happy*.

Her sedate behavior didn't stem from unhappiness, it stemmed from humiliation. Jess was embarrassed about the way she'd behaved at work over the past few months. Rowie's betrayed face burned into her brain. It wasn't that she felt any real loyalty to Rowie, although she didn't dislike her—as much as she'd wished she could. It was just that the one thing Jess always knew she had was her professionalism and the respect of her co-workers. She didn't care if her colleagues liked her, but she worked hard to gain their respect.

And now she'd blown it. She was sure everyone knew that she'd based her decisions on her personal feelings, rather than what was best for the network. She'd acted like the worst type of woman—the woman scorned. And everyone knew it. Or, in moments of clarity, Jess realized *she* knew it . . . and that was more important.

Jess wasn't sure how to rectify the situation. She was a problem solver, yet she was at a loss on how to solve this. She steered clear of Drew as much as possible. She still fantasized about him at night, alone in her bed, but at work she separated the two, something she should have done all along.

He seemed as eager as she was to ignore what they'd done to Rowie. She'd tried to broach the subject once, a few days after his return, but he cut her short.

"I did what I had to do to get my job back," he snapped.

"I could've just fired her. I didn't have to humiliate her."

"Then why did you?" Guilt filled his eyes. "And why did I agree to it?"

They were questions to which she still had no answers . . . yet. Jess knew that in order to put this whole sordid episode behind her, she'd need to face a few truths about herself. She watched as the Bill and Tina montage played live. Mac gave her the thumbs-up sign and Jess nodded. It was the most romantic piece of film since *Doctor Zhivago*.

"Great job, Jess," Taye called afterward. "Almost made me believe their marriage might work."

Jess smiled and felt a weight lift from her shoulders. Perhaps she would be okay.

Chapter Forty-one

Gwendolyn sat on the lounge chair and slowly twirled her wedding ring around her finger. She was strangely quiet for someone whose life was spinning out of control. Despite her wacky façade, she was actually a creature of habit. Change unsettled her, even when she instigated it herself.

The thought of selling Second Site was quite frightening. It had been three weeks since she'd told Lilia and Rowie about her plans. They'd barely spoken to her since, and there were moments when she truly regretted her decision. The shop had been a part of her life for so long that she couldn't imagine what she'd do without it. Not that she was going to change her mind about selling. She had too much pride to back down, and although she knew that was a ridiculous reason to go ahead with the sale, she also believed it was time to make a stand. She was sick of making all the decisions. She was tired of being the strong one, the one who held everything together. She was exhausted. She felt old, and as much as she used that as her trump card, she wasn't old. William Walters certainly didn't think she was old.

And that was disturbing her as well.

Just when she'd thought certain parts of her life were over, along came a man . . . a very attractive man, who made her feel quite . . . alive. It was most inconvenient, given her tendency to focus on death.

She stared at the gold band on her ring finger. She'd taken her wedding vows so seriously that even now it pained her to consider breaking them. She stood and walked over to the mantel. Her fingers stroked the second urn.

"I miss you, Dorian."

They'd been married for thirty years when she found him dead in the garden from a bee sting to the neck. She had known from the moment she first laid eyes on him that she would lose him long before her own time.

She also knew there wasn't a goddamn thing she could do about it.

So she rushed Dorian off to City Hall a week after they met, determined to suck dry every ounce of happiness she could from their union. She dug up all the flowerbeds and its bee-attracting plants, for although she didn't know the exact date of his demise, she had foreseen the route it planned to take. She charged into the ring with destiny, gloves-up and ready to fight. But it didn't help, because the hands of Fate stretched far and wide.

When destiny finally caught up with Dorian Cunningham and stung him on the neck, Gwendolyn knew she had tried her best to avert it. She had no regrets, only sorrow. And a daughter and granddaughter who shared his blood, his genes, in whom she could see glimpses of the man she loved and lost. Gwendolyn had loved Dorian the only way she knew how: completely. And to her, an hour of that was so much better than a lifetime of mediocrity.

Of course, Dorian was used to his spiritual body now and able to pop from one realm to the next. And while she was grateful for his spiritual presence, the physical void hurt. But the thought of existing without him at all was unbearable, so Gwendolyn made the most of the strange life/death they shared, and Dorian continued to be a force in her life. She'd always felt her life was complete. She had her work and her family. She had her man, even though he was dead. But all women complained about something.

Bit-by-bit things were changing. Rowie didn't need her anymore. The shop was up for sale. And to top it off, she'd met this man, this kind, funny man, who was certainly no Dorian, but *was* alive. ALIVE!

She thought about William for a moment and smiled. She liked him so much. He was smart, loyal . . . quite willing to be flexible in thought. And they were on the same page in so many ways. Both of them had experienced true love and still grieved its loss. Both agreed they could never replace their deceased spouses. Yet both had been flirting like teenagers. And she was enjoying it, despite the fact that it scared the bejeebers out of her.

Gwendolyn walked into the entranceway and stood in front of the hall mirror. Her hair was still naturally red, her skin still reasonably smooth, her teeth all hers. She ran her hands over her bust. It had defied gravity and age and remained firm. She turned to the side and stared at her profile. Her bottom had dropped slightly, but certainly wasn't large. Overall she was holding up rather well. Why wouldn't a man find her attractive? Why shouldn't she flaunt it? Why shouldn't she phone him?

And then she glimpsed the ring on her finger and knew why.

"You're still a damn fine-looking woman, Gwen."

Gwendolyn spun around and stared at her husband. "I was just . . ."

"No need to look so guilty." Dorian chuckled. "I know what you were about to do. You were about to blow a chance at a bit of happiness."

"What on earth are you talking about?"

"He's a good man, love. It's okay to like him. It's okay to live."

Gwendolyn began to cry. "He's not you."

"Yeah, well, I'm a damn difficult act to follow." Dorian's eyes softened. "Ask him out, sweetheart. Have some fun."

Gwendolyn stared at her husband's transparent form. "You've started to pull away, Dorian."

"No . . . I'm here, if you need me. It's just that you don't need me as much now." Dorian drifted toward his wife. "Now dry those eyes and call him. Go on."

"Really? You don't mind?"

"I don't mind," Dorian assured her. "I see our future from here. We'll be together again. But in the meantime, be happy."

Gwendolyn grinned. What the hell, she would! She marched over to the phone and began to dial. She would ask William out. For dinner. Or a show. Or simply have him around for sex.

Gwendolyn let out a throaty chuckle. No, William was the type of man who needed to ease into it slowly. She didn't want to scare him off. She'd have to romance him a bit. Yes, she'd definitely have to take him out for dinner first.

"You're right, Dorian. It doesn't change how I feel about you. But sometimes I'm just so tired of waiting to join you." Gwendolyn turned to Dorian but he was gone. And for once, it didn't hurt that much.

Chapter Forty-two

Rowie sat with the phone in one hand and Jack's business card in the other, trying to build up the courage to dial his number. She turned it over a few times, and then realized there was no need for her to feel guilty anymore. The shop was up for sale and she needed to get another job.

What the hell! She dialed, asked to speak to Jack, then waited while she was transferred through.

"Rowie?" Jack's voice was warm and welcoming. "I'm thrilled you called."

"Hi Jack . . . I'm not sure if you heard about what happened at USBC . . ."

"I got a few versions, but none of them matter. What matters is where you want to go from here. Any ideas?"

"Not really," Rowie admitted.

"How about we meet next week to discuss your options?"

"That would be great."

"And in the meantime, I'll put my feelers out, okay?"

"Thank you. I really appreciate this, Jack."

They arranged a time and then Rowie placed the phone down and wandered through the garden and into the shop. She was feeling much more positive about the future. She had mixed feelings about her grandmother's decision. On the one hand, it meant she was completely free to pursue her own thing, without her grandmother nagging her to return to work. But on the other hand—thank God she only had two hands—she couldn't imagine life without the shop. What would it be like living in The Grove, knowing she couldn't duck next door anymore? And what *would* her mother do?

She watched her mother now, sitting quietly behind the counter, her small hands wrapped tightly around a pricing gun. She was armed and ready to fight for her shop. Rowie followed Lilia's gaze and noticed three men in suits walking up the Shamanism to Yoga aisle. Rowie pulled up a stool beside her.

"Who are they?"

Lilia's voice sounded constricted. She always carried her stress in her throat. "The real estate agent and two potential buyers."

"Don't worry, they don't look like the type to buy a New Age shop," Rowie assured her.

"It's the space they're looking at, not the shop."

Rowie and Lilia sat quietly and watched the three men. They looked completely out of place in their expensive suits and shiny shoes.

"Lots of character. Make a great nightclub." The agent oozed that substance common to real estate agents worldwide.

"A shot bar could go there," mumbled the first suit. "Over near that ugly elephant thing."

Lilia visibly blanched, as did Ganesha, although only the Shakespeare women noticed.

"The whole place needs chrome," snapped his slightly shorter clone.

They all paused in front of a mural depicting the tale of Demeter and Persephone.

"That'll have to go," announced the shorter suit. "Who is it?"

His friend boomed with laughter. "Looks like that chick you picked up at the Hudson last week."

"Can't we do something?" moaned Rowie. "This is awful."

"Fight fire with fire." Lilia slipped off her stool and glided over to the three men. "What do you think, gentlemen? I'd be thrilled if you bought the place. I'd trust you to look after them."

"Them?"

"Why yes, Shirley Ann and her sister Rodica." Lilia fluttered her eyelashes, and continued in an almost hypnotic voice. "I'm riddled with guilt over selling. It's taken years for them to trust us. They're going to feel so betrayed when we leave."

Three wary stares.

The larger suit looked almost frightened to ask, "Are they . . . neighbors?"

"Neighbors?" Lilia burst into peals of Oscar-worthy laughter. "No, no . . . they're the sisters who were murdered here not long before my parents bought the shop. Quite tragic." She lowered her voice. "They were discovered, chopped into tiny, tiny, eensy, weensy little bits. It took us years to get all the blood off the walls. And I'm telling you, they weren't pleased to be dead. They smashed things, chased our customers away . . . but they've mellowed a lot. Ever since our coven cast the Spirit Soothing Spell last Halloween." Lilia peered up at the three men and smiled. "But I'm sure they'll be thrilled if you take over."

"I think we've seen enough," snapped the larger suit.

"You're not kidding," muttered his clone.

The real estate agent followed the men as they sprinted out the door. "I have another place in Tribeca . . ."

Lilia and Rowie collapsed with laughter.

"They ran," squealed Lilia. "Like scared little mice. Big, brave men."

"Did you see the look on the real estate agent's face?" Rowie wiped tears from her eyes. "That was very naughty, but oh, so funny. Gran won't be pleased at all."

Lilia became serious again. "I don't really care at the moment. Selling the shop is the nastiest thing she's ever done. And that's a long goddamn list."

"It's my fault," said Rowie. "Perhaps she's tired of running it . . ."

"What about me?" Lilia's eyes flashed angrily. "I could learn."

"But you . . . I didn't know you were interested."

Lilia shrugged and ran her hand over the counter. "I haven't been interested in much for a long time. But that's going to change, Rowie. I can feel it. The winds of change are coming."

Rowie watched as her mother sauntered out the back. Suddenly a warm wind blew in from nowhere, and swept all the papers off the counter. Lilia was wrong. The winds of change weren't coming; they were already here.

Chapter Forty-three

Rowie rang Petey's bell and then straightened the bagua mirror on his door while she waited for him to open it. Petey lived in a part of the Lower East Side that still had ugly gray streets and dingy shop fronts. Being a Libra he needed a semblance of beauty and balance in his surroundings, but being eternally broke he rarely had it. His job as a youth caseworker for a small social service agency was rewarding, but it didn't pay much.

Petey's ground-floor apartment was a feng shui disaster. Opposite a parking garage, it had a gas station on one side and a view of a car wrecker from the back window. Add to that an empty basement underneath and you had a place bound to give Lillian Too a heart attack.

Rowie and Angel had been horrified the first time Petey had shown them his new digs.

"Bloody hell," Angel exclaimed. "Who'd you rent it from, the Addams Family? This is as welcoming as a flat in Kabul."

Petey dismissed her concerns. "I bought a new book on feng shui . . ."

"Honey, it's a book on demolition you need. Even the Chinese can't help this dump."

Petey, however, remained optimistic. "Every problem has a cure in feng shui."

"Well not unless you open a crystal shop in your living room. I'm sure feng shui has its cures, but this apartment doesn't have a common-cold kinda problem. It's not even viral, fixed with a bagua mirror and some rest. This is architectural terminal cancer. The geographical equivalent of Ebola. Feng shui bird flu."

Rowie rushed to Petey's defense. "Oh shut up, Angel. What do you know about feng shui anyway?"

"About as much as the guy who built this monstrosity, darling."

From then on, whenever Angel visited Petey, she did so singing the song "Ain't No Mountain High Enough," only the words were changed to "Ain't no wind chime big enough."

Petey swung open the door and welcomed Rowie with a big hug. "Come in."

Rowie wandered into the living room and was surprised to see how much it had changed since her last visit. A few rugs, throws and lamps, some paintings and picture frames. "It needed a woman's touch," Petey whispered. Rowie nodded, but it wasn't the décor that had changed the room; it was the love that filled it. This was a happy home now.

Georgette stuck her head around the door. "I thought I heard the bell." She gave Rowie a kiss on the cheek, and Rowie was surprised to see how different she looked. She had lost a bit of weight and most of her hair, although she tried to disguise that with a scarf, but the most obvious change was her face. Georgette looked radiant. Her skin, her eyes, her smile—this was a woman in love.

"I'm so glad you could come over," she said.

The doorbell rang again and a minute later Petey led Angel and Shin into the room.

"Wow," said Angel. "This place looks great. No need to sing my song."

"Georgie has a good eye for decorating," Petey explained. "She's made a few changes."

"A few?" Angel laughed. "She's a bloody magician."

Georgette had worked some magic in the kitchen as well, because dinner was a macrobiotic extravaganza, served with a simple explanation: "Petey and I are sticking to a healthy diet for now."

Dinner started with a chickpea and vegetable salad, followed by a miso soup thick with vegetables. Next came a leek pie, then poached pears with raspberries and lemon sauce for dessert. Georgette sipped on lemon-mint tea while the others washed the meal down with an organic pinot noir.

"This is a nice drop," said Shin. "Where did you get it?"

"I ordered some organic wines over the Internet," Georgette explained. "They're quite inexpensive, especially when you consider the cost to the environment."

"We need to rebalance everything," Petey added. "The planet, our bodies." He glanced sideways at Georgette.

"Shall we all join hands and sing Kumbaya now?" teased Angel.

Petey laughed. "Yeah, I know we sound like old beaners."

"It's important you keep healthy," said Rowie quietly.

Angel—it was always Angel—broached the subject that was on everyone else's mind. "Tell us, Georgie, so we can support you both, what's happening with this cancer thing?"

Rowie almost spat her drink everywhere and held her breath waiting to see how Georgette reacted.

Georgette's face was still for a moment, and then she broke into a huge grin. "Thank God someone brought it up." She laughed. "It's like the elephant in the room, don't you think? It really needs to be confronted." She explained what to expect as her disease progressed, if it progressed. There was always hope. She certainly believed in miracles now.

"I tried to talk Georgie into going traveling with me," said Petey. "I thought we could go looking for a cure. I've heard some amazing reports about Sai Baba, and some healers in Asia. But she made me realize that her best chance is here, surrounded by people who love her."

Rowie watched as Petey and Georgette stared into each other's eyes, and hated herself for feeling jealous. The woman was fighting cancer. One of her best friends was in love with someone who might die. And she was envious? She'd suffer a horrible death and come back as a cockroach for having such thoughts.

Yet that one look . . . just to have that, even for a moment.

"So did you have your boob taken off?" Another straight-to-the-point question from Angel.

Georgette glanced at Petey. "Should I show them?"

Petey nodded and Georgette got up from the table.

"Oh shit no, you don't have to show us," shrieked Angel.

Georgette laughed at everyone's horror and lifted her T-shirt over her head. She stood before them, naked from the waist up, a hand covering her remaining breast. Her body was boyish in build, would have been even with the missing breast, and she stood proudly, waiting for everyone to react. It didn't take long before their mouths dropped open in amazement.

"Oh my God," said Angel. "I thought you were going to show . . . this is . . . incredible."

Georgette's breastless left side had been tattooed into a colorful garden of flowers. Sweeping up and across her shoulder and down her back, as though caught in a wind, were a sprinkling of petals and tiny butterflies. Rowie, Angel and Shin moved in closer, immersed in the art. Hidden among the flowers were a number of exquisite faeries, their tiny faces laughing at the amazed onlookers. Drifting near her heart was a single red balloon.

"It's the most glorious thing I've ever seen," Rowie whispered.

"My body's worth celebrating," Georgette explained. "I'd already decided against reconstruction. Petey loves me the way I am, but I still couldn't look in the mirror and be comfortable . . . happy with what I saw. I can now. I'm a work of art."

"It's unbelievable," Angel said. She looked up at Georgette, her face filled with admiration for her new friend. "You come across all quiet and reserved, but you've got balls of steel, girlfriend."

"There's no point being in the theme park unless you ride the roller coaster," said Georgette. "That's why I decided to love Petey, even though it would've been safer not to."

Rowie watched as Angel glanced at Shin, and Georgette smiled at Petey. Boy, was she the odd one out. She wasn't on the roller coaster. Hell, she didn't even have a ticket for the theme park. Her life was more of a long line, waiting for tickets. While she was happy for her friends, their joy only exacerbated her own heartbreak.

And her heart *was* broken.

She missed Drew. Or perhaps she missed the thought

of Drew and the potential between them. Whatever it was, it hurt. But most of all, she missed the hope. All her life, Gwendolyn and Lilia had promised her the search would be over the minute she experienced blissful nothingness. All those first kisses that were shattered by visions, nice guys destined for other women. It wasn't easy, but there had always been a glimmer of hope that the next man she kissed would be the one it took a lifetime, rather than a moment, to know.

That glimmer had been extinguished. Her search *was* over, and there was nothing blissful about what lay ahead.

Chapter Forty-four

Drew looked at the blonde sitting opposite him and smiled as he pretended to find her interesting.

"So I broke into his flat and sprinkled alfalfa seeds all over the floor, gave the place a good watering, turned the heat on and left. He came back a week later and the place was a big goddamn salad bar." She guffawed before turning serious again. "No way was he going to get away with it. No one dumps me, you know what I'm saying?"

Loud and clear. Drew nodded and stared at his beer. It seemed the safest place to look. He wished she'd stop waving her overinflated boobs in his face. For something so large to defy gravity in such a way was truly off-putting.

"I always watch your show."

Drew glanced at his watch. Was it rude to cancel a date half an hour into it? "I would hardly call it a show. It's only a spot on the news."

"I love the traffic report," she said breathlessly, licking her already wine-stained lips.

"I do the weather."

"Oh." She giggled. "Shows how much attention I pay to what you say."

Drew was throwing himself back into his bachelor ways, trying to exorcize Rowie from his mind, from his heart. He refused to be destroyed by another woman. It was best to get straight back on the horse.

Although with this date, he was taking the horse analogy too literally. She didn't laugh. She whinnied.

He'd been out every night for the last couple of weeks, to clubs, bars, and parties. He'd been to an industry party and a photo of him with a couple of models made the paper the next day. It looked like he was having a blast. But he wasn't. The women didn't interest him. None of them were Rowie. None even came close.

"And so I thought, what the hell will I do? I'd never had that problem before. What do you do when your nail technician dies?"

Drew suddenly felt tired. She was boring, superficial and had the IQ of a baked bean. He regretted agreeing to meet her and made a mental note to let his friends know he had no intention of dating for a while—a long while.

"No idea," Drew said, pretending to care.

"Luckily everything turned out for the best because my new one is even better than the dead one. Look." She held out her hand and twiddled her fingers in front of his face, proudly displaying her nails. They were just like her: long, loud and thick-looking. They would definitely come in handy if you couldn't find a bottle opener.

"How about we go back to your place for a nightcap," she suggested.

Drew motioned for the check and resisted the urge to run for the nearest exit. Was this what was in store for him? Mindless encounters with women like this? She had the class of a Vegas hooker! In the past he may have taken her up on her offer, just for the hell of it. But that was before he met Rowie.

"What do you think?" she whispered.

Drew paid and turned toward ole Buoyant Boobs. "I think it's a lovely and very tempting offer . . . but I've got an early start tomorrow."

Chapter Forty-five

Rowie and Lilia had barely uttered more than two words to each other all morning. It was Autumn Equinox, usually a time for celebration. But neither of them felt like celebrating. Instead, they unpacked a box of books and tried to ignore what was happening around them.

For days, a constant flow of potential buyers had paraded through the shop, and all were more than willing to share their inane opinions on how to make the space better.

"A gentlemen's club. I'm talking high class . . . with topless waitresses."

"That's right, a dating agency for men and blow-up dolls . . . although this place may not be quite right . . . it's a bit strange, really."

"We'd paint the walls black and turn it into a radical feminist bookstore."

"I'd keep it like this. I don't know anything about psychic readings, but it shouldn't be too hard to learn."

But none of the potential buyers were as obnoxious

or as disturbing as the couple Lilia and Rowie were watching right now.

Bobby Burger was a well-known figure, thanks to his TV commercials and burgeoning business. In the past five years his burger chain, Burger Boy, had expanded quickly and was snapping at the heels of Burger King. He was now looking to expand into New York, and was overseeing potential premises himself.

Bobby was tall and large—obviously a big burger eater himself—and dressed like Hoss from *Bonanza*. His wife, Sally-Sue, was well known for her faith in the Lord and the donations she made to overseas Baptist missions to help spread His word.

Rowie felt physically ill as she watched Bobby Burger march around the shop. She could almost smell the rump steak on the man. Surely *this* wasn't what her grandmother wanted! Personally, she'd rather burn Second Site to the ground than let this man get his hands on it.

"I don't know, Bobby," Sally-Sue flitted close to her husband. She didn't like the place one iota. "That other place in Chinatown was nice. Good Christian owners."

"Looked goddamn Buddhist to me," Bobby boomed.

Sally-Sue paused and took *Tantric Sex For Dummies* off a shelf. "What on earth . . . ?"

"An excellent book for beginners," Lilia offered.

Sally-Sue glared at Lilia and shoved the book back on the shelf.

Lilia gave a snicker and turned to her daughter. "Her root chakra is completely blocked."

"It's a prime spot," slimed the real estate agent. "There's a serious lack of burger joints around here."

"Too many goddamn vegetarians," Bobby barked. "Gotta put a stop to it."

"Did you know it takes eight barrels of oil to get one

cow to market?" announced Lilia loudly, to no one in particular.

The real estate agent ignored her and groveled further up Bobby's posterior. "I'm a fan of your Mega Burger, sir."

Bobby Burger gave the real estate agent a hearty slap on the back. "That's my favorite too, son. The Burger Boy specialty. Five beef patties on a sesame-seed bun."

Lilia pulled a face. "Eoow! Did someone say bowel cancer?"

Sally-Sue glared at Lilia. "This place is strange, Bobby."

"Won't be strange when I gut it and shove my Burger Boy logo out front."

Rowie couldn't take it anymore. "I need some fresh air."

"I'll come with you," said Lilia.

Neither of them noticed as Gwendolyn entered from the back room and watched them leave.

Chapter Forty-six

Rowie and Lilia wandered through Central Park. It was beautiful at the moment, with the reds and oranges of early fall splashed across the trees. Rowie lifted her face and let the sun shine on it. She loved the park. It exuded a lightness that stemmed from being full of people in search of relaxation. It was also home to countless earth creatures, if one knew where to look.

"What horrible people," Lilia moaned. "Did you see his hat?"

"We can't let them buy the shop."

"It's not up to us."

"Perhaps they won't want it."

Lilia picked up a small pebble and ran her fingers over its edges. "They want it."

Yeah," said Rowie. "I figured they would."

Drew and Jack were jogging. Neither of them liked it, but they did it anyway, twice a week, at lunch. They started near the Plaza, then jogged into the park and past the entrance to the zoo. Jack was no marathon runner, but that suited Drew, who was still building strength in his leg.

"I had a call from Nike," puffed Jack. "They've got this new all-weather shoe."

"If they pay, I'll play."

Jack glanced sideways at his friend. "For someone who just got his life back on track you're . . . gloomy."

"I'm fine." Drew shot Jack a big, fake grin. "See?"

They dodged a group of children and a kamikaze squirrel before heading past the Wollman Rink.

"Does this have anything to do with the pretty redhead?"

"She screwed me over, Jack. I was just returning the favor."

"Word is she didn't know she was getting your job."

Drew was silent for a moment. "Who told you that?"

"I ran into Mac."

Drew stopped running and stared at Jack. He could hear the carousel behind them. He stretched for a moment while Jack bent over, trying to catch his breath.

"I've really got to exercise more," Jack wheezed.

Drew was surprised. He took off his sunglasses and searched Jack's face. "She really didn't know?"

"Nope."

Drew's eyes glazed over. "But she still took it."

"Yeah, well, you made that easy for her, acting like an ass. You should know I'm going to represent her."

"What? Why?"

"Because she's a hot property. She's good for business. And most of all . . . I like the girl. She came by the office a couple of days ago. She's a great kid." Jack took a slug from his water bottle. "And no point in looking at me like that, Drew. You're not my wife. I can represent whomever I want."

"Fine."

"Sulker."

"Am not."

Jack's face lit up. "Wouldn't you like to see her again?"

"Nope."

"It could be easily arranged." Jack seemed easily amused.

"I'll pass."

"Pity." Jack grinned. "Because she's over there."

Jack boomed with laughter as Drew's heart shot into his throat. Rowie and her mother were a few feet away from him, headed for the carousel.

"Don't say anything," Drew pleaded, but it was too late. Jack was already calling out to them.

"Rowie . . . Rowie. Hey, what a coincidence."

Judging by the look on Rowie's face, she was as horrified as Drew by the coincidence—if one were to believe in coincidences. But Jack only noticed it for a moment, because then he laid eyes on Lilia . . . and his world stopped.

For only the second time in his life, Jack Witterspoon fell madly in love.

Rowie thought she was going to be sick. The last thing she needed right now was a face-to-face with Drew. She wasn't mentally prepared. Even worse, she wasn't wearing any makeup.

"Hello, Jack . . . Drew . . ."

Drew nodded, while Jack introduced himself—rather shyly—to Lilia.

"Jack Witterspoon, lovely to meet you." Lovely? It was goddamn mind-blowing.

"Oh, you're the one helping Rowie find a job," said Lilia.

She's heard of me, Jack thought. Now if only I can

think of something witty to say. "Yeah," he said. And then he fell quiet.

Rowie's eyes searched Drew's. "How are you, Drew?"

Drew slipped his sunglasses back on. "Good . . . great . . . you know."

Yes, she did know. She'd read the papers. He obviously missed her as much as one would a head cold, and had moved on to much blonder pastures. There was an uncomfortable pause, and Rowie looked at Jack, urging him to fill the silence. But he seemed as tongue tied as she. "We were just going on the carousel," Rowie explained.

"Lovely," said Jack.

"The horses are hand-painted," Lilia said, to no one in particular.

"Is that so?" said Jack, way more interested in that information than most men would be.

Rowie began to edge her way toward freedom. "Anyway . . . nice to see you both." She turned to Jack. "I'll fax the management agreement back to you in the next couple of days."

Jack tried to think of something businesslike to say. "Cool."

"Well . . . goodbye." Rowie started to walk off, each step an effort as she felt Drew's eyes boring into her back. How she wished she had the graceful, fluid movements of her mother, or even the sexy swaying rhythm of Angel. Instead she had been endowed with the lumbering gait of a drunken truck driver and was known to trip on a regular basis.

"Rowie?"

She turned, grateful for the chance to stop and compose herself. "Yes?"

Drew smiled at her. "I . . . um, nothing . . . thanks. I'll see you around, okay?"

"Sure," she nodded, "like a donut . . ." WHAT! Like a donut? What sort of moron would say "like a donut"? Rowie took her mother's arm and rushed off before she heard Drew collapse on the ground with laughter, because that was what she would do if some idiot with a bumbling walk said something as ridiculous as "like a donut" to her.

It was genetic. Lilia always said the most ridiculous things and now it was obvious the defect had been passed on to Rowie. She could remember the day she had been teased mercilessly by a girl at school who had told everyone that Rowie rode a broomstick. Rowie had arrived home in tears, her face smudged with the dirt the girl had pushed her in, the back of her dress torn.

"Just look her in the eye and tell her she's a silly duffer," Lilia advised.

"A what?"

"A silly duffer."

"What's a silly duffer?"

"Someone who says silly things."

Gwendolyn, who'd overheard Lilia's solution, pulled Rowie to one side and told her that the silly duffer route should only be taken if she wanted to subject herself to more ridicule.

"Then what will I do, Gran?"

"Tell her you've cursed her and unless she starts being nice to people she'll grow warts on the end of her nose."

The following day at school the girl confronted Rowie as she ate her lunch.

"Where's your broomstick, witch?"

Rowie was an unusually obedient child. Even if she had tried, it would have been impossible to rebel against such an odd and open-minded family. Perhaps conservatism was the ultimate rebellion. So being as compliant as she was, she attempted to follow her mother's advice first. "Oh leave me alone. Don't be a silly duffer."

The girl looked as though she was going to burst with glee at being handed such valuable ammunition. "What did you say?" she said, guffawing like the donkey she resembled.

Rowie glared at her, her tiny body tense with rage. "I said, me and my grandmother put a curse on you last night and if you don't start being nice to me . . . to everyone . . . then you're going to wake up with warts all over your face."

The girl froze and the guffaw subsided as a look of pure fear flickered across her eyes. Then she turned, ran, and stayed away from Rowie for the rest of the year. Rowie would still be riddled with guilt over frightening the girl like that, except that the girl's fake niceness eventually developed into genuine niceness, her popularity ensuring her the title of class president in their senior year. She was generally considered to be the kindest girl ever to grace the halls of Lincoln High, and Rowie liked to believe she had had a hand in that.

Drew watched Rowie bounce off—for that's how she walked, with a slight bounce that he found incredibly sexy. In fact everything about her was incredibly sexy, even her cute, kinda dorky sayings. *Like a donut!* Part of him just wanted to forget everything that had happened between them and start again. "That was uncomfortable," he mumbled.

Jack's eyes still looked glazed. "Yes, lovely . . ."

"She looked . . . tired. Don't you think?" Perhaps she was pining for him, and unable to sleep. Drew allowed himself a little fantasy about forgiving her and then giving her something to tire her out. Twice.

Jack gave his head a shake and pulled himself together. "Well . . . wow . . . her mother's lovely."

Drew stared at his friend and started to laugh. "You dirty dog, you liked her."

"What's not to like? She's an attractive woman."

They were both quiet for a moment as they watched the two women collect their tickets and disappear into the carousel. Both men suddenly felt edgy, uneasy . . . bereft.

"Let's keep running," said Drew.

Jack was already legging it.

Rowie and Lilia mounted their favorite horses and watched as Drew and Jack ran off.

"That was uncomfortable," Rowie said.

"About time," Lilia whispered vaguely.

The organ music blared and the carousel began to move. Lilia gave her horse a pat. He was white with colorful trimmings and always seemed to be pulling at his bit.

Rowie relaxed back on her horse, a dark brown mare with a more docile nature. "We haven't done this for ages."

The carousel picked up speed.

"Shall we lock Gran up in a nursing home?" Rowie giggled.

Lilia hung her head backwards. "I wouldn't be that cruel . . . to any nursing home. Hang your head back, Rowie!"

Rowie knew what was coming. It was a silly little tradition they'd had since she was a child. She hung her head back and waited for her mother to speak.

"Life's like this carousel." Lilia laughed. "Full of ups and downs while you go around in circles. Fun while it lasts, but the ride will eventually end."

Rowie smiled. Few things remained constant, but those that did were lovely.

Chapter Forty-seven

Rowie looked around the Shiva Cafe and regretted coming. Angel always talked her into the craziest things, but a speed-dating night had to take the cake.

"Stop looking so miserable," Angel hissed. "How often does a girl get to date twelve men at once, unless she's a slutty cheerleader?"

"I'm not into team sports," Rowie said. "So Shin is okay with you coming here?"

"Absolutely. He said you need to move on from Drew."

"I have," Rowie lied. But in her heart she knew she hadn't . . . and perhaps couldn't.

Angel linked her arm through Rowie's. "C'mon. It's not like you have to see any of them ever again. Try to have fun."

Rowie grabbed a drink from a passing waitress. Angel was right. She needed to move on. Or at least try to.

"Holy hell, check out the bum on that guy," Angel whispered.

Rowie checked it out and decided it was fairly average, but then she was way more selective than her friend. Angel's tastes were eclectic and spanned the whole spectrum. As far as she was concerned, if a man made her laugh out loud, then he was worth a shag. If asked to describe her taste in men, Angel would usually say something like, "A pulse, a sense of humor and over the legal age limit . . . but I'm open to offers."

For Angel, finding the right man was the same as finding the right haircut. You experimented, tried different colors and styles, until you eventually woke up with something that resembled what you had always hoped for. As with that perfect haircut, you'd never wake up with the exact same man you went to sleep with. Something similar would usually suffice. Perfection was impossible and the older a woman got, the less likely it was that she'd airbrush her men. There would always be flaws. The trick was finding that someone whose flaws were least annoying. Therefore, Angel saw love as a process of elimination. And eliminate she had, right into the arms of Shin Higaki.

Rowie believed finding love took patience. And faith. With her gift, she had no choice but to believe that. Also, she'd prefer to date someone attractive . . . to her. Not a complete ogre. Not every girl wakes up to George Clooney. The idea was to wake up to someone who didn't startle you. Who didn't make you wish for sharper teeth and an edible arm. Love may be blind, Rowie thought, but I'm not.

The cafe was overflowing with women who dressed by the Coco Chanel book of rules. The men were all shuffling about, pretending to be cool and uninterested. If they were so uninterested, why bother coming at all? Probably the same reason she came—because they'd run out of other options.

Sven, a tubby, balding blond in a kaftan and Chinese

slippers, called for everyone's attention and explained the rules. "Each woman is to sit at her own table, which will be her nest for the evening, her own little goddess cave. All you handsome gods get to move around from table to table every five minutes. It's all based on Tantric mating rituals I learned on a commune in Poona . . . without the sex. That can happen too, but please wait until later as I don't feel like hosing down the tables. See this big donger?" he said, referring suggestively to a large oriental bell. "When you hear it, time is up . . . and I don't care if the woman you are sitting with is your future wife and she is more interested in your big donger than mine. You hear it, you move it. Got it? If you click with someone, swap numbers, or arrange a date, or promise to meet later. If you hate someone, then grin and bear it, please. It's only five minutes. I bet you all sat through *Titanic* and that was three hours of torture. This, in comparison, is only a little prick . . . or perhaps from the ladies' perspective anyway. That's it, so hang on to your panties and let's get started."

All the women rushed for a table.

"Come on, Goddess, that's your nest there," said Angel, pointing to an empty table against the back wall.

"This is so embarrassing," Rowie moaned. She was starting to lose her nerve.

"Oh bullshit. Just take a deep breath and go with the flow." Angel laughed as she sauntered off, swaying her hips to a silent but catchy rhythm.

"Go with the flow, go with the flow," Rowie repeated under her breath, like a mantra.

A waitress distributed glasses of wine, while Sven made a big deal of circling the participants with a leering smile. He made his way to the bell, lifted it and gave it a dramatic shake. A loud clang vibrated throughout the room. All the men scattered like sailors on shore leave. Rowie was startled when a brown-haired guy in glasses and a suit threw himself into the seat opposite her.

"How's it going?" he said in a businesslike fashion, thrusting out his hand to shake hers, "Keith Allen, corporate lawyer."

Rowie, who figured this was how it was done and was desperately trying to go with the flow, shook his hand. "Rowie Shakespeare . . . weather woman."

"Weather woman, eh? So do you like your men hot . . . or cool?"

Oh God! "Genuinely amusing and not prone to clichés."

"Yeah? Interesting." Keith yawned. It was obviously anything but.

"So, corporate law . . . that's interesting," Rowie lied.

Keith grinned, relieved the conversation was back in an area he was comfortable with: himself. He began to talk about his job, then his salary, which led to how his wife had cleaned him out when they divorced.

He didn't mention that he'd slept with his wife's sister, which had ultimately led to the divorce. Rowie just knew that. It was times like this that her clairvoyance came in handy. Clarity around men like Keith Allen was a blessing.

Keith stared at her for a moment, his eyes dropping to her chest. "So . . . what are you up to after this? We could go back to my place." He sniggered like a schoolboy who had just seen his first copy of *Playboy*.

Rowie glanced down at her watch. Three minutes down, two to go. This had to go on record as the longest five minutes in history. She had read in *New Science Magazine* that time was speeding up. Obviously the writer of that piece had never met Keith Allen.

"You know, for a night*cap*." He emphasized cap—

although Rowie had no idea why—and raised his eyebrows suggestively.

Yeah right, sounds about as appealing as a bowl of dog vomit, thought Rowie. "Well, that's really tempting, Keith, but I'm the first person you've met tonight and you've got eleven to go. I personally think you will hit it off with that girl over there."

Keith looked at the blonde to which Rowie was referring. "The one with the huge hooters?" he asked, beads of sweat breaking out on his forehead.

"That's the one."

"How can you be so sure?" He gulped.

"Just by the way she's been staring at you. I don't want to stand in the way of such attraction."

"Don't worry, you won't!"

Finally Sven's donger came between them and Keith raced toward the blonde without as much as a backward glance. In his place sat a pleasant-looking guy with ginger hair and a splattering of freckles across his cheery face.

"Hi, I'm Dean. It's always a treat to meet another redhead. It's natural, isn't it? You can never be sure nowadays."

Rowie nodded, relieved that he seemed nicer than the previous offering. "I'm Rowie Shakespeare. Nice to meet you."

Dean leaned forward and whispered conspiratorially, "This is all a little weird, isn't it? Who dragged you along?"

"My friend, over there," she said, pointing to Angel.

"The living Rubens?" He grinned.

"Yep, straight off his canvas and into the lives of unsuspecting American men."

"She should carry a warning on her forehead."

"In my experience, most men would ignore it anyway." Rowie laughed. "So at the risk of sounding trite, what do you do, Dean?"

"I'm a photographer."

"Sounds glamorous."

"I'm a food photographer, so unless you find photos of fruit platters and chocolate deserts glamorous, you'd probably be disappointed."

"Well, I'm not sure about fruit platters, but I am quite obsessed with chocolate." Rowie felt relaxed. He seemed nice.

"You're *the* Rowie Shakespeare? I used to watch you on the news." He seemed impressed and not the slightest bit put off by it. "I bought some of Edgar Cayce's books at your shop once. It's interesting stuff. So what can you tell about me?"

Rowie took a sip of her wine. "I don't do readings after hours."

"Why not? Man, I'd love to be able to do it. Come on, give me a prediction. Anything."

"Sorry, I don't like reading people when I'm out socially."

"I can understand that, but this is different. Come on," he pleaded. "Give me something."

"I don't think I should."

Dean wasn't quite so laid-back anymore. "Come on. I'm cool with whatever you say. One little thing."

Rowie felt like a woodpecker was hammering at her.

Dean leaned back in his chair and opened his arms wide. "Hit me with whatever you've got."

Without thinking, Rowie blurted, "You are a loving, intelligent man, but if you continue using cocaine you will destroy everything."

They spent their final two minutes in silence.

Things went downhill for Rowie after Dean stormed off. Next came Dennis, a strict Catholic who asked her if she would be willing to convert if they married. She couldn't resist telling him she was a Pagan and would practice Catholicism only if he allowed her to acknowledge the Pagan holy days as well. Dennis spent his remaining three minutes clutching the crucifix around his neck and lecturing her about heresy.

After that, she met Mark, who was married with two kids but failed to mention it; Daniel, who was gay but hadn't yet acknowledged it; Paul, who came across as a real charmer but one glance at his aura told her he hit women; Mr. Cohen (yes, that's how he introduced himself), who was nice enough but had a piece of spinach stuck in his teeth; and Hiro, who, although sweet, was only interested in talking about Angel.

Finally Sven's bell let out its final death peal and the torture was over.

"So how did you do?" Angel was clutching a pile of business cards.

"Oh wow, what can I say?" groaned Rowie. "Tonight really ranks up there with the final flight of the Hindenburg for a great night out. What about you?"

"Eight out of twelve cards, five offers to meet later tonight, and one proposal of marriage if I convert to Catholicism. All crap, don't have to be psychic to know that." She tossed all the cards but one into the trash, and waved it in Rowie's face. "Hiro Maruyama, graphic designer, very cute. You should call him. I don't think you've ever tried sushi before."

"Well, you know what they say: You should try everything once," said Rowie.

"Yeah, except incest and folk dancing. Let's take off, shall we?" Angel gave Rowie a hug as they left. "Look at it this way, darl. You can cross twelve more men off your list. And I go home knowing the guy waiting there is definitely the one for me."

Rowie sighed. It was typically sweet of Angel to put a positive spin on a dull night, but it just made her realize how much she missed Drew . . . and how that fact wasn't going to change anytime soon.

Chapter Forty-eight

Jack paused outside the shop. *What was he doing?* It was nuts. He met some woman for all of five seconds and was suddenly compelled to chase her home. Crazy! Or was it? Because she'd certainly made an impression when they met yesterday and had invaded every thought since.

He was fairly levelheaded when it came to the fairer sex. He'd been madly in love once and married once, to two different women. The love affair had been brief and incredible, the marriage longer and costly. Since then he'd dated a number of extremely nice women, but none had ever made him feel the way Lilia did in the short time he spent with her.

Best to confront it, really.

He checked his reflection in the shop window. He'd gained a few pounds recently. He'd discovered a fabulous little gourmet chocolate shop near his apartment and they sold Mozartkugeln. And his hair needed a trim. Perhaps he'd wait and drop by later.

How ridiculous! She'd already seen him mid-jog,

sweating like a Kentucky Derby entrant. He strode into the shop and looked around. It was a charming place, filled with interesting books and knickknacks. He was tempted to spend time shopping, but he was on a mission and needed to find Lilia before he lost his nerve.

Jack noticed a display of carved wooden sticks and stood behind them while he searched for Lilia. He spotted her across the room, speaking to a bookish-looking customer. She was obviously a regular because Lilia called her by name.

"But you weren't, Ethel," Lilia said.

"But what if I were Napoleon?" Ethel said.

"Everyone thinks they were important in a past life," Lilia said. "It helps them deal with the fact that they're nobody now."

"Is that how you feel?"

Lilia shook her head. "No. I was Eleanor Roosevelt."

Ethel's eyes nearly popped out of her head. "You're so lucky."

Lilia pointed down one of the aisles. "The Reincarnation section is over there, Ethel, next to Raw Foods. Go and check it out."

Ethel walked off, and Lilia turned toward Jack, as though she'd been expecting him. Her gaze dropped down to his shoes and she smiled. Perfect.

"Hello," said Jack.

"It's a fertility stick."

Jack realized Lilia was talking about the carving he was holding. "Is that so?"

"Tradition says you pass it on to your children."

Jack placed it back on the table. "I don't have any kids."

Lilia looked surprised. "Oh, I must have misread your energy."

"It probably needs a cleanse," Jack joked.

Jack and Lilia stared at each other and smiled shyly.

"I'm not sure why I'm here," Jack said. "I just . . . when we met . . . I feel like I know you. Like we've met before."

Lilia nodded. She felt the same. "Perhaps we have. Another life . . ."

"Another time . . ." Jack finished.

They grinned like love-struck teenagers. The space between them was like taffy: thick, sweet and pulling them in.

"Will you have dinner with me?" Suddenly Jack felt embarrassed, exposed. He knew nothing about this woman. "You're probably married, or busy . . . or not interested . . ."

Lilia cut him off. "I'd love to have dinner with you. Tonight. Let's not waste any more time."

Rowie was in front of the TV with a pint of Ben & Jerry's and a bottle of wine. The Grove was quiet, with both her grandmother and mother out for the night. Rowie had been surprised to answer the door earlier to find William standing there, in his best shirt, holding a bunch of stargazers and looking a little nervous. Suddenly her grandmother appeared on the stairs, dressed to kill in a fabulous red gown and gold wrap.

"William and I are off on our date," she announced, passing Rowie the flowers. "Don't look so surprised, Rowena. It's not our first." And with that she hooked her arm through William's and slammed the door behind them.

A date! With William?

Rowie was about to rush upstairs to tell her mother when Lilia floated past her and out the door with barely a goodbye. Rowie had no idea where her mother was going, as her dates rarely made it past a greeting at the door, but she too was dressed to impress. Rowie glanced down at her grubby T-shirt and old sweatpants. Life wasn't fair. There was only one thing to do.

Crack open a bottle of wine.

Rowie lay on the couch with a merlot and watched TV. On some level she was aware of the millions of people having a great time around Manhattan—including her mother and grandmother—while she was at home alone on a Friday night. She tried not to think about Drew, his intense stare, his muscular back . . . the fire inside her when they kissed. She plowed her way through the wine and tried to concentrate on *The Ghost Whisperer*. But her mind kept drifting back to *Aspasia*. To a reunion with Drew on *Aspasia* . . . a long, hot reunion with Drew on . . . oh, damn it!

Rowie took another swig of melancholy. Was she destined to fantasize about Drew forever? Would she ever meet anyone who compared? Didn't have to be psychic to know that the answer to that was a big, fat no.

The front door opened and Rowie glanced at the clock—9:15. Still early, so probably her mother home after another failed date. She relaxed back into the sofa when she heard Lilia . . . *and a man*, giggling . . . whispering . . . Rowie bolted upright. What the hell?

More giggling. More whispering. Oh God, was that kissing?

Then suddenly Lilia *and Jack* crept past the living room door.

Rowie spilled her drink all over the floor. "Jack?"

Jack backtracked and stuck his head into the room. "Rowie . . . evening."

"Jack." She was stating the obvious now.

"You've spilled your wine."

Rowie glanced at her wine-stained feet. "Yes."

Jack didn't seem the least bit embarrassed. "Got

your fax, thanks. There are some potential job offers I need to talk to you about."

"Oh."

"Come on," Lilia whispered from the other side of the door.

Jack gave Rowie a nod. "We'll do lunch. Good to see you."

Rowie stared at the empty door for at least ten minutes. How would she ever process that? She decided to not even try. Instead she switched off the TV and headed upstairs to bed. It was best if today came to an end—quickly.

She swung open her bedroom door and flicked on the light, only to find Lilia rifling through her drawers, dressed in nothing but a royal blue negligee.

"Do you have any condoms?"

Rowie passed her mother a packet of Durex and a stern warning. "I want you to know . . . I might never recover from this."

Chapter Forty-nine

Morning already? Rowie had barely slept. She tossed and turned and tried desperately not to imagine what her mother and Jack were up to. *Eeeww . . . banish the thought!* She knew she'd been raised to be quite free-thinking about sex, but that meant sex for her. Not for her mother.

Or her grandmother.

Rowie finally admitted defeat at around one A.M. and went downstairs to get a drink, preferably alcoholic. Halfway down the stairs she heard a strange slurping sound.

What on earth! A burglar wearing wet galoshes? A giant slug?

Rowie felt her way in the dark to the umbrella stand and grabbed a weapon. Then, creeping and shaking, made her way to the living room, flicked on the light and found her grandmother kissing William on the sofa. Really kissing . . . like two horny teenagers.

"Oh . . . hello dear." Gwendolyn yanked her blouse down.

"Hello . . . Gran . . . William . . ." *Don't mind me while I vomit.*

"Is it raining?" Gwendolyn asked, referring to the umbrella.

Rowie glanced down at her weapon of choice. It would still come in handy if the two old fogies continued kissing like that. She excused herself and returned to bed. The Grove was like a frat house after a keg party.

Morning didn't bring any relief from the geriatric love fest. Rowie dragged herself out of bed and padded downstairs, only to find Lilia and Jack already up and giggling over breakfast.

"Morning," Lilia said cheerily. "Sleep well?"

"Like a baby. Awake all night." Rowie poured coffee and sat at the table, opposite Jack. "So, Jack, this is weird."

Jack obviously didn't think so. He was beaming. "Rowie, with your permission, I'd like to see a lot more of your mother."

Rowie couldn't resist. "I thought you saw a lot of her last night."

"Heavens no!" squealed Lilia. "We kept the lights off." Jack and Lilia burst out laughing.

Rowie felt like an intruder in her own home. "I think I'll drink this in my room."

"Rowie, I've had a lot of calls about you," Jack said. "Offers are flooding in. Can I set up some meetings?"

Rowie turned back to Jack. "In light of . . . everything . . . are you sure representing me wouldn't . . ."

Jack interrupted her before she could continue. "Not at all. I'm an ace at separating business and pleasure. My friendship with Drew is proof of that." He raised a hand to ward off interruption. "And no, representing you doesn't compromise my friendship with Drew either. So, should I set up some meetings?"

"Okay. Go ahead."

Lilia placed a plate of scrambled tofu in front of Jack, and suddenly had his full attention again.

"Scrambled tofu? Are you veggie too? Come here, woman!"

Jack pulled Lilia onto his lap. "You're delicious."

Jack and Lilia kissed passionately over the plate of tofu. Rowie watched for a second, and then slipped out the door before her eyeballs melted.

Chapter Fifty

Rowie was in the shop alone, wandering around, silently saying goodbye to some of her favorite nooks and crannies. Her grandmother had accepted an offer from Bobby "Beelzebub" Burger. The papers were about to be signed, and they would have six weeks to clear the shop. Then it would be over.

Rowie knew she should embrace the change. New doors were opening, and life was certainly presenting her with some exciting opportunities. She was meeting with Jack today to go over a contract for a fantastic job—her own show. The very thought made her want to kick up her heels. But then she'd remember the fate of the shop and her heart would feel heavy again.

She could barely imagine how her mother was feeling. Thankfully, Lilia had Jack now. They both did. He'd been with Lilia every night since their first date two weeks earlier, and already it was hard to imagine life without him. He'd turned out to be a blessing in disguise, for both her career and her mother. He was certainly the one thing keeping Lilia afloat at the moment.

Rowie wandered back to the counter and opened a box of crystals. For as long as she could remember, sorting stock had been a chore. All of a sudden, it meant something to her. Her grandmother had already canceled all the regular orders. They weren't buying any new stock. Rowie lifted a piece of rose quartz from its packaging and gently stroked it. She was surprised at just how sad she felt.

The bell jangled and Rowie quickly pulled herself together. No point in getting emotional now. Perhaps her grandmother was right: If she'd felt this loyalty to the shop beforehand, then there'd be no need to sell it.

The customer stalled just behind a shelf. Another first timer, thought Rowie. "Can I help you?"

The customer stepped into view and smiled nervously. It was Jess. Or an alien who looked like Jess, because the real Jess would never wear a nervous smile or a pink shirt. Both made her look soft and pretty.

"Hi, Rowie."

Rowie didn't say anything, which seemed to annoy Jess. She sighed and crossed her arms. That's more like it, thought Rowie. Not an alien.

"The thing is . . ." Jess shuffled from foot to foot. "I decided to drop by . . ." She dropped her arms by her sides and suddenly looked quite vulnerable. "I came to apologize." Jess waited for Rowie to say something, but she still didn't, so Jess continued. "I'm not usually like that. Not at work. My heart got in the way of my head."

Rowie softened. She understood totally. "Hearts do that sometimes."

There was an uncomfortable pause. Jess wasn't used to admitting she'd been wrong, and she was burning with embarrassment. She picked up a crystal.

"What's this one for?"

"Moving on," said Rowie. "You can keep it."

"I told Drew how he could get his job back. About how he short-circuits your powers," Jess admitted.

"Yeah, I figured that. But ultimately it was his decision to use that information and hang around the studio."

Jess fingered the crystal. "See, the thing is . . . I was so busy thinking I'd lost my chance at true love, I didn't realize I was messing up yours."

"I don't want to be with someone like him anyway. Not after what he did to me." Rowie could feel her nose growing.

"We all make mistakes, and he's a good person, Rowie. But you know that." Jess suddenly looked relieved. "That's all I wanted to say. So . . . goodbye." She offered Rowie her hand to shake. "And good luck."

Rowie took Jess's hand, but instead of shaking it she turned it over and began to trace a finger over the palm. "Let's see what other changes are in store for you." Rowie smiled. "Do you like French men?"

Jess was back at her desk a couple of hours later, reeling. Not only from Rowie's predictions—a French man, a job opportunity, and a daughter—but also at how much better she felt after apologizing. Being nice wasn't so hard after all. Jess wasn't ready to start doing volunteer work at a soup kitchen, but she was proud of her behavior. Brutal business decisions were one thing, and she had no problem making them, but manipulating co-workers because of her feelings for a man was a mistake she'd never repeat. She was finally ready to forgive herself now and move on.

"Jess . . . I need a word with you."

"Sure. Sounds serious."

Mac seemed agitated. "It is."

Jess broke out of her reverie. She followed Mac into his office, certain that Mac's desire to have a little tête-à-tête with her was a bad sign. She could feel something *vraiment important* about to occur. Perhaps he'd been told the truth about her professional faux pas. Yes, that's it. And now she was about to pay. She knew it, and she wasn't even psychic.

Mac closed the door. "This isn't easy for me," he began.

Jess slumped into a chair. "It's okay," she mumbled.

"Lou Jenkins from the Paris bureau hasn't been well. He's decided to retire. Bought a freaking vineyard or something. Your name came up. Obvious choice, really, with your background, and ability to speak the lingo. It won't be easy for me to lose you. I like working with you, despite some of the shit you've pulled recently. This is a great opportunity, Jess. It's a small office, but two years in Paris and you could be heading London. So what do you think? You want the job or not?"

"Paris, France?" Jess asked in an uncharacteristically small voice.

"Yeah, France, unless Paris has moved and no one told me."

Jess glanced at her palm and began to cry. "Yes, Mac. I'd like that very much."

Drew was stepping out of the elevator just as Jess was stepping in. He was going to keep his greeting to a polite nod until he noticed she was holding a box of belongings. He held his hand on the door to stop it from closing.

"What are you doing? Did you quit?" Perhaps she'd been fired. She looked like she'd been crying.

"I've been offered a job at the Paris office . . . effective immediately."

"Wow! Congratulations. Do you speak French?"

Incredible! He really knew nothing about her. "Fluently." Jess placed the box at her feet. "I saw Rowie today."

That had his attention, although he faked disinterest. "That's nice."

"It *was* nice. She's nice, Drew . . . weird but nice." Oops, she couldn't help herself. Oh well, complete change didn't happen overnight. She pushed the "door close" button, but Drew stopped it again.

"I need to tell you . . ." He searched the elevator for words. "What happened between us . . . I didn't mean to . . . you know . . ."

Jess laughed at him. "That was eloquent."

"It had nothing to do with you. I didn't mean to hurt you. Or anyone really."

"Me either," said Jess. It was okay now. "It just wasn't meant to be. Simple."

"I should've considered your feelings before I . . . you know . . . . with Eva. I'm sorry. But I can't apologize for Rowie."

"You shouldn't have to," Jess admitted. "Besides, right now, I'm more upset about the way I've acted at work . . . because of a guy!"

"Not just any ordinary guy!" Drew grinned, but Jess didn't laugh. "That was a joke."

"Impeccable timing."

Drew stuck his hand out. "Friends?"

"I don't think so. But not enemies either." Jess smiled. "You're lucky, Drew."

"Why's that?"

"The search is over for you. Don't blow it." She stared at him for just a moment, taking one last snapshot in her mind "Au revoir, Drew." She pressed the button again and this time Drew stepped back and watched the doors close. He leaned against the wall, deep in thought. *Was* the search over for him? After everything that had happened between them, could he and Rowie work it out?

A workman approached him and gave a cough. "It's a sign, buddy."

"Excuse me?"

The workman pointed at the wall behind Drew. "You're leaning against a sign. I've gotta remove it."

Drew realized he was leaning against an old promotional sign for Rowie. He stared at her face, into her eyes. He read the tagline for the show.

Let a little magic into your life.

The workman lifted the sign and carried it into the elevator.

Drew began to laugh. "It couldn't be clearer than that."

Chapter Fifty-one

Rowie was in Jack's office, going through a proposal for a new job. It was perfect. It was exciting. And best of all, she was sharing the moment with Jack. As much as she'd been surprised when he and her mother first got together, she'd fallen in love with him too. He was a great man and she was thrilled he was with Lilia.

"It's a half-hour show, once a week," Jack explained. "You present different aspects of the occult through interviews and reviews."

"It looks like fun."

"It will be. And they really want your input. They want to demystify psychic phenomena." Jack smiled at Rowie. He adored the girl. He adored her mother. Hell, he adored Gwendolyn, even though she could be a huge pain in the ass. He returned to the proposal. "Plus they want a live feed each morning, with you predicting the weather. I know the shop is closing, but you can do it outside The Grove."

"It all sounds great." Rowie flicked through the pages. "This is definitely the best offer."

"Apart from the one from *Playboy*." Jack laughed and threw his hands up in the air. "Joke! Whoa, Lilia would kill me."

Rowie fell silent for a moment. "I'm worried about Mom."

"She'll be okay. Today will be tough, but I'm looking after her." Jack looked at Rowie and she could see the love shining in his eyes. "I'm not going anywhere, I promise."

Lilia sat quietly in the garden. The ground was covered in a carpet of red leaves. She pulled her sweater sleeves down over her hands. There was a real bite in the air. Lilia loved fall. It was her favorite time of year.

She could see her father drifting nearby, but his presence was little comfort today. There was nothing she could do but wait. She looked at the stone archway that joined both the shop and house gardens to make one sprawling Eden. She would have to perform some rituals to get the fey folk to relocate to The Grove's side. And quickly. Once the contracts were signed, the Burger Boy energy would begin to permeate the place and the veil between the worlds could close.

Lilia felt renewed, with a sense of purpose, and decided to begin immediately. She stood up and made her way over to the herb garden. She needed to brew a tea and make an ointment. She picked some nettle and thyme. She picked some marigold. It wasn't a full moon but she'd just have to improvise. She had ginger, hollyhock and hazelnuts inside. She'd seen a four-leaf clover here a few days ago . . . where was it? There. And finally, a snap of moly—which may or may not exist.

She straightened and stretched out her back. She wasn't able to save the shop, but she as sure as hell would save the faeries.

* * *

Gwendolyn was in the Edgar Cayce room with Bobby, Sally Sue and the real estate agent. There was no turning back now.

"Another autograph right here," the agent guided.

She scrawled her name and waited until the agent turned the page.

Sally-Sue was not a happy camper. "It's a bit creepy here, Bobby."

"Nothing a bulldozer can't fix, sugar pie."

"Another signature here."

Gwendolyn felt sick, but signed her name again." Her fingers clenched the pen. She wasn't feeling well. Her chest felt tight. Something was . . . oh dear . . . not really an appropriate time for a . . .

Gwendolyn shot through a tunnel into the future. She found herself standing in the middle of a Burger Boy. There was a huge poster of a happy cow, dancing into a burger bun. She looked around, frantic. She wanted to shake off the vision, but for some reason she was finding it difficult.

A cheery teenage boy was standing behind the counter, smiling at her with a robotic grin. "Welcome to Burger Boy's 700th store. Despite my working conditions, I'd love to take your order."

I can't believe I'm contributing to this, thought Gwendolyn as she pushed her way out of the fog and back to reality.

Sally-Sue was looking at her warily. "How can there be light in this room if there're no windows?"

Gwendolyn pressed her fingers against her throbbing temples. "Magic." *You ignorant woman, isn't that obvious?*

Sally-Sue was starting to feel hysterical. One hand clutched at the crucifix around her neck while the other grabbed Bobby's arm. "Honey, you don't think this place is haunted, do you?"

"No such thing as ghosts."

Gwendolyn's hand flew to her mouth. Blasphemer.

"And if there is a spook or two around here," Bobby boomed, "Father Patrick and a bucket of holy water will soon fix it."

Gwendolyn clutched her chest. Something wasn't right. Breathless . . . can't breathe. Pain, pressing. Help. It hurts. Stop. Make them stop. The pain shot up her arms. She tried to call out.

LILIA. ROWIE.

She began to fall forward . . . forward . . . the floor shot up and hit her. She lay there. Helpless . . . cold. And then, thankfully, everything went black.

At that very moment, the teapot slipped from Lilia's hands. She froze and a second took ten to pass. The fey folk whispered urgently, telling her to hurry. The sound of the teapot smashing roused her. And then she began to run.

Rowie and Jack were saying goodbye when Rowie sensed her grandmother passing. She clutched hold of the doorframe. Her hand shot to her forehead.

Jack looked horrified. "Rowie . . . are you okay? Rowie . . . what's wrong?"

She began to sob. "Oh no, no, Gran! It's Gran."

Jack grabbed Rowie's hand and sprinted to the elevator.

Drew was trying to flag a cab. He was getting more and more frustrated each time another one passed him by. Why did he feel a sense of urgency? He'd waited this long for Rowie. Would five extra minutes really matter?

Finally, a cab pulled over and he jumped in. "The Village," he said. "And hurry."

* * *

Gwendolyn felt fabulous. She was floating around, staring at her body with a sense of complete detachment. The real estate agent was calling an ambulance. The scene below her was muted and dreamy, yet she understood everything with complete clarity.

"It looks like a heart attack," the agent yelled into the phone.

Bobby gave Gwendolyn's lifeless body a poke with his foot. "I hope she doesn't die before signing the contract."

"Should we pray for her Pagan soul, Bobby?"

"Don't be ridiculous."

Suddenly the room disappeared, and Gwendolyn was sucked through a tunnel. Or was it different layers of reality? Whatever it was, it was familiar. She'd made this journey before, and she'd make it again.

She became aware of people around her: family, friends, guides, all there to welcome her home. Her senses exploded and she turned to the Light. It was so welcoming and bright. She couldn't wait to step into it.

But first, before it, stood Dorian. "Hello, my love."

"Dorian." Gwendolyn dissolved into him and rejoiced in her infinite form . . . until she heard a voice. A small voice. An important voice.

"Mom!"

Dorian released her. There was a huge roar and suddenly Gwendolyn was aware of the constraints of her body, aware of Lilia holding her, begging her. . . .

"Don't you leave me, Mom. Don't you dare die."

Jack screeched to a stop outside The Grove. There was an ambulance and a crowd in front of Second Site. The crowd parted as the paramedics came racing out of the shop. Rowie ran toward the stretcher and her grandmother.

"Oh Gran, please no . . ."

"You go with Lilia," Jack yelled. "I'll follow."

Rowie climbed into the ambulance, and into her mother's arms, and then they both turned their attention to Gwendolyn. The driver slammed the doors shut and ten seconds later the ambulance roared away.

Drew was paying for the cab as the ambulance passed. He still wasn't completely sold on the idea of precognition, but somehow he just *knew* that that ambulance was carrying Rowie. Fear turned his blood to ice. He sprinted down the road and spotted Jack getting into his own car. "Jack!"

Neither seemed very surprised to see the other.

"It's Gwendolyn," Jack explained as he started the car and screeched into the traffic. "She goes on and on about dying, but no one believes her."

"She seemed full of life."

"She's stubborn. Could die . . . out of spite."

Drew turned to his friend. "What are you doing here?"

"It's the strangest thing, Drew. I'm in love with Lilia."

"That's not so strange. I'm in love with her daughter."

They both nodded. Nothing more needed to be said.

Chapter Fifty-two

Time ticks by differently in a hospital waiting room. Lilia and Rowie sat side by side . . . waiting, watching the clock move at an outrageously slow pace. Sometimes it seemed to go backwards.

A sob caught in Rowie's throat. "Why didn't I . . ."

"Rowie, please don't."

"But she always said . . ."

"I know."

"We didn't . . ."

"Believe her. I know."

The doors opened and Gwendolyn's doctor walked in. A grim look marred her pretty features.

Lilia's hand flew to her heart. "Oh Goddess. She's gone?"

"No, oh no," the doctor comforted. "She's okay. Apparently my ex-husband is going to marry his bimbo, but your mother is fine."

"What happened?" asked Rowie.

"A heart attack, but there doesn't seem to be any damage to her heart. She's healthy. Could live to a hundred."

"One hundred? You don't know how happy I am to hear that," cried Lilia. "Despite how annoying she'll be."

Rowie was reeling with relief. "Can we see her now?"

The doctor nodded. "Sure. Not for long, though. She needs her rest."

Rowie and Lilia clutched each other all the way to Gwendolyn's room. "She's okay, she's okay," they both whispered like a mantra.

Lilia knocked lightly and they stepped inside. Gwendolyn was propped up on some pillows, reading a nurse's palm. The nurse withdrew her hand, but Gwendolyn ignored Rowie and Lilia and grabbed it back.

"You'll meet a lovely dentist before long," she promised. "He'll help fix those teeth. Oh, fabulous, triplets!"

The nurse looked faint. "You have visitors," she said as she bid a hasty retreat from the room.

"Are you two just going to stand there all night?" barked Gwendolyn.

Rowie and Lilia took a couple of steps toward the bed.

Gwendolyn looked triumphant. "I hate to say I told you so. Luckily, I'm organized," she declared. "Prepared!" All of a sudden Gwendolyn burst into tears. It was their cue. Lilia and Rowie ran to her and scooped her into their arms.

"I don't want to die," Gwendolyn wailed. "All the promises and Post-it notes . . . I didn't really think . . ."

"Nor did we. You scared us, Mom."

Gwendolyn looked panicked. "I'm not ready. I mean, I thought I was. The silverware has been distributed, but there's so much I haven't done yet."

"The doctor says you'll live for years," Rowie promised.

"I want to live . . . really live. Without the Post-it notes."

"You can now." Lilia kissed her mother's cheeks. "You have plenty of time."

"I saw the other side, and it was lovely . . . but I'm not finished here." Gwendolyn's face crumpled and she cried with such sorrow. "I spent so much time wanting to be with Dorian, I didn't see that I was wasting my time with you."

"I'm so sorry," said Rowie."You do too much. I haven't been there for you. If I'd taken over like you asked . . ."

Gwendolyn stroked her granddaughter's hair. "No, love. I haven't been there for you. You have every right to find your own path."

"I'm a Shakespeare. The shop was my path."

"No. Only part of it."

"Now it's too late." It was Rowie's turn to cry. "Mr. Mega Burger will destroy our beautiful shop . . . our history."

Gwendolyn grabbed a tissue and wiped her eyes. "No, he won't."

"Of course he will," Rowie said. "You've met him. He's vile."

Gwendolyn composed herself. This decision had been the easiest of her—lovely, and very much valued—life. "We're keeping the shop."

"What?"

Gwendolyn looked apologetic. "I can't sell."

Lilia threw her arms around her mother. "Oh thank you, thank you."

Rowie was surprised by the huge wave of relief that engulfed her. "Thank Goddess."

"A Burger Boy!" snorted Gwendolyn. "Over my dead body."

All three women look horrified for a moment and then burst out laughing.

"Almost *was* over my dead body," Gwendolyn hooted.

"Oh that's so awful, Mom."

Rowie grabbed Gwendolyn's hand. "I promise I'll learn how to run the shop."

Gwendolyn shook her head. "No thanks. It keeps me young."

"But it's my duty," said Rowie.

"You know why so many Shakespeare women took over the business? Because they wanted to. That's your duty, Rowie. To do what you love. To have the freedom to choose. That's what countless Shakespeare women fought for."

Lilia cleared her throat. "What about teaching me the business side of things?"

Gwendolyn stared at Lilia, surprised.

Lilia was determined to be heard. "I know I have my head in the clouds a lot, but it's only because everyone expects me to," she said. "It's time I expand my horizons. Besides, Jack thinks I have quite a head for business." Lilia paused for a moment. "What do you think?"

Gwendolyn slowly nodded. She was impressed. Finally! "I think it's an excellent idea, Lilia."

Rowie wasn't quite sure where that left her. "What about me?"

"You find your own job."

"Really?"

"Yes, really."

Rowie was finally able to share her excitement with her grandmother. "Actually, I've been offered my own TV show, Gran."

Gwendolyn looked taken aback for a moment. "And you didn't tell me?" And then she shook her head. "Well, of course not. Probably too scared." She grabbed Rowie's face between her hands and stared at her with such love. "I'm thrilled for you. And very proud."

"That means a lot to me, Gran."

"I also think you should get that gorgeous man back."

Rowie's smile faded. "Drew? No, that's over."

"It can't be." Gwendolyn was adamant. "It's destined."

"What have you always taught me? Destiny is only a map . . ."

Gwendolyn and Lilia joined in: "You still choose which road to take."

"You're on the wrong road without him," said Gwendolyn. "Now go! I need my rest . . . I also need to call my boyfriend and tell him to buy me some chocolates and flowers." Her face lit up like a young girl's. "I've got quite a crush on him."

Lilia and Rowie blew Gwendolyn kisses.

"We'll come back later," Lilia promised.

"I love you, Gran." Rowie was smiling as she slipped out the door.

"Lilia!" Gwendolyn called.

Lilia paused at the door. "Yes, Mom?"

"Are you in love?"

Lilia's eyes lit up. "Yes. I never thought I'd find it again. After Rowie's father . . ."

"Then love really is blind."

Lilia felt like she'd been kicked in the stomach. Why would her mother try to hurt her now? "I thought you liked him."

"I do. Very much." Gwendolyn had a sly smile on her face. "Do you know much about him?"

"Only what he tells me . . . my gift doesn't work that well with him."

"Have you ever seen him naked?"

"Mom!"

"Don't be coy with me, dear. I know you've been at it like rabbits. I'm just amazed you haven't seen . . ."

"Seen what?" Lilia demanded.

"His tattoo, Lilia. It's not a past life you know him from."

Chapter Fifty-three

Time ticks by differently in a hospital waiting room. Drew and Jack sat side by side . . . waiting, watching the clock move at an outrageously slow pace. Sometimes it seemed to go backwards. Eventually they stood and paced the room. It was cliché, but made them feel like they were doing something.

"I'm sure she's fine," said Drew.

Jack gave a nod. "Yes . . . tough old girl."

Suddenly Rowie rounded the corner and gave Jack a huge grin. "She's okay."

Jack slumped into a chair. "Thank God."

Rowie felt someone watching her. She turned and noticed Drew in the corner. Heat filled his eyes and slowly but surely he moved toward her.

"What are you doing here?"

"Taking control of my destiny." He kept moving.

"I thought you didn't believe in destiny."

And moving. "And then I met you."

Rowie wasn't ready for this. "Wait . . . stop . . ."

Drew didn't. He kept moving her way. She noticed a wheelchair nearby, so she grabbed it and hurled it at him.

Drew leapt out of its way, shocked. "What the hell are you doing?"

"You can't just waltz in here, 'Oh I believe in destiny now.' "

"But I do. Nothing has made sense since I first kissed you. I can't explain you, Rowie . . . and I've realized, I don't have to."

Rowie placed her hands on her hips. As much as she wanted to forgive him immediately, she needed to hear one more thing. "It's not enough."

"What more do you want? My soul?"

"An apology."

They glared at each other for a moment, both refusing to back down, until Drew couldn't stand it any longer and grabbed her. His mouth crushed down on hers. Rowie felt the anger drain from her body as a different heat took over. Her arms slid around his neck as she dissolved into him.

"Nothing," she sighed.

"Everything," he whispered.

"Will it ever work?"

"Who knows?" And then he thought he'd better check. "Do you *know?*"

Rowie shook her head. She had no idea . . . and it was lovely.

Drew grinned, relieved. "Me either. I can't predict the future."

She searched his eyes. "And everything that's happened between us?"

"It's in the past. All I know is what I feel right now. I love you. I don't want to spend another second without you."

There was a long hospital-waiting-room pause . . . and then Rowie smiled. "Then don't," she said.

Drew swept Rowie into his arms and they kissed. A feeling of utter joy filled him, and he laughed and twirled her around. There was no way he'd ever let her go again.

"We'll let the future take care of itself." Rowie was finally happy to do so.

Jack watched them and felt like doing a happy jig. About time, he thought. And then he saw Lilia marching up the corridor and his own heart skipped a beat. He smiled at her, but she didn't smile back. Something was wrong. Something had happened. No, not now, thought Jack, not when everything else was so right.

Lilia walked up to Jack and without uttering a single word, removed his jacket.

"Hey, whoa . . . whatcha doing? Honey, not here," he said. Had she gone mad? He tried to turn it into a joke. "Wow, you want me to turn the lights off?"

Lilia dropped Jack's jacket on the floor. She unbuttoned his shirt cuff and pushed the sleeve up to reveal a tattoo of a mermaid.

The mermaid.

"Blue eyes and a mermaid tattoo," she whispered. The heat of the Beltane fires from so long ago surged through her veins. She stepped back, reeling.

Rowie and Drew stared at the tattoo, shocked. They immediately understood the implications.

"Jack's the missing urn!" said Drew.

Rowie shook her head, confused. It didn't make sense. Jack? "A mermaid?"

Drew turned to Lilia. "How did you miss that?"

"Lights off, Drew," she explained. "I breast-fed Rowie for two years. I prefer to wait until I'm totally comfortable."

Jack was completely confused. "Did I miss something?"

Rowie turned to her mother. She had to be sure. "The fires of Beltane?"

Jack realized what they were talking about, what he had always, on some level, known. "That was you, Lilia? The May Queen mask? No wonder I . . ." And then thirty years of longing filled his eyes. "I never thought I'd find you again."

Lilia broke into the most beautiful smile and stared up at the man for whom she'd waited three long decades. "We always knew we'd find you, Jack."

Jack stared at Lilia. She was the one, the one woman he had been with so briefly, yet loved for so long. How had he missed it? How had . . . *what?* Did she say . . . *we?* The whole room seemed to shift. He turned to Rowie. "Is she . . . are you?"

Both Rowie and Lilia nodded.

Jack stalled for a moment, shocked . . . and thrilled. How could something so bizarre, so outrageous, feel so right? Rowie stared at him, silently pleading for him to say something, anything. Finally, he reached out and tenderly stroked her cheek. "No wonder you're so familiar," he whispered.

Rowie had to agree.

Epilogue

The Grove's annual Yule party was in full swing, Shakespeare style. There were Witches, psychics, healers and dozens of friends currently in spirit, in both the dead *and* alcoholic sense.

Rowie wandered through the rooms chatting with old friends and checking that everyone had a drink. She noticed the transparent forms of Isabel and Grandpa Dorian drifting near the stairs. They had discovered a genuine affection for each other and were now spending time together until their soul mates joined them. She squeezed through a corridor and saw Officers Washington and O'Hare drinking bourbon while they chatted with a woman who channeled Picasso. The woman had given Gwendolyn one of her most recent paintings, and declared it should be worth a flipping fortune.

Rowie stopped to chat with some of her new work colleagues. Her show was a success and she loved every minute of it. The heady popularity she had experienced at USBC had settled and she now had a loyal audience for her Monday night show and weekday morning report.

She excused herself and headed out to the garden. It was covered in a light dusting of snow and looked like a magical fairyland. Taye, Michelle and Mac were standing around the bonfire chatting, while Sunny, his wife, Min and their granddaughter danced to the Celtic band. Despite the snow, the garden was warm, and they were all laughing and wiping sweat from their brows.

Rowie sighed with happiness. How she loved this garden and the magic it housed. How she loved her home. She'd be moving out in a few months. She and Drew had agreed to spend the warmer months on his boat, but during the winter they would live at The Grove. Balance. It was perfect.

The Grove was so full of life and love lately. William was always dropping by, and Jack had quickly married Lilia and moved in. He understood Lilia's need to remain in the rambling old house.

And then there was the new life headed their way.

Rowie walked back inside and discovered Angel, Shin, Petey and Georgette all sitting around the kitchen table.

"Don't you look gorgeous," said Georgette.

Rowie glanced down at her black top and deep green velvet pants. She felt great. Glowing. "You should talk, Georgie. You look wonderful."

Georgette was wearing a pink sweater that showed off the color in her cheeks. She was going from strength to strength. She still had one more course of chemo to go, but was feeling positive. She'd already defied the doctors' predictions and intended to continue doing so. Petey was hopeful. He refused to consider, even for a moment, that he would lose Georgette. He was just thrilled to be loved by such a beautiful, smart woman.

Angel and Shin had recently announced they were moving to Tokyo. Rowie had been inconsolable for about ten minutes until Angel promised it would only be for twelve months and an excellent opportunity for Rowie and Drew to visit Japan. Angel was already embracing all things Japanese. Tonight she was wearing an incredible blue top with kimono-style sleeves, and her hair was heaped on top of her head and held in place using chopsticks.

Rowie pulled up a chair with her friends and started shoveling some chips into her mouth. She was always hungry lately.

"Wild party, Rowie." Georgette giggled.

"This is nothing," said Petey, deadpan. "Wait until they sacrifice the goat."

Georgette's eyes bulged in horror, and Petey burst out laughing. "I'm kidding."

Rowie turned to Angel. "So when are we going to see this book of yours?"

"I haven't even seen it yet," said Shin. "I'm not completely certain it exists."

Angel gave him a playful punch. "You'll all see it soon," she promised. "It's nearly finished."

"I'm proud of you for writing it," said Petey. "What's it about?"

"I've written about what I know," she said, gesturing to the scene around them.

Petey ruffled her hair. "It'll be a short book then."

Drew pushed his way through the crowd and over to the table. "Here's the gang." He slipped his arms around Rowie and kissed the top of her head. "How are you feeling?"

"I'm fine." She laughed. "Stop asking."

Drew noticed the empty bowl of chips in front of Rowie. "You'll get fat." He laughed. "And I can't wait." His hand slipped down and rested on her still flat stomach. He gave it a rub. This had been a surprise, albeit a wonderful one, conceived during their first weekend together—so much for condoms—and discovered during their first weekend back together.

"She's sleeping," whispered Rowie.

"How on earth could *he* sleep with this racket?" Drew chuckled.

"She."

"He."

"Here we go again." Angel laughed.

"We really should settle this, once and for all," Drew said.

Everyone looked at him in shock.

"You said you didn't want to know," said Rowie.

"I've changed my mind."

"But we're not due for an ultrasound until—"

Drew interrupted. "Oh come on, there's another way to find out."

Rowie laughed. "Oh boy, the scientist has changed his tune. Are you sure?"

Drew nodded. "Positive."

"Okay," Rowie jumped to her feet. "Let's find out."

Gwendolyn was channeling a past life as a royal and holding court in the living room. She was regaling everyone—not for the first time—about her near-death experience.

"It was a revelation," she announced. "It taught me about living, as well as dying."

William watched her and smiled. She was a vision in red. He'd been relegated to working the punch bowl. Not that he minded. He quite liked it when Gwendolyn bossed him around. And besides, the punch was delicious. It was an interesting concoction that reminded him of . . . his youth. He took another sip. He couldn't work out what was in it and Gwendolyn refused to divulge the ingredients. The recipe for Shakespeare's Secret Punch had been handed down from each generation along with the family name and bright red hair.

William caught Gwendolyn's eye and she gave him a wink. Who would have thought that he'd be standing in the middle of a haunted house, watching his witchy girlfriend conjure up tall tales about the world of Spirit? How incredible that one can feel so at home in the strangest of places.

Jack squeezed onto the couch beside Lilia. "How's my second favorite girl?"

Lilia rolled her eyes. "You'd think Rowie was still a baby, the way you mollycoddle her. I feel quite left out." She obviously didn't. She was beaming.

"I have a lot of time to catch up on," Jack explained. He looked at his wife lovingly and then searched the room for his daughter, the child he never even knew he had until two months ago.

There she was, pushing her way over to them. The light of his life, looking radiant.

"Drew wants to know," she said when she reached them.

Lilia and Jack looked at each other in surprise, then nodded and headed for the stairs. Rowie grabbed Gwendolyn.

"I need you," she whispered.

They made their way to the attic, where Lilia, Jack and Drew were already sitting.

Gwendolyn immediately understood what they were up to. "There's no point. It's definitely a girl."

"Yes, Mom, but none of us are sure. Don't you think that's strange?"

Gwendolyn threw her arms up in mock defeat. "Fine, let's look . . . but six hundred years of tradition says it's a girl."

"Let's make sure, Gran."

The five sat at the séance table and Lilia shuffled the cards. They could hear the strains of music and laughter three floors below.

Lilia held the cards. "Please tell us about the baby." She spread them across the table: The empress, the world, the priestess . . . and then . . .

Drew was no tarot card reader but even he understood what was before him.

Everyone stared at the cards for a moment and then looked at each other with joy.

"There you go," said Jack, proud as punch.

"Wonderful," said Gwendolyn. She glanced at her daughter. "What do you think?"

"Oh my!" said Lilia. "Lovely."

Drew and Rowie gazed at each other and nodded. "Perfect."

And it was.

Christie Craig

Divorced, Desperate and Delicious

Ever since photographer Lacy Maguire caught her ex playing Pin the Secretary to the Elevator Wall, she's been content with her dog Fabio, her three cats, and a vow of chastity. But all that changes when the reindeer-antlered Fabio drags in a very desperate, on-the-run detective who decides to take refuge in her house—a house filled with twinkling lights and a decorated tree. (Okay, so it's February, but she has a broken heart to mend, a Christmas-card shoot to do, and a six-times divorced, match-making mother to appease.) For the first time in a loooooong while, Lacy reconsiders her vow. Because sexy Chase Kelly, wounded soul that he may be, would be an oh-so-delicious way of breaking her fast. Now, if she can just keep them both alive and him out of jail....

ISBN 13: 978-0-505-52730-1

Unlucky

Jana DeLeon

Everyone in Royal Flush, Louisiana, knows Mallory Devereaux is a walking disaster. At least now she's found a way to take advantage of her chronic bad luck: by "cooling" cards on her uncle's casino boat. As long as the crooks invited to his special poker tournament don't win their money back, she'll get a cut of the profit.

But Mal isn't the only one working some major mojo. There's a dark-eyed dealer sending her looks steamier than the bayou in August. Turns out he's an undercover agent named Jake Randoll, and for a Yank, he's pretty darn smart. Smart enough to enlist her help to catch a money launderer. As they race to untangle a web of decades-old lies and secrets amid a gathering of criminals, Mallory can't help hoping her luck's about to change....

ISBN 10: 0-505-52729-4
ISBN 13: 978-0-505-52729-5